Love & Candy

ELIZABETH FAMOUS

Dedication

For my mom,
My champion,
My inspiration to
do things differently

Chapter 1:

Standing in line at lunch, breathing in disinfectant mixed with oregano, Samantha tried to ignore the boys behind her doing karate kicks as the regret and nausea welled up. Regret over not being able to think of her dad the same way again. Nausea over a man she'd never met, named Anton de' Medici, whom her mom once knew.

Samantha couldn't grasp the idea of her mom having sex with someone other than her dad. Actually, it was hard to get her mind around the idea of anyone having sex, even, or *especially,* herself. Notwithstanding plenty of sex education at home, where she'd learned about penises and vaginas as a toddler, she still had trouble picturing the act. On dull Saturday nights watching TV with her sisters, she'd conjure the image of a guy lying on top of a girl, partially undressed, and in a bed, then the mechanics would come to mind, her cheeks would start to burn, and she'd become so self-conscious she'd have to stop.

With lunch tray in hand, Samantha looked across the aisle at some students lined up waiting for the vice principal to evaluate their class trip permission slips. Her eyes were drawn to a tall girl with dark red lipstick and a green lollypop moving in and out of her mouth.

That's when she first noticed him. It was like being blindsided on the soccer field. Feeling short of breath, she leaned against the tiled wall behind her.

Since starting 9th grade, she'd prided herself in avoiding the epidemic of boy-craziness overrunning the freshman girls at Darcy High. But he, as he ambled into her line of sight with a sly smile, was something else. Her eyes riveted, she tried to balance her lunch tray without spilling anything.

He approached the girl with the lollipop from behind, reached around her waist, and grasped a mesh cord dangling from her lacy Goth dress, cinching it tighter. In a voice like Kurt Cobain's during his classic MTV Unplugged performance, he droned a line from a song about the smell of "sex and cannndy" as his beautiful face brushed against her straight black hair. He didn't have perfect pitch or a singer's voice, but he pulled off the lyric with charisma. The casualness of it, normalness of it, made it seem like he was some sort of music buff.

The Goth lollipop girl laughed encouragingly at his serenade. Turning to face him, she hooked her thumbs through his front belt loops and poked him with her hip. It could have been so crass, like every other flirtatious display she'd witnessed at school, but somehow it wasn't.

His face was a Grecian ideal of symmetry realized in flesh. A straight, proportioned nose. Sunken cheeks that emphasized his cheekbones as he grinned. A jaw that contoured sharply at his chin. Skin glowing with a sheen more lustrous than any woman wearing make-up. And deep-set eyes of fiery blue that locked onto Lollipop-girl with an intensity that made Samantha blush.

He wore jeans, like everyone else, but they fit him like a rock star: loose in the front, more snug in the back. A black T-shirt framed his lanky torso and angled shoulders. He was tall, maybe six feet like her dad. On his head was white-blonde hair, haphazardly tucked behind his ears and hanging to the nape of his neck.

But it wasn't just the way he looked. If she had seen him in a photograph, her experience would not have been nearly so dramatic. It was the way he moved, slowly and confidently with his head slightly arched to the side. It was his lazy grin, so mellow and at ease. He stood erect without seeming like a poser or show off. None of the guys in her classes carried themselves with such confidence.

In a low voice, he said to the Goth girl, "How'd you get home last night? Do the walk of shame?"

"No," she insisted. "How about you? Where'd *you* go after the party?"

"I don't remember," he said with a smirk.

"Hmm, I figured."

He glanced downward at her spiked boots for just an instant.

Samantha wiped perspiration from the back of her neck. She had noticed handsome men before, but nothing like this. He was exponentially more daunting than the asexual husband she'd daydreamed about last year when writing an essay on how she envisioned her life as an adult.

Even so, it was shocking to feel instantly drawn to a guy she didn't know. Not only was he several years older than her -- looked at least five years older -- but he seemed to have a girlfriend. If this was sexual attraction, her previous thoughts on the subject were overly rational. She had thought one needed to get to know someone before feeling overwhelmed by his presence. She hated how her classmates focused almost exclusively on looks when it came to the opposite sex. She didn't want to be shallow, but her reaction was undeniable and seemingly out of her control.

A petite freshman girl standing in line in front of her must have noticed her open stare. "That's Delaney Troy. He's on the soccer team." The second sentence was spoken as if it said much more than the fact that he participated in the phys. ed. department's soccer program.

"I play soccer," Samantha mumbled, meaning only that she played on the school's girls' team. Over the summer, she'd decided to try out for a sport, and soccer seemed like a fun choice. Although she didn't have much experience, this was not a problem. She fit right in with the rest of the female players at school.

In contrast, the boys' team was renowned throughout the state of Connecticut. Dozens of placards announcing its successes were front and center in the wall-sized trophy case across from the gymnasium. Team members formed a clique idolized by the general population of the school.

The girl who knew Delaney's name introduced herself with a simple, "I'm Ally." She was dressed flamboyant and punk, with flower-shaped patches sewn onto her khaki pants, nothing like Samantha's conservative friends from middle school.

"I'm Samantha. Samantha Montclare." She grinned cautiously. "His first name is *Dell-eh-nee*?"

"A totally whack name for such a gorgeous guy, huh? He goes out with Nicolette Hunter … Junior Homecoming Queen."

"She was homecoming queen?" asked Samantha, looking across to the black-clad lollypop girl with whom Delaney was chatting inaudibly.

"No, that's Mairin. She's actually a friend of mine, or my sister's friend really. He goes out with her *and* Nicolette. You've probably seen Nicolette. She's captain of the cheerleaders."

"Both of them? He has two girlfriends?"

"Sick, huh? He's a total player."

"Really?" said Samantha, looking at seemingly poised and self-respecting Mairin. "I can't believe she'd go out with him if he's dating someone else."

"Yeah. No surprise she and Nicolette have issues. Last year they were screaming at each other at this party. I heard it was a major scene."

Normally Samantha had zero interest in who was voted this or that, or who was at this or that party, but, as she watched Delaney rest his elbows on the table where the vice principal was stationed, she didn't have to pretend to be following Ally's account.

"Mairin told me he doesn't want a girlfriend, wants to be able to hook up with whoever. He messes around with other girls too, not usually from our school. At Darcy, he's only doing Nicolette and Mairin. I guess it's too bad for the rest of us."

"That's …" said Samantha. "Wow, I can't believe that." She was repulsed, yet fascinated.

"They say he's a wicked lay," Ally laughed, without awkwardness. Motioning toward two guys who'd joined Delaney, she added, "That's Brian Woodberry and Trevor Thomas from soccer."

Samantha nodded but the names of the other boys didn't register. She only noticed Delaney, who was smiling at Mairin, his eyes shining. "I'm surprised Mairin doesn't insist he be faithful."

"Yeah, well, she likes to keep her options open too. You should have seen her at the mall the other day. She was totally styling this guy in a business suit. He must have been about twenty eight or something. He looked all uncomfortable and stuff, but she said the minute they were alone he asked for a BJ."

Alone that night, Samantha decided she admired Ally's blunt, no-nonsense attitude and was pleased to be making friends, instead of just losing them. Ally's slang references to sex were not foreign. Samantha was often forced to listen to provocative banter at school. But an abbreviation for oral sex had never come up in her own conversation before.

She was accustomed to associating with a reserved crowd of overachievers. But high school was an upheaval. Her middle school friends had little to say to her since the first week of school when she'd offered them unsolicited advice, insisting they *ought* to care more about spending time with each other than scoping out guys. This tore a rift.

"Why do you like him?" she had complained to a longtime friend who was busy with a new boyfriend. "He seems kind of boring and gross, always talking about getting drunk. You always said you wanted someone smart. He's not even in a regular math class."

Samantha thought about Mairin, who dressed with verve and seemed perfect for the role of sex in his rendition of "Sex and Candy." She didn't think of herself as unattractive, but she also didn't think of herself as anything like wild Mairin. She was medium height, about 5'5" but still growing. Her wardrobe consisted of jeans, hooded sweatshirts and sneakers, nothing like Mairin's racy attire.

Samantha also thought of Nicolette, the other girl Ally mentioned. At a recent pep rally, every first-year student in Samantha's vicinity was gaping at the squad leader wearing a gold 'Nicolette' necklace. Standing in front of seven other cheerleaders with a self-satisfied smile, she was a walking -- and jumping -- stereotype: statuesque with long blonde hair, opal skin, and a toned stomach. Samantha hadn't been able to understand why it was mandatory for her, and the rest of the non-cheerleaders, to watch Nicolette and company dance around and elicit whooping from guys in the crowd. And why would anyone, even someone as impossibly good looking as Nicolette, choose to expose her underwear by kicking and twirling in a short skirt?

In all probability, *he* had sex with both of them.

Chapter 2:

Darcy High's soccer coach periodically gathered the girls' and boys' teams for co-ed practice. Telling the girls they hadn't improved after weeks of workouts, he scheduled the first co-ed match-up of the school year, explaining to Samantha and her teammates that the experience of being "outclassed" by the boys was going to allow them to get some much-needed pointers.

Samantha was excited by the prospect of seeing Delaney in action, yet skeptical of the coach's intentions. He spoke of his "boys" so adoringly that she wondered if he was actually setting up a rout, either for his own amusement or to give the guys an unneeded ego boost.

Sitting on the hard basketball court waiting for the coach to appear, Samantha's pulse perked up as Delaney exited the locker room with some other guys. He was dressed in blue practice shorts and an oversized white jersey scrunched at his waist.

With a sluggish gait, he followed the others who filed over to where the girls were huddled quietly under a dangling basketball net. Delaney and a friend of his, whom Samantha had seen him with in the hall, exchanged a couple words, then broke away from the pack and strode across the gym to where the cheerleaders were practicing. As Delaney approached Nicolette, she clapped three times, her hands aligned in a praying position. Samantha couldn't see the expression on his face as he spoke to Nicolette, but his stance was stoic.

Eventually, Coach Simmons arrived and, noticing the wanderers, called out, "Troy…Thomas…will you please join us?"

For a moment, Samantha wondered if Ally had gotten his name wrong.

"Would you be so kind as to take a seat?" snapped the coach as the two straggled back.

Delaney sat down not five feet from Samantha. Ignoring everyone else around her, she studied his mid-length hair, tied at the base of his scalp with a black rubber band, a few strands escaping the bind and falling to his jaw line. She noticed his legs and arms were a soft tan color, dusted with blonde hair.

Soon she found herself surmising that he was naturally blonde, then blushed, feeling herself perspire. She frowned at the thought she couldn't control her body. She'd experienced physical reactions before when thinking of him while alone in her bedroom. But she tried to assure herself it did not mean that, on some primal level, she wanted to have sex with him. It was merely another uncomfortable side effect of puberty.

They headed outside. After a short jog and some warm-up stretches, the mixed group was divided into defense and offense to practice passing and shots on goal.

The skill, quickness, and tenacity demonstrated by the boys left Samantha riled up with envy. And it didn't take long to recognize Delaney was their star.

His primary position was striker, yet unlike other forwards Samantha had seen, he showed flashes of brilliance at midfield and defense, executing well-placed long passes and making dangerous tackles. He fluidly changed directions to avoid defenders, weaving around them. Sprinting with possession of the ball, he lunged at full speed as he set up for a kick. Over and again, he led charges to the goal, peppering the goalkeeper with sudden shots from unexpected angles. Most impressive to Samantha was that he never looked down. His eyes were always alert, scanning the playing field as his feet dribbled the ball. It was as if the ball was attached to his foot with an elastic band.

As she waited to take a crack at playing offense, Samantha strained to hear every word he said. He spoke most often to the guy the coach had called 'Thomas' yet the other kids called 'Trevor.' Trevor had a Caesar haircut, a pleasant all-American face, and a laugh like a frat boy. When he put too much on a pass and the ball took off, Delaney, his intended recipient, called out, "Come on, man, I'm over here," and stood motionless as he watched the ball sail past his reach, not wasting energy on an impossible play.

"I can't help it. The little girls are distracting me," Trevor replied with a chuckle as he headed off to retrieve the ball.

Delaney blinked slowly and smiled, showing straight paste-white teeth.

It wasn't long before the coach began hollering about the girls' off-target passes. "That's how you're supposed to pass the ball!" cried Coach Simmons, referring to a low, ground pass demonstrated by one of the boys.

Many of the girls seemed dazed and star-struck in front of the older guys, giggling as they were nudged aside. There were no JV soccer teams at Darcy and the boys' team was made up of juniors and seniors, while, due to attrition, the girls were 14, or 15 like Samantha. As the coach herded the girls for some elementary instruction, a couple of the guys broadcast their boredom, "What the fuck is this?"

Delaney said nothing, merely looked off into the distance where the cheerleaders were chanting. "We're the best … of all the rest …"

Samantha felt deflated.

Her enthusiasm rebounded when Coach Simmons set up for a scrimmage with mixed teams. Delaney was named captain of the blue team; he picked five guys, including the boys' team's first-string goalie, and five girls, whom he merely pointed at, not knowing their names. Samantha was picked for the opposing team.

As the match kicked off, Delaney was near the center line when a girl about half his size received a pass. He caught up with her and scooped the ball away with gentle finesse. The muscles in his legs strained against his skin as he twisted. Samantha looked down at the dirt smears on her own less-contoured legs.

As play continued, stealing became unnecessary. Girls started conceding the ball, languidly passing it to a male teammate or carelessly losing it to the opposing team.

"Let them have it. I don't care," said one girl, flapping her hands in resignation.

Samantha was determined not to be an easy target, but first she had to get the ball. The guys on her team weren't bothering to pass it to her, or any girl. She couldn't stand being ignored, and avoided like an obstacle on the field, so she ran after every loose ball, occasionally checking to see if Delaney ever looked her way. No, not that she noticed.

Eventually, the coach improvised a new rule, "Every other pass to a girl or it's the other team's ball."

Samantha got the ball just outside the center circle and immediately tried a shot on goal. It didn't go in. As she jogged back across the halfway line, she saw Delaney and Trevor say something to each other, then glance at her.

Almost out of breath, Samantha was served the ball in the air. As she got control, she saw Delaney coming at her out of the corner of her eye. He confused her by leaning to the left and then poking the ball from the right. She chased after him but didn't catch up.

Undeterred, when she next got the ball she was able to pass it forward. But her team couldn't get anything past the other team's goalie. Even after two open shots.

At midfield, she was passed the ball with Delaney on her back. Wedging her body between him and the ball, she blocked him with extended arms, looking around for a free teammate. Several seconds ticked by, then she flailed at the ball, losing her balance and falling backwards. The ball rolled out of bounds.

As she brushed the back of her thigh, damp from the turf, Delaney stepped toward her and offered his hand. Normally she would have been too shy to look him in the eye, but she was tired and irritated so she looked. Up close, his skin radiated, and his blue eyes pierced through her.

She righted herself and noticed a strange expression on his face, like he was thinking that she should know when she's conquered. Yet he didn't say a word and neither did she. For only a moment, she thought about the feeling of his warm, rigid hand around hers, but the action of the game quickly refocused her. The coach called for a thrown-in.

With a duffle bag embroidered 'Darcy Soccer' and a backpack so full of books it wouldn't zip, she was on her way to meet her mom across the street at the middle school where her sister Gretchen had afterschool band practice. Her eyes located Delaney. He was with Nicolette and their friends standing in the parking lot next to an older-model black car. She heard some laughter and saw Delaney touching Nicolette's arm and pulling her against his side. Nicolette was wearing an emerald blouse with low neckline that made her breasts look large against her slight frame. The strong color of the top in contrast with her fair skin and fair hair made her look like a Raphaelian angel with translucent halo.

Samantha tried to imagine what it might be like to be someone who could tempt him. Someone taller and prettier, with a grown-up body and an outgoing personality. That must be what he wants if he's with someone like Nicolette. She looked both ways as she crossed the street and said to herself, "Parents who aren't perverts would also be a plus."

Since first noticing Delaney, Samantha found not just Ally but lots of kids talked about him and Nicolette, usually with a mix of lust and envy. She heard that Nicolette's parents owned a construction company, lived on an estate in the wealthiest part of Darcy, let her have her own platinum credit card, and picked her up in a metallic-gold Bentley.

Traversing the empty middle school parking lot, she looked down at her small, size-A breasts, which had not a bit of pointiness to them. She felt hopeless yet drawn to him at the same time. During the ride home in the backseat of her mom's car, she tried to formulate a list of reasons why a guy might prefer someone like her to Nicolette. She came up with a short list but it was a struggle.

Chapter 3:

Normally, when she got home, she would unwind by watching music videos with her sisters. Half the time they'd end up doing some wacky dancing. Even if one insisted on changing the channel to a grating sitcom rerun, Samantha would crash with them, listening to gossip about friends at school. That evening, despite arriving home exhausted, her mind was racing.

From the back patio, the trees looked gloomy with spidery leaves collected under them. The jungle gym, set up by the hedge that separated their lawn from her grandparents' next door, was dimly lit, like a skeleton left over from her childhood. She and her sisters used to play house by throwing a blanket over its highest bar. Back then, their make-believe family drama involved a mom trying to control a couple of screaming, misbehaving brats.

All summer they used to run wild outdoors, hardly wearing shoes, except flip-flops. Bug bites and scrapes covered their legs. Her face sunk as she thought of the many Sunday afternoons she'd spent kicking around a soccer ball with her dad. The jungle gym served as a goal. Her dad's parents, sitting in the lighted house next door, would never be able to guess what she was now thinking about their eldest son.

Samantha had always been close to her father, Robert Montclare. When reading *To Kill a Mockingbird* in 7th grade, Samantha had told her teacher that Atticus reminded her of her own dad. "That's quite a compliment!" her teacher replied. A 41-year-old architect, his disarming smile made him a favorite among his daughters' friends as well as the female designers with whom he worked.

Up until high school, Samantha had thought of her dad as a model for the perfect man: a loving husband and father, with a witty streak to boot. Her peace of mind was contingent on their one-on-one chats. Almost every evening, an hour after dinner, he'd wander into her room to hang out for a while as she did homework. She could discuss anything that was bugging her, which included complaining about something he'd said or done. Weightier issues had taken over of late, but he addressed even the most insignificant facets of her life with insight.

After a long day of shopping for a trip to the Cape May seashore, she, at 12, had asked, "How come Mom said we can't buy two-piece bathing suits yet they make them for babies?"

"It has to do with, uh, social convention," Robert replied. "Just like little girls can run around on the beach without shirts while young women can't -- at least not in this country. You can blame it on patriarchy, which I know you enjoy." He laughed. "If the average Joe would find something suggestive, we don't want you to wear it until you're old enough to handle attracting that sort of attention."

"Why shouldn't we wear something just because of what some stupid guy thinks? That's not fair."

"No, it's not, but your mom and I have to be practical."

"But if we lived in a place where the average guy thinks pants are suggestive, would we have to wear skirts?"

"We'll decide on a case-by-case basis. And, you know, Samantha, the bikini Stephanie wanted to try on was nothing like the two-piece a baby might wear. It wouldn't work for swimming … and sunbathing is bad for your skin."

Samantha wondered if it was odd for her dad to be interested in what his daughters wore to the beach. Some of her friends' dads weren't so involved in day-to-day decisions. Then again, that's what made him so great as a dad.

She felt her fingernails dig into her skin. She'd been catching herself reevaluating her memories of her dad ever since her parents' momentous disclosure.

Four weeks earlier, Stephanie had uncovered an enigma while searching for a yellow nightgown in their parents' bedroom closet and immediately summoned the troops.

A thin leather volume could be seen inside the half-opened side drawer of their mom's special keepsake case that stayed in the back of her closet. The one they'd been forbidden to touch because the contents were extremely fragile.

"Let's just take a peek," Stephanie said, looking at her sisters as she opened the soft-covered book.

Samantha opened her mouth to speak but she was interrupted.

"Look!" Stephanie pointed to the words 'orange-flavored condom' on the center of the page.

Samantha reached out to hold the page steady as Annabelle, the youngest, insisted on taking a look. The surrounding sentences mentioned something about a trip to Santa Barbara and a novelty shop. The diarist, who was clearly their mom, said, "It was so embarrassing. I picked up an orange packet on the counter not realizing what it was. He insisted on buying it."

Samantha did not see a man's name on the page.

Stephanie was gleeful. "It's a sex diary!"

Annabelle smiled as one eyebrow shot up questioningly, "What are orange-flavored condoms for?" At nine, Annabelle enjoyed embarrassing their parents at family gatherings with sex-related questions about soap opera storylines, "Don't you think they would have used birth control?"

"They're for reproduction," 11-year-old Gretchen answered matter-of-factly, her wide eyes belying equanimity. Despite Samantha's dislike of the phrase, Gretchen was called "the shy one" amongst their neighbors. Thanks to their parents' and grandparents' sociability, Samantha and her three sisters were known locally as the cute Montclare girls.

"For reproduction?" Stephanie laughed derisively as she folded the diary and placed it in Samantha's outstretched hands. "Did hunters and gatherers have artificial orange flavoring?" Despite her mere 13 years, Stephanie was self-assured and eye-catching, even with adult men. A thoughtless dinner guest recently singled her out as "the fairest of them all" in front of Samantha, Gretchen and Annabelle.

"We shouldn't have gone through her stuff," said Samantha softly, tidying up the drawer and preparing to close it with the diary inside.

"I know it's naughty … but what does it do?" pleaded Annabelle with a grin.

The sound of commotion in the driveway caused them to disperse. Annabelle and Stephanie ended up in the latter's tiny bedroom discussing the possible purposes of orange-flavored condoms.

Samantha helped her dad unload kitty litter and then decided to check up on the gathering in Steph's room. She peered in and whispered, "Poor dad. It must be hard to be the only guy in the house. He was worrying about whether you dingbats have enough tinted acne medicine -- they forgot to get it -- and you're up here talking about how guys use condoms."

"Maybe it wasn't dad who got it for her." Stephanie giggled, springing off her bed.

"Of course it was," Samantha protested. She and her sisters had heard all the stories. Their dad was their mom's first serious boyfriend. Their mom, Catherine, tried to be candid when discussing sexual matters with them. Sometimes, under an onslaught, she could be goaded into telling about personal experiences, such as her anxious decision to have sex for the first time after she and Robert had been dating for three months.

Samantha told herself it was wrong, but she couldn't conquer the temptation to check out more of what her mom had written. A few days later, she was alone in the house and guiltily walked into her mom's closet. It's not like she'd tell anyone about what she read or act differently if she found out a couple of her parents' secrets.

Opening the diary near the beginning, she read, "The teachers cafeteria is horrible. It's an old kitchen with a greasy table set up in the middle. Most people smoke instead of eating. I wish I had someone to go to lunch with, or an office so I could be alone."

The journal obviously described the time when her mom had taught grade school in Manhattan. A few months into her tenure, she ran into Robert on the street, after not having seen him since high school in Connecticut. Their parents were friends and they'd known each other since they were kids. They immediately started dating.

Skipping forward in the journal, Samantha noticed the unfamiliar name 'Anton' repeated several times on a single page, but the content was just stuff about grading papers and Anton's views on plagiarism. Flipping to the last quarter of the book, her breathing accelerated as her eyes located the name 'Anton' again. But the surrounding sentences were banal stuff about plans for a business trip to Milan.

She couldn't recall her mom ever mentioning someone named Anton, at least not as someone special to her. Starting to break into a sweat, Samantha chose a page from the middle of the text. It again contained an 'Anton,' but she was pleased to see one 'Robert' also. It was an account of a dinner where the conversation had turned to how her mom dressed. "Why does it matter that I never wear skirts? I don't understand why he brought it up." Unsettling as it was, the 'he' obviously referred to this Anton person.

There has to be more about Dad, Samantha thought, wishing she had more carefully perused the pages surrounding the part about orange condoms.

She flipped again and located a description of a visit to her grandparents' house next door. "They have all the same mahogany furniture. Just as I remembered. Robert mentioned that time I bumped into the table with snow globes on it. Robert's dad was so nice. He kept saying how happy he was to see me again." Anton's name was nowhere to be found, and Samantha was somewhat relieved but still curious.

Approximately thirty pages from the end of the text, she opened the diary and read, "When Anton got home from work, I told him about the pregnancy test."

She slammed the book shut.

She was going to get in big trouble and have to watch her dad's face morph into a heart-wrenching frown, but she needed an explanation. Everything will be okay, she told herself. There has to be an innocent explanation. Then her chest muscles squashed her lungs. *Oh my God, what if Dad doesn't know about this?*

She leapt for the phone.

Her mom's voice was immediately comforting. "He's going to be late tonight, Sam. What's the matter?"

"Uh, I'm sorry, but could you please come home? I really need to talk to you. *Right away.*" She tried to control her trembling.

"Okay." Catherine gasped. "I'll call your dad."

"No! Uh, please just come home. Don't call Dad." Samantha knew her mom would be panicky the whole drive home but was fairly certain she hadn't caused enough alarm so as to make driving risky.

Catherine Fisher Montclare was by profession a school administrator and did competent work at the board of education where both her father and father-in-law once served. Delicate and youthful in appearance, with blonde hair she usually wore pinned up in a twist, she was soft-spoken and self-effacing. Every woman at the PTA was willing to co-chair with unassuming Catherine.

As an often-bruised teenager with a temper, Samantha couldn't discount the power of her mom's conventional femininity. Neither she nor her sisters could resist their mom's gentle admonishments. But Samantha felt a pang of fear as she thought of her mother's weaknesses. Her inability to make a decision without first talking over every detail with her husband. Her need for his constant reassurances about everything from what she bought for dinner, to her haircut, to her decision to use the U.S. Postal Service over UPS. She was so emotional and so serious about being emotional.

Samantha heard her mom call upstairs, toss her heels with a thud, and mount the steps.

She greeted her with a sob, "What pregnancy test?"

Catherine froze, her eyes brilliant with confusion. "Did something happen to you? Samantha? Are you okay?"

"Who's Anton?" Samantha erupted, her voice harsh and an octave higher than normal.

The twenty minutes that followed were a blur of barely coherent effusions, during which little information was successfully conveyed by Samantha or her mother. For the most part they talked over each other; however, Catherine did clearly articulate several times, "Your dad and I love you very much." And amongst her stammering was the statement, "Anton is a very special person ... I think it's very important ... we really should talk about ... him."

In consequence of a text message request for haste, Robert arrived home a half hour later to find Catherine and Samantha stable yet exhausted and confused looking. He was rarely at a loss for words, but their shocked, tear-stained faces seemed to take away his ability to speak for a moment. He pulled at his tie, obviously striving to construct an optimistic visage. "What is it?" he asked with a crease of worry under his eyes.

Chapter 4:

That evening marked the beginning of a series of marathon discussions regarding a jarring bit of information Samantha's parents had withheld from her for the first fifteen years of her life: someone named Anton de' Medici was most likely her biological father.

As she breathed in the crisp humid air, Samantha's mouth twisted as she thought of her mom and dad sitting on her bed, on either side of her, alternately hugging her as she sat with crossed legs, hanging her head.

They had seemed so upbeat about it all!

"We really don't want you to feel bad about this, Sam," Robert had reassured her.

"I don't understand how he could be...? How could...? How could *he* be with mom if she was dating you and then you got married and then you had me?" She looked up into his eyes, squeezing her eyebrows in bewilderment.

"That's true," he said. "We had been dating -- I was at Columbia for grad school and your mom was teaching -- and we *were* very serious.

Actually, we had been talking about marriage for a while. I knew at that point that we would eventually get married but I wasn't in a rush.

"I met Anton at an architectural show and we talked for a while. I mentioned that I grew up in Connecticut and now worked and studied in Manhattan, and he told me a little about his family in Rome and Florence and that he was an investment banker, running his family's banking firm. I suppose I was effusive talking about my girlfriend -- how amazing she was -- and he asked to meet her."

Samantha seethed. Why couldn't he find his own girlfriend?

Her mom got up to fetch an old photo. It was of her parents and Anton sitting on a couch, her mom in the middle looking so young. Anton looked surly with dark hair and, she begrudgingly admitted, a handsome face. He wore a blazer while her dad had a collarless shirt and a smile. Robert looked outdoorsmen-like with sandy brown hair. Samantha saw much more of herself in him than in Anton.

"That's the only picture we have of the three of us," Catherine said, leaning her face against Robert's shoulder as she sat down.

"But just because you were friends, how does that mean…?"

Robert patted Samantha's upper back while reaching his other arm around Catherine. "It was a gradual thing, nothing overnight. Your mom, Anton, and I started spending time together. We went to dinner, and we talked about our families and very personal stuff as well. Eventually, things developed.

"We decided we all wanted to live together. Anton already had a place on the Upper West Side. It was hardly a normal sort of, uh, arrangement. I know it must be hard to understand, but the three of us had a sort of relationship, much like any other relationship between a man and a woman but with three people instead of two."

Catherine looked up meekly and sniffled. "You look a little like him, your eyes especially. We always knew. In the hospital, when you were born, I looked at Robert and he smiled, and we both just knew."

"You've never said anything about it… to anyone?" Samantha asked, her voice straining. "How can you be sure? You didn't do any tests, did you?"

"There wasn't any reason to, Sam," said Robert. "We both wanted you so much. We were married; legally you were ours. No questions asked. And, more importantly, Anton agreed that we should be your parents. We called him from the hospital when you were born and told him what we suspected. When you were about two we found out your blood type, which confirmed what we already knew."

Catherine smiled tremulously. "We talked to each other about it all the time … when we were alone. We smiled about it all the time. My mom bought you some shape puzzles made for three year olds, and you could do them when you were only ten months old. My mom laughed when Robert told her that you couldn't possibly take after my side of the family." Catherine rubbed her eyes. "We were so happy, Sam. You were our perfect baby; we were so happy to have you. I'm sorry if we messed up by not telling you sooner. I think we were scared that if we told you when you were young you wouldn't be able to believe that it doesn't affect things … that it would make you feel you were less *ours* than your sisters."

Samantha looked across the yard to her grandparents' rectangular pool, which she and her sisters had always considered their own as long as they found an adult to watch them. When they were young, they staged cutthroat naval battles with rafts and beach balls. Their dad served as referee, settling disputes and tending to hurt elbows. Back then, Robert was pure in her mind.

"I wasn't disappointed when I realized your relation to Anton," Robert had told her during one of their long conversations. "I love you the way you are and would never change anything about you, Sam."

Catherine looked at Robert as though she'd heard him say this a hundred times before.

"If I said that I'd prefer you were mine genetically speaking, then I'd be saying that I want you to be a different person, which I certainly do not want."

"But why? He wasn't supposed to be with mom. You were!"

Robert looked pained as he scratched the bridge of his nose.

Samantha wasn't going to let him sidestep the bombshells. "You're not explaining it. I don't understand what you mean. A relationship with three people?"

"I was the one who introduced your mom to Anton, and I liked being around both of them."

Samantha gave him an exasperated look. She watched him as he seemed to contemplate his next words. "It doesn't make sense. Why would you like that?"

"It's not that I wasn't sure about my relationship with your mom. It's just something we experimented with before settling down and having a family *like normal people*." He grinned slightly at his attempt at levity. "Maybe it was crazy, but I felt like I'd be lying to Catherine if I didn't tell her that Anton had a, uh, physical interest in her that actually appealed to me in a very hard-to-explain way. Things evolved, as Anton and I definitely encouraged them to. Your mom was very … impressionable. At first, she was wary of going along with what we asked, but -- "

"But I was so totally and completely in love with you, I couldn't say no to you," Catherine interrupted with a strange grin.

Robert smiled. "She was willing to follow me into a very strange situation. It sounds so odd when trying to explain it to you, Samantha."

Catherine's eyes clung to Robert's. "You told me you wanted to get married but that first you wanted to know what it would be like to be with me around Anton." Turning to Samantha, she continued with wavering voice, "He just wanted to see what it would be like for both of them to be with me…at the same time…but only temporarily…as an experiment. After a while, I felt so much for them both. I felt like I had this…special attachment to them both."

Samantha felt a tear formed at the edge of her eye.

Robert studied her face. "I wish we didn't have to talk about anything that you'd rather not hear about, but I can't let you believe that your mom cheated on me, or that we broke up, or that we weren't sure about each other and took some time off. It was an extreme, youthful thing, but it was also just people spending time together because they enjoyed each other's company."

"But what about me? What about having me?"

"I didn't plan to get pregnant--"

"Women sometimes become pregnant unexpectedly; it's not necessarily a bad thing," Robert broke in. "We were so excited to be having you, from the moment we found out. We'd always planned for the thing with Anton to be short term. The pregnancy just brought it to a sudden end. We always knew we'd get married. When Catherine got pregnant, it was the natural progression of things. I was thrilled that I was going to be your father, and finding out about Anton's connection to you didn't change this one bit. Only a hypocrite would think that way.

"We rushed to plan the wedding and found an apartment in Connecticut, and although we knew that he could be your biological parent, it never worried either of us. And from what he said, it didn't worry him either. When you finally arrived, we realized you were probably going to be much better at math than we were." He smiled, and then said with sincerity, "Samantha, I feel so lucky to be your dad. I admit, I sometimes feel sorry for Anton in that regard. He's missed out on so much."

Samantha had always been a little concerned about the differences in appearance between herself and her three blonde sisters, but not enough to be troubled by it. Yes, she had seen pictures of her dad when he was a young boy with platinum blonde hair and had noticed her brown hair was a few shades darker than his as an adult, but she had assumed that he was the carrier of some genes for darker hair and she was the only one who got them. She had been aided in her beliefs by the glaring fact that no one had ever suspected that Robert wasn't her biological father, not any of her four grandparents or any stranger.

It was easy to assume that she was somehow always a little tan. She was clearly not adopted; she'd inherited her mother's facial features. She simply didn't look distinct enough from her father or siblings to cause any alarm, especially since there was no reason for anyone to suspect that someone other than Catherine's husband was Samantha's biological father. According to Darcy's community-wide estimation, Robert and Catherine were a respectable couple. They didn't drink too much or fool around, and they had four well-mannered daughters.

Samantha thought of her dad's plea for leniency toward her mother. But she couldn't help but blame her, regardless of whether she had been encouraged to become involved with Anton. If her mom had refused to take part, then it never would have happened. Moreover, she shouldn't have gotten pregnant. "Even if it meant I would never have been born," Samantha sobbed to herself.

And as for her dad, how could he be the great husband Samantha always thought him to be if he wanted to be around both Catherine and another man? Samantha struggled to figure out how there could have been some sort of relationship between all three of them. Although her parents had barely touched on the implicit non-heterosexual aspect, it was an essential piece of the story. The idea that her dad experimented in a relationship involving another man was unbearable.

It simply was not possible to think of her dad that way. He rarely talked about anything other than male/female relationships. He was hands-on and affectionate with her mom. He mentioned ex-girlfriends from high school and college, whom he sometimes ran into at parties, which made her mom jealous. He did not act gay. He never said anything about other men that sounded gay. And Samantha watched prime-time TV. She was certain she knew what gay was. Her father was not that.

Lunch used to be the worst part of her day. Face down in a book, Samantha would pretend not to feel alone while sitting with girls she barely knew from English class. However, since first noticing Delaney, things were looking up. She spent the half hour happily spying on him from across the lunchroom.

He always sat at the same table in the juniors-only section, surrounded by his friends, including Nicolette and some other cheerleaders. Just to see him lean back and stretch his legs, like he had mistakenly taken a seat in the children's section of the cafeteria, was enough. She felt no remorse about her lack of productivity.

Often, Ally, who liked to hop from table to table, would stop by. Pulling up an extra chair, she offered food and gossip.

"Delaney and Nicolette were practically fucking on a couch at that party Saturday night. Everyone saw his hand up her skirt…"

"This girl in my social studies class said he was drunk at this party and she made out with him, but I don't know if I believe her…"

"He and Mairin went to check out his brother's band. They were playing at a bar in Stamford. Mairin spent the night at the band house and everybody started calling her a groupie…"

Despite her distaste for following the crowd, Samantha did just that and became a fan of Darcy's boys' soccer. Staying for the guys' games, she sat in the stands with a couple girls from her team and reveled in the speed of the guys' attack-minded formation. Often, with the score lopsided, Darcy's foes would start fouling Delaney intentionally. He took every type of abuse: kicking, elbowing, tripping, holding, and cursing. Yet he never reacted in kind, just looked at the referee with hands out, palms up, asking for a foul call.

Chapter 5:

One rainy Sunday in November, Samantha sat by herself on the deep couch of her family's lofty great room. Her sisters had gone out with friends. Her parents were in the dining room looking through a week's worth of mail. Staring vacantly at the flashing television screen mounted on the wall in front of here, she thought about Delaney.

She didn't know what to say about him to her parents. There was nothing to tell. She'd never spoken to him. Yet he'd dominated her dreams for weeks. Not that she was imagining herself *with him* in any R-rated way, but with an ache in her stomach, she ran her fingers along her temple and tried to imagine what it might feel like to touch his hair. There seemed no chance of getting to know him better. At school, juniors didn't hang out with freshmen.

Samantha could hear her parents stirring behind her, making tea. She got up to grab a magazine, then propped her legs over the sofa pillows. Her thoughts shifted to her parents' enormous lie. She would never again be able to trust them so completely. The stability she'd relied on was now wobbly. What if they decided they wanted to go back to being swingers?

What if they weren't really as inseparable as they seemed and broke up because of the Anton thing?

She'd been trying to share these thoughts with her dad, her usual confidant. At night, her parents would come into her room to see how she was feeling. Mostly they'd repeat what they already said and reassure her about how much they loved her. The other day, when she'd asked her dad to tell her for the umpteenth time that he really truly didn't hate the fact that she was half Italian, he told her,

"I'm happy you're related to Catherine and that's okay, right? So why can't I be happy about your connection to Anton? There shouldn't be a double standard."

Hearing that he, and her mom, liked the idea of her being related to Anton was not comforting. She would rather have her dad tell her that if it weren't for her existence, he'd be really sorry about the whole thing and wish he'd never gone there. But it was difficult to put what she was thinking into words, and she was afraid of saying something unforgivable to a dad who was hers by volunteer.

Part of her wanted to tell him it was unmanly to want his child to be the offspring of another man. She wanted to holler back at him, tell him that his parents, all of the family, would be devastated if they knew. Some of their more conservative relatives, including Catherine's parents, would probably stop speaking to them. Samantha had put her dad on a pedestal and now it was pulled out from beneath him.

Her eyes were drawn to the TV screen in front of her by an announcer's booming voice, "Her escort at the Cannes premiere was Italian financier Anton de' Medici."

It was a nightly entertainment show and there he was, looking like the photograph, walking next to a young actress, in her twenties at most. He was dating a movie star; his hands touching a woman near her own age. He was invading her living room with a conceited look on his face, his appalling figure moving past the camera like he was above it all, too important to notice paparazzi.

Blood flushed from Samantha's extremities as she whipped her head around to glare accusingly at her parents. They were sitting at the dining table, their eyes fixed on the television as hers had been a second before.

After exchanging odd smirks, they got up and walked over to where she sat. Looking composed, Robert eked out a smile, "How ironic." As he took a seat, his face reversed to a frown.

"We've seen him in gossip columns before," Catherine offered, twitching her lips as she perched on the sofa end near Samantha. "He does date well-known women sometimes. Although he doesn't tend toward more serious, long-term relationships ... I often wish he could find someone special and get married but ..." Her mom shrugged. "Did you recognize him from that photo I showed you?"

Samantha wanted to shred the photo. She already cringed at every thought of him and now this. Now she had to deal with his social activities making the news. The month and a half since she had first heard about him had not passed easily, and now all her feelings came to a head as she thought about the new image seared in her memory. She was stunned with pain.

As her parents said something about his choice of a date and speculated about his lifestyle, her thoughts about Anton began to collide with her thoughts about Delaney. It had never bothered her before, not even a little, but suddenly she was crushed by the fact that Anton had nothing to do with her.

He was apparently interested in other young women. She thought of him, 40ish and dating beautiful people, while she, whose grandparents already had started using the annoying phrase "sweet 16," had no chance of dating Delaney, or anyone else for that matter. She thought of how gorgeous Nicolette and Mairin were and how attractive the actress with Anton was. She felt unwanted as a sharp pain cut her stomach. Both Delaney and Anton were unapproachable and somehow superior to her.

During the second half of the match with Forest High School, Samantha got a yellow card for failing to give an opposing player ten yards for a corner kick. She wanted to argue that she was no closer than the other team's player had been when she took a free kick five minutes earlier, but the coach refused to back her up.

"It wouldn't change anything," he said. "We're shutout 3-0."

Benched for the remainder of the game, her eyes drifted one field over to where the guys were playing. From fifty yards out, Delaney untied the game by scoring directly from a free kick. Bending the ball around defenders and teammates, he sent it into the back of the net. While the Forest fans booed, his face burst into an unabashed smile, but he did not run around in a circle with his arms out-stretched like an airplane, as the other team's scorers had done.

When her dad stopped by her room with a cupcake from an office party, she decided to mention Delaney by name. Even if he grinned at her like when she made him watch a silly chick flick, that would be better than the usual arguing about Anton. She told him about Delaney's exceptional soccer playing, adding a dramatic description of him and his beautiful girlfriends.

"It's so embarrassing. I try to stop thinking about him but I can't. I'm an unattractive freak compared to them."

"Wait a minute. You're no such thing." He sounded like he was on the verge of a lecture. "You have so much to be thankful for. Health, intelligence ... good skin. It's insensitive to claim otherwise.

"You could spend your whole life holding beauty pageants in your head and placing runner up, but what's the point? If looks were all important, gorgeous people would always be in great relationships, but they often aren't."

At school Ally informed her that Delaney's friend Brian had been saying something about a girl from soccer always watching Delaney. "I figured he meant you, but don't worry, there are lots of girls eyeballing him."

When Samantha heard that Delaney wrote an article on the MTV music awards for the school newspaper, she perused it so many times, folding and unfolding the pages, that it tattered to pieces.

She wanted to do something ... anything.

Heading out the door of the girls' locker room to wait for postgame announcements, Samantha noticed Delaney sitting alone at the end of the front row of the bleachers, none of his friends with him.

He was chewing gum, his jaw moving under his skin as his eyes wandered. The bone structure of his face was flattering from every angle. There were specks of blonde hair on his lower cheek, evenly spaced.

Her heart was racing. This was her chance. There were only a few people around. She wasn't a maniac, just a fellow soccer player being friendly. She thought of her middle school friends who'd jumped several steps ahead of her while she was still hiding her face during movie scenes with nudity. She thought of what her dad would say about being intimidated by a boy.

Taking a seat, then turning in his direction, she said the first thing that came to mind, "Your name is *Dell-eh-nee*?"

His eyes were hooded as he glanced her way. "Who wants to know?"

It encouraged her that his words were punctuated by a slight smile, but she was a little surprised by his glibness. "I've seen you play, and I just wanted to know your name."

His legs shifted gracefully as he leaned in her direction, the fabric of his jeans tugging against his thighs. "I think you already know my name."

"Uh." She opened her mouth, aghast. Was he insinuating that she was asking a question under false pretenses? Taxing her brain, she thought of the bit of confusion she'd experienced when Coach Simmons had called him by his last name. "Yeah, but sometimes people call you Delaney and sometimes they call you Troy. I guess Delaney is your first name?"

"Yes," he grinned insolently. "Want an autograph?"

"I ... I was just curious."

Softly, but unabashedly, he said, "I've noticed."

A couple of guys were heading their way, and she pretended she had to get something out of her bag as he turned his attention to them.

It hurt, especially when she was alone in her room listening to the radio that night. He was so flip, must have thought of her as another pathetic girl trying to catch his attention. Sad songs on the radio suddenly had poignancy. She used to change the station when they came on.

At lunch on Monday, Ally had updates,

"Mairin was over our house on Sunday. My mom was out and Suzanne got totally drunk on a bottle of vodka they found. So anyway, I asked Mairin if Delaney was going to the Christmas Formal with Nicolette and she was like, 'Probably.' I told her, 'Why don't you ask him?' and she was like, 'I hate dances; they play crappy music.'"

Samantha nodded, attempting a slight laugh. "I tried to talk to him after the game on Friday, but he clearly didn't want to talk to me."

"Really? What happened?"

"Nothing, actually."

"Well, Mairin said they were fucking for, like, hours on Saturday night."

"Wow," said Samantha, feeling gloomy.

"She has a perfect body. She and Suzanne were trying on a bunch of outfits and talking about picking up guys in the city and stuff. They're gonna try to get into some clubs.

"I told her, 'Why don't you share Delaney with the rest of us? I haven't gotten laid in like months.' And she was like, 'If you see him drunk at a party, that's your chance. Just make sure Nicolette finds out, okay? Anything you can do to piss her off.' And I was like, 'So, he has to be drunk to fuck me?' And she was like, 'No, it's just he doesn't want to make it with anyone younger than like 17 and get hassled by some girl's dad. He's almost 18, you know.'"

"Geez, you had a much more interesting weekend than me," said Samantha.

"Oh yeah, guess what! Mairin has two piercings besides her ears. Suzanne was ratting on her about 'em."

Samantha smiled. "Stop, I don't want to hear about it."

Ally laughed. *"He* likes them."

Chapter 6:

Samantha's geometry teacher called her aside one day and asked if she'd be willing to take the geometry qualifying exam early. It was only December; the exam was usually taken at the end of the school year.

"I'm not sure how, but you already know this material, even if, as you say, you've never been formally taught. You're wasting your time in this class. Let's send you down to Mrs. Kurtzle to get the trigonometry textbook, so you can take a look at it over winter break. I think we're going to move you up to her class for spring semester."

As she made her way down to the basement en route to Mrs. Kurtzle's classroom, she thought about what her sisters were going to say when they heard about this one. Gretchen would be complimentary but Stephanie and Annabelle ...

After completing her errand, she turned a corner and saw Delaney standing with Trevor and Brian as he shuffled through a disorganized locker.

So this is where his locker is.

As she got closer, she overheard him say, "Probably wants her. He let her out of taking the midterm." There was articulateness in his speaking voice that allowed her to pick him out from a crowd. It was assured, regardless of the content.

Brian saw her first. He, looking rugged in work boots, smiled like he recognized her, and called out, "Hey, it's Soccer-girl!" They all laughed, although Delaney's laugh was more of an understated chuckle.

Samantha smiled, walking past them self-consciously. Peeking into his locker, she was pleased to see he didn't have any girlie pictures.

She heard Trevor's voice as she began to scale the stairs at the end of hall. "...always running around the field like she's gotta take a piss."

She paused, thinking she heard the words 'little freshman,' but wasn't sure who said them. She would have given anything to hear Delaney talk about her candidly. If she heard him say something negative, that might lift the spell.

Over the next few days, she overheard more people calling her 'Soccer-girl.' A girl on her team who knew a senior on the boys' team told her, "They think it's funny you run after goal kicks as if they're still in play ... and don't touch the ball with your hands even when it's in touch."

Coach Simmons scheduled another co-ed practice. Samantha was determined to hold her own on the field. She had put everything she could into recent all-girl practices. And during weekend afternoons, she'd been in her backyard dribbling around lawn chairs until her legs ached. Lagging behind while the guys played at a whole other level was unacceptable.

Things started badly with the seniors calling to the cheerleaders who were blaring high-pitched dance music nearby. Their dance was synchronized stomping. "Hey. Hey. Are you ready? ... Okay!" followed by eight counts of voguing. Darcy's cheerleaders weren't the type who competed in competitions or did stunts.

In order to keep Delaney and his ilk from dominating the scrimmage, the coach insisted on five passes before goal shots. Samantha raced around the midfield, keeping herself open and successfully attracting the ball. Delaney was on the opposing team, but for a while he wasn't able to challenge her before she passed to a teammate.

In great position, she received the ball in the penalty area and was about to take a shot at the goal when Delaney, helping the defense, came from behind her and blocked the shot. She hadn't seen him coming and staggered from confusion. Ignoring her loss of balance, he sprinted back towards the other side of the field. All she saw was the number 11 on the back of his un-tucked jersey.

The coach's assistant asked, "You weren't fouled, were you?"

She shook her head, no.

It wasn't long before she was facing Delaney again. He came toward her with his familiar haughty expression, not meeting her eyes. Assuming she couldn't outmaneuver him, she strained her neck, desperate to find someone open to a back pass. Just as his foot closed in on the ball, she wound up and kicked the ball as hard as she could right at him.

He ducked but the ball grazed his cheek. There was no one behind him, no mistaking her action for a failed pass.

What happened next was foggy.

People were yelling and she wasn't sure why. Delaney stumbled a few steps backward, then regained his balance and turned to glare at her, his face saying, 'What the hell is wrong with you?'

She noticed some of the guys laughing while others had angry looks. One said something about her trying to injure their best player.

Her abs curled tight as she realized the coach had blown the whistle and was walking toward her. Senses on full alert, she was concerned that one of Delaney's teammates might kick a ball at *her* head, and with a lot more force.

Delaney himself looked quite calm now, his face displaying only incredulity.

When Coach Simmons arrived, he questioned, "What's going on here? Montclare? Troy?" The other kids gathered round, talking loudly amongst themselves.

"I have no idea," said Delaney dryly. "I was going for the ball and she tries to knock my head off."

"No, I didn't mean to -- "

"Is there a problem here?" the coach asked, looking back and forth between the two of them. "Because if there is, I won't have a problem separating you two."

"No," said Delaney firmly.

"No, I -- " said Samantha, flustered.

"You're not supposed to kick the ball at the other team, Montclare. Maybe you should try for the net."

"Okay. I'm sorry." She glanced at Delaney as she said 'sorry.'

"Yeah, whatever." His friends laughed at the twang in his voice.

As her heart rate returned to normal, the coach called to restart the game and she turned to hide her face for a moment of privacy.

At the end of the next day, she lugged her backpack down to the basement and found him by himself, on his knees, reaching to the back of his locker.

Walking up to the opened locker door, and not waiting for him to look up, she said, "Hi."

The night before she hadn't been able to stop thinking about what had happened. The image of his sweaty hairline, simmering eyes, and momentary scowl were hard to wipe from her mind. The way he handled the situation made her want him more. But she'd been totally in the wrong.

He leaned back on the balls of his feet and looked at her, his unkempt blonde eyebrows slanted in a frown. No less than she expected.

"I just wanted to tell you that I'm sorry about losing my temper yesterday at soccer practice. I really didn't mean to hurt you or anything. I...I just get really frustrated. Our team has lost every game, you know. And you keep stealing the ball from me. But still, I shouldn't have aimed for your head. I'm sorry."

As he listened to her speech, his mouth bent into a wry grin. "Forget about it. It's no big deal. I don't mind if you try to hit me, as long as I can do the same."

"Oh. Well, I shouldn't have … and I won't do it again."

He seemed to find her earnestness amusing. "No, it could be fun. See if you can knock me down."

"No, I shouldn't have done it."

"But I give you permission."

"No," she said, shaking her head with a hint of a smile.

"Coach doesn't care. Believe me; he has more important things to worry about." He grinned. "Take your best shot."

She lost hold of all appearance of seriousness. "No, I'm not going to do it again. I'm sorry," she insisted with a big, shaky smile.

"So, I can't retaliate?"

"Um, you don't have to."

The final bell rang. "Yeah, you guys really do suck. Maybe you should go out for badminton or something. Your team is hopeless."

"No," she insisted. "I want to play a real sport, not something lame … like cheerleading."

With a squint, he nodded his head. "Yeah, okay, whatever. See ya around."

Nicolette and her cheerleader friend Brynn were primping in front of the full-length mirrors of the girls locker room. Twisting to check out her backside, Nicolette had on a bra that looked like the upper half had been cut away and a thong that disappeared into the crevice of her butt.

Eavesdropping, Samantha tried to dress while hiding under her long soccer jersey. They were talking about an acquaintance of theirs.

"She looked so fat. What was she thinking? She, like, totally couldn't pull it off," said Brynn, adjusting the black ribbon that held up her underwear.

Brynn was one of Delaney's crowd from lunch. A self-proclaimed size zero, she was admired by girls at school who believed in anorexia. Yet, she seemed flat-chested next to Nicolette. As would anyone, thought Samantha. Brynn was often seen with Trevor in the halls, leaning against his shoulder, saying stuff like, "I'm so tired. Hold me up."

Nicolette pulled a lotion bottle from her shiny pink bag with 'Dior' imprinted on the side. "And she was trying to tell me her knock-off Louis Vuitton was real, as if I couldn't tell."

Brynn motioned towards Samantha while pulling a mass of straightened hair into a ponytail. "What's that girl's name? The one over there." She wasn't bothering to lower her voice. "Trevor calls her Soccer-girl, and she's always giving Del weird looks."

Samantha felt a surge of adrenaline. She was only ten feet away, sitting in front of her locker.

"She's some kind of jock/nerd combo," Nicolette scoffed. "Wearing sports bras under her Nike t-shirts and carrying around five textbooks. Someone told me she was trying to chat up Del at his locker the other day."

"I dare you to say something to her," whispered Brynn.

Out of the corner of her eye, Samantha spotted Nicolette taking a step toward her.

"You're friends with Mairin's friend Ally, right?" she asked, with a voice that echoed off the cinderblock walls. "They call you Soccer-girl."

Samantha squeezed the edge of the bench beneath her, not sure if she should pretend not to know she was being spoken to.

"I should warn you that you don't have a chance with Delaney," began Nicolette, still undressed as she bent forward to rub lotion on her knee.

Samantha looked up.

"He only fucks Mairin because she's so available. And he wouldn't let you suck his dick."

Samantha stared with slack jaw.

"We know you have the hots for him," Nicolette announced. "It's laughable." Her mouth stretched wide on the word 'laughable.'

Barely able to raise her eyes to Nicolette, Samantha said with an unintended whine, "You're not a nice person."

Nicolette and Brynn broke into scornful laughter. "Oh no, I was hoping we'd be friends."

Samantha hung her head, knowing her comment was childish. The rest of the girls in the locker room were now looking at her. She was stuck on the image Nicolette had thrust upon her brain. So he does stuff like that with girls he likes only marginally? If you meet a minimum standard, which she didn't rise to, you're granted the privilege of degrading yourself. With a deep breath, she looked up, wanting to fight back.

"Nobody needs you to *lead* them in cheering. They can cheer without any help. If you like soccer, join the team. Girls don't have to just sit on the sidelines rooting for the boys."

Nicolette's smile faded into a sneer. "Don't take it out on us that you couldn't even make the color squad. I'm sorry you're an ugly loser who nobody talks to, but it's just the way it is. All the guys I know are creeped out by you."

The words were too hurtful. Samantha couldn't go on. She stood up and wobbled away, taking refuge in a handicap bathroom stall. Grabbing some scratchy toilet paper, she rubbed at the tears pouring down her cheeks and thought about pulling the cord labeled, "Pull for Assistance."

She'd never cried at school before.

Chapter 7:

Samantha managed to survive the final week of the fall semester of her freshman year without another altercation, save for an argument on the bus with Stephanie over whether she'd become moody since starting high school.

The day after Christmas, Samantha, her sisters, and her dad went outside to attempt to sled on the back lawn spotted with snow.

"Oh yeah," Robert said, as he positioned Gretchen on her new plastic toboggan. "I wanted to remind you. That old friend of your mom's and mine is coming to visit after dinner. I want you all to be polite even if he's not up on the latest songs."

"Are we going to play charades?" asked Annabelle, who was doing jazz jumping jacks.

"Probably not. We'll just sit around talking."

Samantha kicked at an icy clump of snow.

When she had first found out that her parents had called Anton to tell him about seeing him on TV, she was furious. When they had tried to get her to speak to him on the phone, she yelled, hoping to be heard on the other end,

"Why would you have anything to do with him?"

After that, her parents relentlessly pleaded his case. "He's feeling guilty for having made such a bad first impression," Robert told her. "You need to meet him, if only to convince yourself he's not a sociopath."

"He apologized, Sam," insisted her mom. "He said he never wanted you to see him like that ... or, uh, think of him as ...."

"He's always been respectful of Catherine and me as your parents," said Robert. "Blood ties are important in his family, but he's never done anything to interfere in my relationship with you. He always refers to me as your dad. We wouldn't allow him to visit otherwise."

Following her dad into the kitchen, Samantha found her mom looking agitated as she poured olive oil into a sauté pan, splashing it onto the countertop. "Can you set the table, Rob? Oh, Sam, give me a hug. I'm so ..." She smiled nervously. "How are *you*?"

Samantha shrugged and wrapped her arms around her mom. It felt different hugging her now that they were the same height. Catherine's fruity perfume triggered memories of parties when she was a little girl and had been allowed to stay up past ten. Her mom would place trays of hor d'oeuvres in front of guests, and her dad would walk around asking people about their kids.

Samantha's sisters were out of earshot, so Catherine spoke openly to Robert. "Do I look okay? What is he going to think of me?"

Samantha had heard her mom begging for compliments before, but never in an allusion to Anton.

Robert smiled and shook his head. "I think you look great. And don't forget he's older too." Playfully patting her back, he added with an odd smirk, "Besides, it only matters what I think, right?"

Her parents smiled at each other as if they were doing a love-at-first-sight movie scene. They'd been having cutesy exchanges for several days now.

Last night, they had gone to bed with Robert teasing Catherine about a silly comment she'd made in front of his boss.

"I was nervous. I can't think straight when I'm nervous," her mom had said.

The president of Robert's architectural firm had cordially mentioned, "You can see three states from up here," as his ten guests looked out from the cupola tower of a newly built estate.

"Including Connecticut?" Catherine asked.

Stroking his chin and looking like he wasn't sure what to say, Robert's boss replied, "Of course, my dear. We're *in* Connecticut."

As Catherine knocked over a pile of dirty cookware stacked in the sink, Samantha scrutinized her mom's innocent face and slim-yet-grown-up proportions. She was wearing flat-front slacks and a chiffon top in muted pink. She didn't look like a person one would associate with threesomes.

When Samantha was younger, she used to crawl into bed with her parents when she was frightened there were bad people lurking outside her window. It was so warm in their bed and her mom was so relaxed, not at all fidgety as usual.

Samantha had imagined that when they were alone together her mom was really clingy and her dad smiled a lot and said sweet things to her. They held each other and kissed in front of her and her sisters. She figured that they did pretty much the same thing behind closed doors.

Now Samantha wondered if she'd gotten things wrong. There was probably a lot she didn't see or understand.

Anton arrived at 8 pm in a town car with a driver. Robert went to get the door and Samantha tried to look uninterested as she stood with her genuinely indifferent sisters. Annabelle and Stephanie were already asking how long they had to stay downstairs despite the novelty of a chauffeured car in the driveway. Catherine held back behind them all and looked like she was trying to blend in with the furniture.

Anton was dressed in a three-piece suit with a tightly bound tie. There were symmetrical shadows on his razor-scraped cheeks and his thick hair looked freshly trimmed and brushed. What a fop! He looked like he was coming directly from the opera, although Samantha was grateful that he carried himself like the opposite of a flamboyant stage performer.

His behavior was formal like his attire. He shook her dad's hand, then greeted Catherine with a slight nod. In response, she demurely raised the corners of her mouth. As Robert introduced Samantha, sharp ebony eyes flashed at her. She focused her own brown eyes on the carpet. Anton offered her and her sisters each the same calm and aloof greeting, "Hello, I am glad to meet you."

Samantha noticed he had the slightest accent and was not smiling as he asked after everyone's health like a gentlemen caller in a Regency novel. She frowned, savoring her dislike of him. He had none of her dad's easy likeability, and yet he could never be mistaken for someone shy like her mom or Gretchen. She would never have survived with him as a father. She should be thanking her lucky stars, not complaining about his visit.

She looked to her sisters to confirm her opinion. Annabelle and Stephanie were nudging each other, starting to show signs of mirth; they had no idea what this stuck-up man was doing at their house.

Her dad was the only one who seemed capable of normal social behavior and politely offered drinks. Her mom looked pale and abruptly turned toward the sitting area as Annabelle pranced after her. Gretchen, who was always wary of visitors, sat next to Samantha. Stephanie joined them after an elegant twirl.

Anton took a seat across from Samantha. Leaning back, he stretched his leg under the edge of the glass and steel cocktail table. It occurred to her that he probably thought of himself as an impressive man. As he listened to Robert inquire about his family's health -- "How's your father doing?" -- Anton's manicured index finger briefly touched the ridge of his streaked black eyebrow. His replies were minimal. His thoughts seemed elsewhere. Then Annabelle interjected,

"So, how's the weather in old *Paris*?" She pronounced the word 'Paris' with a Hollywood French accent.

Anton gave Annabelle a perplexed look, his eyes coming alive. "I have not stayed in Paris recently, but I assume there is a weather forecast online."

He spoke to Annabelle like she was a miniature adult, which Samantha knew her sister would love. But before Annabelle had a chance to enter into an attempt at witty repartee, their dad interrupted,

"Mr. de' Medici is Italian, not French. You know that, Annabelle."

"Oops, my mistake. So sorry. Pardon me," she replied with fussy politeness.

Stephanie joined in. "We had such a delightful trip to Firenze last spring. We lunched at the most charming café."

Anton grinned faintly as he scrutinized Samantha's sparkling 13-year-old sister, but Robert was not smiling, "You've never been to Florence and shouldn't pretend that you have."

"We've been to the Italian village at Disneyworld. And that's just about the same thing, right, Mr. Anton?" Annabelle offered.

To this, Robert gave his stern look that meant, "You'd better cut it out." Samantha first became familiar with this look when she was three and liked to kick her toys against the walls.

Robert, who was sitting on an ottoman, glanced behind him at Catherine who was nestled on the matching armchair with her legs in a fetal position. He reached back and ran his fingertips along her wrist. Anton sat completely still as his gaze wandered: first it touched on her mom and dad looking at each other, then it examined the layout of the house, which Robert had designed. His parents had given the plot as a wedding gift and construction started after Robert put together a blueprint from previous sketches.

"Your daughters are interested in visiting Italy?" Anton asked as his eyes paused on Robert and Catherine.

"I think they'd like to see the Renaissance art," replied Robert.

"Stephanie has a poster of Botticelli's Birth of Venus on her bedroom wall," Annabelle said excitedly. "She's naked. Not Stephanie, Venus," she added, with comic timing.

Stephanie retaliated. "Annabelle runs around the house without any clothes on every time she gets back from swimming class. She's a part-time nudist."

Samantha felt herself blush, but she noted that Anton looked un-rattled, maybe even slightly amused.

"Thanks for sharing," Robert said sharply. "But divulging private information isn't a competitive sport." In a more friendly tone, he addressed Anton, "Speaking of sports, Samantha and Annabelle are serious athletes. Samantha plays on her high school's soccer team and Annabelle dances jazz, ballet and hip hop."

"Gretchen and I are lazy bums," added Stephanie.

"No, actually, all four of the girls dance, although Annabelle is the only one taking classes currently. Gretchen likes painting and is interested in international affairs. And Stephanie -- " Robert paused and looked at Stephanie who was tossing her hair with a flicker of merriment in her eyes.

"Stephanie is brash and bold and a world-class showoff, but we put up with her."

Stephanie feigned surprise, then conspicuously rolled her eyes.

Anton looked taken aback at Robert's partiality, and Samantha saw him studying her dad. Her mom, who was grinning at Robert, captured Anton's gaze for a moment, but he quickly looked away.

"Samantha's so gifted at math, they're having trouble finding a class that challenges her," continued Robert affably. "Next year, as a sophomore, she'll be taking calculus."

Samantha did not want to be the topic of conversation and started throwing darts with her eyes.

Robert ignored this. "Samantha, tell Mr. de' Medici about the soccer teams at your school. It's really shocking how they treat the boys and girls so differently."

Samantha gave him a look that screamed but only mumbled, "No thanks."

Her dad began for her, "The boys' team gets all the attention. The pep rallies are just for them. They play their home games in a brand new stadium. The cheerleaders only perform routines at their games. It would probably be better if they got a separate coach for the girls' team, maybe a woman."

Stephanie, grinning ear-to-ear, added, "Samantha is in love with a soccer player with long blonde hair, but he only dates cheerleaders."

Samantha wanted to reach over and knock the grin off her face. She hadn't realized her sisters knew anything about Delaney.

"Stephanie, again, that's a bit personal, don't you think? Not to mention, 'love' is a very strong word," said Robert with a frown.

Looking at Stephanie, Anton seemed to want to say something. There was a pause. "I assume your parents want you to marry successful men who do more than play soccer."

Samantha's sisters laughed without restraint at the absurdity of a guest giving them marriage advice, but Samantha only frowned, even as she noticed her dad trying to restrain a smile.

"I don't think there are enough investment bankers to go around," Robert replied.

Samantha cringed, shifting in her seat. Maybe it would be better if her dad didn't do all the talking. Why had her mom and Anton said nothing to each other?

"But you must want them to marry well-educated men of some means," said Anton.

Robert glanced at Catherine, clearly trying to get her to smile or say something.

"I want to marry a rock star," Annabelle shouted as she stood up and started to demonstrate her own musical abilities by rapping the lyrics to an upbeat pop song about a breakup.

Anton looked openly amused as Robert got up to grab Annabelle and whisper something in her ear.

After things calmed down, Anton said nonchalantly, "At the very least, they should avoid men who are looking to move up in the world."

"So they should marry rich but avoid men who want to do likewise," Robert retorted.

"Yes."

Samantha felt incensed. How dare he come to their house, for the first time, and presume to tell them what to do with their lives. She suddenly recalled an offhand story her parents had told her about a wedding in

Anton's family between his twenty-year-old female cousin and a rising executive in the family company. The two must have been set up.

"What about you?" Catherine began with a shaky voice. "Are you making sure not to spend a lot of time with women who like your money?"

Samantha looked at her mom with admiration, but then she noticed her dad looked concerned.

"I don't think our children have cause to worry about being pursued by gold diggers," Robert said as he squeezed Catherine's hand.

Anton said nothing.

Catherine, looking at her lap, flicked her eyes at Anton and said, "But, what about ...my ... question?"

Anton looked at her with detachment. "Excuse me. I assumed your question was merely rhetorical." His voice was steely. He didn't even look at her directly, just a nod in her direction.

He's mean to her. This was not something Samantha had expected. Yes, her mom had said something about him rarely answering her calls or letters over the years. She'd said that he thought she was too emotional. When on occasion he did call, he spoke primarily to Robert and only briefly thanked her for pictures of the girls which she'd sent overseas. But it was worse than that. He was out-and-out cold towards her mom.

Samantha began to see things from her mom's point of view. He was thousands of miles away, perhaps cozying up with some other woman, while her mom went through 18 hours of labor to have a baby they'd conceived while fooling around in an illicit relationship, which he'd certainly never want anyone in his highfalutin family to know about. And now he was mean to her.

With the help of a little bribery involving extra computer time, Robert convinced Samantha's sisters to head upstairs and look up Florence on

Google Earth. Samantha didn't move. There was no way her curiosity would allow her.

Robert said something about getting dessert and they all moved to the dining table. Catherine sat at one end and Anton sat at the other. Robert, after refilling wine glasses, pulled out a chair for Samantha and then sat down across from her.

They were quiet with only the sound of glasses touching the table. Then Anton looked at her mom for a moment and abruptly offered, "To answer your question, men should be financially self-sufficient; the same is not required of women." He then looked upstairs to the open hallway lined with bedrooms where the younger girls had retreated.

"That kind of chauvinism isn't very popular here," Robert said with a dry smile. "Samantha is an excellent student; she plans to go to Yale and be quite self-sufficient." Turning to Samantha he added, "Anton went to Christ Church College as an undergraduate."

"She's also a very kind person," Catherine urged.

Samantha looked at her parents wondering how they'd suddenly transformed into a couple of raving lunatics. They were never so tacky in front of company. They never bragged about her and her sisters, or talked about them like they were the center of the universe.

Samantha noticed Anton was looking at her. She could only imagine what the expression on her face looked like as she glared at her parents. "*Please* don't talk about me."

"You're being so chatty yourself; you need to let us get a word in," said Robert.

Catherine closed her eyes and said in a soft, mournful voice, "Things haven't been easy for Sam recently."

Samantha felt her heart thumping.

"I'm sorry, Sam. I shouldn't say anything."

Samantha nodded. Did her mom actually intend to start one of their nightly chats about her troubles?

Catherine abruptly stood up, her chair screeching against the floor. Then she sat back down and was still for a moment. "I can't do this. I can't just sit here and pretend like there's nothing to talk about." She glanced at Anton. "I know Samantha doesn't want me to talk about anything, and *you* definitely don't want me to talk about anything, but I can't. I can't do it."

Although she was not talking to him, Robert answered gently, "What do you want to talk about, Cat?"

She took a quick look at Robert and then Anton. "I can't sit around and pretend like nothing happened. Maybe the two of you can act like you never cared about each other, but I can't."

Anton looked stern and displeased.

Sounding alarmingly emotional, Catherine continued, "Things at school are so hard for Sam right now. I keep thinking of how miserable I was in high school. She's had trouble with her friends. And, there's this soccer player. Words cannot describe him. She feels so unpopular. You two, of all people, should help her!"

Samantha closed her eyes and bit her lip. She thought of running to her room, then she stopped herself. She had known all along that this was going to happen. Of course her mom was going to start freaking out. And the fact that Anton was acting like a stranger who had come to sell life insurance just made her twice as overwrought as anticipated.

"You shouldn't put pressure on her to be more popular than you in school," Robert said emphatically, yet with a tender look. "And she can be interested in whomever she chooses."

"It's true. She's much stronger than I ever was. Even now, I'm too weak to deal with all of this." She swung her arms open at the two men and then hung her head. "But she's tough ... and she's so smart."

"Cat, we shouldn't make a big deal about this. Not *now* anyway."

"Robert, I don't understand ... How do you just act as if there's nothing to be said? Like there's nothing to talk about?"

"I'm willing to talk about whatever anyone wants to talk about," he replied. "As long as Samantha's okay with it."

Feeling like an outside observer, not a real participant, Samantha shrugged at her dad, unwilling to speak.

Catherine looked despondent. Samantha felt charitable and smiled at her which seemed to immediately lighten her mood, "I'm sorry, Sam, but I just don't understand why they --" Looking at Robert she asked, "Why is it you have to protect him from me?"

"He can take care of himself," replied Robert. "Say whatever you like to him."

From her peripheral vision, Samantha saw that Anton looked fascinated by her parents' exchange. No annoyance showed on his face.

Exhausted looking, Catherine's eyes touched on Anton, then lowered to the table, "I would like to know that you would have been there for Samantha if she had needed you."

Anton immediately answered, "What is the point in talking about the hypothetical?"

Catherine looked braver as her eyes stayed on Anton's face. "I'd like to know that ... if something had happened ... you would help with Samantha ... if she needed you."

"Does she need something? A boyfriend? I'm not sure what you want me to do."

Samantha felt a sting. "I don't need anything from you, thanks."

"Maybe we should go back to discussing the girls' soccer team," said Robert sarcastically, with a pained look on his face. "Samantha is actually doing quite well, despite her parents' sometimes bizarre behavior."

There was a long pause. It seemed like a random thought, but Samantha found herself surmising that Anton and her parents used to have these three-way conversations often.

With the slightest grin, Robert's gaze focused on Anton, "I'm sure Samantha appreciates your offer to help her acquire a boyfriend, but I don't think she necessarily has the same tastes as her mom."

Wide-eyed, Samantha studied her dad's posture. His shoulders square, he leaned back in his chair with some haughtiness of his own.

"I will keep that in mind," Anton replied in a low voice.

Hearing a sniffle, Samantha turned to see her mom was crying.

"I know you never really cared much about me." Catherine raised her hand to her mouth, looking at Anton, but not sounding as self-pitying as her words. "I know that now, but at the very least, I wish you would say something about being there for Samantha."

Anton finally looked unsettled. "No, what you want to hear is that I would have stepped in if Robert had not followed through on his commitment to you, so as to afford you the prospect of choosing between us."

"Talk about hypothetical. You know that's ludicrous," said Robert. "She is not, and never has been, on any sort of ego trip. She was sincerely broken about never seeing you."

"No, Anton, I knew you would not allow yourself to be stuck with me. I felt lucky that somehow Robert thought he'd be happy with me."

"Maybe you should concentrate on making him happy instead of worrying about what would happen if he was not around," Anton replied.

Samantha looked on, astounded by the anger behind his words, all directed at her fragile mother.

"She does make me very happy," said Robert, "and I feel incredibly fortunate to be with her. And one of the reasons I love her is that she's not the kind of person to just forget about people who've played a part in her life, no matter how unreceptive they may be."

Anton shook his head and, with his most earnest voice of the evening, said, "I do not mean to suggest that I do not want a connection with your family, Robert. I have always appreciated the photographs and messages. And it was not my intention to insult your wife. But I do not see the point in dredging up the past."

Catherine's eyes had turned red, contrasting sharply with her otherwise pastel coloring. "I just wish Samantha didn't have to deal with all this mess. It must feel like some sort of rejection to her."

"Rejection?" Anton snapped. "It was my understanding that you and Robert were going to have a nice little American family and that I could assist you in this by getting out of the way."

Robert answered, "As she said, Catherine is merely wishing for some expression of regard from you."

"Exactly what sort of expression?" Anton asked, looking exasperated.

Robert turned to Catherine.

"I'd like you to be more interested in our kids," said Catherine, sounding impulsive. "All of them," she added.

"I am," Anton said. "I will arrange for them to visit Italy in the summer, if you like. You can all tour the museums with our art historian." His voice became formal again, "I assure you that I wish you and your lovely daughters all the best."

Catherine rallied as Anton got up to leave and smiled in his direction. Samantha could tell she was worried that he would never visit again because of her outbursts.

When Anton reached out his hand to Samantha, she shook it. His fingers felt stiff and hot.

"Hopefully, we will meet again soon."

"Yeah, maybe," said Samantha.

Chapter 8:

Fumbling with a postcard-sized slip of pink paper containing her new class schedule, Samantha came across Delaney walking with Nicolette outside the art department. In profile, his face was an exhibition of unstudied apathy. But she thought she saw a trace of sadness in his eye. If not sadness, at least some kind of ache. Maybe he was injured while skiing over winter break.

He was wearing a maroon T-shirt with grey edging at the neck and dark-blue jeans, which were tighter than the ones she usually saw him wearing but still on the loose-fitting end of the spectrum. Samantha loved the way his clothes didn't cling to his body or accentuate bulges. They suggested his lean shape without outlining it. For all his exquisiteness, he looked like he'd dressed for the first day back in five minutes.

Lying on her side in bed at night, covers forming a tent over her head, she heard his gravelly voice and replayed in her mind every word she'd ever heard him speak, dwelling on the time he'd jokingly asked permission to knock her over with a soccer ball. With a feeling of longing in her lower abdomen, she tried to imagine what it would feel like to have him lying behind her with his long limbs wrapped around her. She thought about whether it would be physically possible to have sex with him in that position, without looking at his face or body, just curled up in his arms. Then she wondered how she could possibly want to have sex with him if she had no idea what sex feels like.

It would probably sting one hundred times worse than using a tampon for the first time. It didn't seem physically workable for a guy's penis to be forced inside the tight muscles between her legs. The moral of her mom's tale of losing her virginity had been that sex hurts a lot the first few times and only gradually gets better.

At lunch, she caught up with Ally over hamburgers. "Did you get any cool gifts for Christmas?"

"I got this furry clock from my sister," replied Ally. She was wearing what looked like a segment of a chain-link fence around her neck. "What about you?"

"I got a nice bracelet from this weird friend of my parents," said Samantha. "I don't really know why he gave me a fancy Christmas gift. He never did before."

"Guess what! Doug and I are gonna borrow his dad's car and go to Coney Island, as soon as the weather's okay. Why don't you ask someone and tag along?"

Raking her fingers along her scalp, Samantha wrinkled her face into a sarcastic grimace. "Who do you suggest I ask?"

"Well, stud muffin had an interesting Christmas. According to Mairin, him and a bunch of his friends went to this lounge in the city, and he was, like, dirty dancing with these Greenwich Village girls."

"In front of Mairin?"

"No, she wasn't there. Just heard about it." Ally dragged a potato wedge through a pool of ketchup. "He's going to the '90s Dance with Nicolette.

Do you want to go with me and some friends? A bunch of us are riding together."

"Sure! I'm in. But how are we going to dance to grunge?"

Sixth period was trigonometry. Samantha arrived early and sat in the front near the door. She didn't recognize any of her classmates, most of whom were juniors, then Delaney walked in with Brian. He did not look in her direction, nor seem to notice her, as he headed to the back row of the half-sized classroom. She hadn't considered the possibility that he'd be on an advanced math track.

Soon after, Nicolette and her cheerleading second-in-command Meghan slid past her, hips swaying with a haughty gait. They were in full game uniform. The breeze of perfume they created reminded Samantha of walking through department stores with her sisters and being the only one who refused to be sprayed with samples. Staring at the thick wired notebook in front of her, Samantha heard a masculine voice behind her,

"Fuck me! ... Soccer-girl ... in *this* class."

She twisted her head and saw a hulking kid she knew from the boys' soccer team who'd run you over if you got in his way. Samantha thought about giving him a dirty look, but then, out of the corner of her eye, she saw Nicolette brandish a boney finger,

"Oh look, Del, it's your little dyke friend. She's a math genius." Her laugh was self-congratulatory, showing more admiration for her own cuteness than the cuteness of what she said.

Delaney glanced at Nicolette for a moment, then returned his attention to Brain who was sitting next to him. He didn't look in Samantha's direction and didn't act like he heard what was said. Whenever she encountered Delaney with his friends during school hours, and they shouted something about Soccer-girl and started laughing, his attention always seemed to be directed elsewhere.

"Soccer-girl doesn't approve of cheerleading," continued Nicolette. "It's too girly for her. She prefers to look like a total zero." As she crossed and uncrossed her bare legs, the heels on her feet dangled by a thread of leather.

Samantha trained her eyes on the blank chalkboard in front of her, glancing down at her zippered sweater, jeans, and sneakers. She considered getting herself transferred back to geometry if she was going to be taunted like this the entire semester. The easy A+ would be fine with her.

Things got better after their teacher, Mrs. Kurtzle, stopped closing her ears to the drone of chatting students and looked up from her notes, calling the class to order.

Samantha did not raise her hand, but she was called on four times, more than anyone else. Each time she immediately gave the correct answer. Presumably, she was being tested to see if she did the catch-up reading she'd been assigned over break. She would have preferred to remain unnoticed, but, regardless, she was not going to pretend not to know things.

She resisted looking at Delaney and thereby calling attention to herself. However, her ears perked up when the class was working silently on a practice problem and Mrs. Kurtzle interrupted,

"Mr. Troy, is that you? Perhaps you'd be willing the share your insights with the class?"

"No thanks."

Samantha hadn't heard his voice in the first place and wondered why his talking in class warranted a comment while his friends flaming her made no impression. She was reminded of the unjust way punishment was meted out at Darcy. Smoking a cigarette in the bathroom, even if you were of legal age, got the same five-day suspension as punching someone.

Five minutes before the end of class, Mrs. Kurtzle wrote on the board,

$$\sin(3x) = 0.5$$

and announced, "This is extra credit for Friday's quiz. Any ideas how to solve it?

The question bounced around the room for a minute, with kids saying things like, "Can you divide the whole thing by three?"

Suddenly, Brian called out, "'Bet Soccer-girl can do it."

Half of Samantha's classmates found this comment amusing. Mrs. Kurtzle again seemed oblivious. Yet after another minute, she looked at Samantha and asked, "Ms. Montclare, do have a suggestion?"

"Um, there are a few ways to solve it, I think." Imagining superimposed graphs, she hoped she was not going to be asked to draw them on the chalkboard, dreading the thought of being scrutinized from behind by Delaney and his friends. "Do you want me to give the answer?"

Mrs. Kurtzle seemed to hesitate. "Uh ... Ok." She peered over to see if Samantha had written anything on the ruled paper in front of her.

"X has an infinite number of ... values. 10, 50, 130, 170, 250 ..."

The bell started ringing, interrupting her, but no one got up from their seat. They were all staring at Mrs. Kurtzle's face. Finally, she spoke, "Yes, well, for Friday you need to be able to show *how* you arrive at those ... answers."

In her bedroom she walked to the bookshelf where she'd placed the Tiffany box Anton sent. It sat next to the shiny Christmas-red ribbon it had been wrapped in. Trying to re-tie the satin strip, she found it slipped out of a bow with the gentlest tug.

The terrifying unknown was no more. Anton was not a demon come to destroy her life. He was human. Seeing him undergo her dad's blunt logic and a dose of her mom's overt emotionality had made him less scary, more flesh and blood. It also helped to see her sisters' self-possession in the face of his imperiousness.

There had been a look between her mom and Anton, during one of the few times their eyes had met, that gave Samantha some pause and kept her awake several nights. But she was happy that her dad hadn't changed into a gay version of himself. *He's not a frustrated New Yorker who ended up in the suburbs raising girls.*

Before Anton's visit, it had seemed so disloyal the way her mom talked about her feelings for him. But maybe she was forced to care for him, regardless of the fact that he's a jerk, because she had sex with him, because she got pregnant. Her dad assisted in her mom's wish to talk about the past and alluded to her relationship, *their* relationship, with Anton. Somehow her parents were strong as a couple, even when dealing with something like this.

Chapter 9:

As Mrs. Kurtzle walked around the room returning graded quizzes, she announced that their Trigonometry class would be participating in a sex education seminar, which would "meet sporadically, every couple of weeks or so." Samantha gaped at the news, not caring how she might look to the senior sitting to her left and blocking her view of Delaney. Sex ed with Delaney and Nicolette? She would rather take an organic chemistry exam daily.

The first day of the seminar was a Friday. A twenty-something history teacher named Mr. Franks came to lead the discussion. He was new to the school but already had a reputation as young and hip. He began by explaining that this would not be regular sex education like they'd experienced before in health class, but more of a discussion group where they'd get a chance to participate.

After writing a slew of textbook terms relating to sex on the chalkboard, he asked with a grin, "Does anyone know a synonym for this word?" He was pointing at 'vagina.' There was a sprinkle of nervous laughs.

"Anyone?" asked Mr. Franks after waiting a minute.

Brian called out, "Yes, but you don't want me to say it."

"Quite the contrary, I want to talk about the popular equivalents for these clinical terms, even if they're considered vulgar."

"Cunt," someone called out, which was followed by open laughter.

"Yes, that's a slang term for vagina that's considered offensive." Mr. Franks began walking around the room. "But what do you think makes the word offensive?

"Is the string of letters C-U-N-T inherently vulgar? Perhaps the word is in bad taste because of the negative intentions behind its use, or the context in which it's used, or maybe it's the people who use it who make it offensive."

Returning to his handiwork on the board, Mr. Franks continued, "Do any of you regularly use the word 'vagina?'" He scanned the room, looking each student in the eye, including Samantha. "I doubt it. It sounds forced. It's used by doctors, or people in sex ed class, or your parents trying to talk to you about sex."

Mr. Franks went on to argue that words are considered offensive not because there's anything inherently wrong with them but because of the way people use them. Often words like 'cunt' or 'fuck' are used in contexts where they're meant to connote something base or smutty, or even abusive. This philosophical discussion led Mr. Franks to conclude that words relating to sex are too often thought of as dirty or degrading. "People should discuss sex in a way that treats it as the vital part of life that it is."

A student asked if this meant they could use the word 'fuck' in class, and Mr. Franks smiled indulgently, "Maybe, if you're willing to start a new trend and use it without antagonism. We could try. However, I warn you that other teachers may not feel the same as I. And I suspect that few of you could manage to use offensive language in a positive way. Does anyone want to give it a try?"

"She has very lovely tits," Brian called out, followed by a glance at Nicolette.

Everyone laughed and Mr. Franks exclaimed,

"That's a perfect example. You laugh because it sounds so odd. But, think about it. Isn't it disturbing that it's difficult to find mature, complimentary language to talk about sex while it's easy to find words for the purpose of insult? Calling someone a synonym for penis is, for some reason, an affront. Why isn't it a compliment?"

Stephanie was manic all weekend. One of the girls in her class had told her that she was thinking about taking things to the next level with her fourteen-year-old boyfriend. Samantha sat on the petal-shaped rug on the floor of Stephanie's room as Steph argued with their mom over whether she should be allowed to date.

"I think you should try to talk her out of sex," said Catherine, wrestling with a fitted sheet for Stephanie's mattress. "I'm sure she doesn't really want to do that. She's not old enough to appreciate it or deal with the consequences."

"Don't worry; I told her not to do it," Stephanie insisted. "So did everybody else. Her dad told her he'll send her to Catholic school if she tries anything, so her mom and dad know she's getting serious." She clearly didn't want Catherine to even think about calling the girls' parents. "Her boyfriend's a real deadhead, anyway ... likes to skateboard into walls."

Catherine tugged the sheet over the fourth corner of the twin-sized bed. "As for you, Steph, going on a date won't make you feel older or more grown up. It would just be something to tell your friends about."

"But I need to know! How old do I have to be to date?" demanded Stephanie, tossing the pillows back onto the bed and then jumping on top of them. "You gotta tell me now…ahead of time…so I'm ready! You'd let Samantha go on a date, wouldn't you? You have to let me when I'm her age or that's discrimination."

"You can hang out with boys, get to know them, without dating," said Catherine as she crawled onto the bed next to her second daughter. Samantha thought of how strongly they resembled each other.

After some screaming from Stephanie, her mom was asked to tell the story of her own dating history. Samantha had heard the story before, but to hear the events described in her mother's fanciful language was fairy-tale charming.

Catherine's earliest memory was of a backyard BBQ at her parents' old house next to the horse farm. Her mom goaded her to say hello to five-year-old Robert Montclare and then scolded her the rest of the afternoon for pulling her sunflower dress up over her face and refusing to utter a word to him. "He's such a polite little boy, he said 'hello,' he said 'please' and 'thank you.' But *you*, where are your manners?"

When they were both eight, after Christmas caroling, his parents invited all the carolers back to their home for iced gingerbread angels and hot cider. When her brother began tugging on her scarf like it was a noose, Robert interrupted, inviting her, and her alone, to play with his model railroad set. He wasn't bossy like other boys, but gently, slowly explained how to put the caboose back on the track when it derailed. She was soothed by him. He gave her a precious feeling of comfort.

Whenever she saw him at elementary school, he'd talk to her, ask her how her dog Millie was doing or if she'd learned any new card games. At his parents' social events, she followed him around. He never treated her like a nuisance, even when the other boys teased him for letting a girl in his room. In high school, during computer lab, they discussed issues like gun control and global warming after finishing their regular assignment. Her fondest memory of high school was watching him smile at her as she rambled on with her wishy-washy opinions. Everybody at school liked him, he was so easy to get along with, and he was in tons of groups like debate club and yearbook.

When they were in 12th grade, he was at her house for a youth mentors meeting, and, during a moment alone with her, he said, "We should go out sometime."

On their date, she tried to say all the right things and not act so painfully shy. He was so unlike her parents who were always finding fault with her. He didn't act like there was something wrong with her, or give her strange looks when she had trouble getting her words out.

Yet, despite a promise to do so, he didn't call for a second date.

After that, she saw him with other girls in the hallway at school and felt sick. They were awkward around each other when their parents corralled them for a picnic at Seaside Park. When he wished her congratulations at their graduation, she heard a distraught inner voice, "Those are the last words he'll ever say to me."

The few times she dated other guys in college, she felt like she was under scrutiny the whole evening, never at ease. Pushy guys who tried to put their hands on her were terrifying. Sometimes she'd see someone with a haircut like his, or she'd read something that sounded like something he'd say, and the memories would rush back. She'd feel the sting of his rejection afresh. When she made it home for holidays, Robert didn't attend their parents' parties anymore. She was waiting for her parents to break the news that he'd gotten engaged to someone poised and sophisticated.

After a quick year of graduate study, she began teaching at a private grammar school in Manhattan. It was a struggle to stand up in front of a room full of people, even children. She was self-conscious in general, but in the classroom she worried about having trouble explaining something or accidentally saying something embarrassingly incorrect. Sometimes, she would start to sweat and turn red.

She split the rent with four hairstylists with whom she had little in common. But she made some friends at work and tried to get out a bit. When there wasn't anything planned, she used errands as an excuse to loiter at places like the local bookstore.

Then one day, on the corner of 79th and Broadway, she passed Robert on the street and they instantly recognized each other. His face burst into the biggest grin imaginable. He said he wanted to know everything she'd been up to. Then, he asked her to meet him for dinner. "On second thought, are you busy? We could take a walk now."

They talked as if there weren't any hurt feelings. He was in graduate school studying architecture and had a project downtown, a 5,000 square foot loft, which he was very excited about. Everything he said was so refreshingly sincere. No pretense. No air of superiority. As she walked up the five flights to her apartment after giving him her phone number, she was giddy with excitement and didn't feel the slightest bit winded as she used her keys to unbolt the three locks on her apartment door.

During their first official grown-up date, over tuna steak and red wine, he broached the subject of their one trip to the movies in high school,

"So, were you mad at me after we went out that one time in high school?"

"No," she whispered. 'Mad' probably wasn't the right word.

"I just thought you were kind of angry with me after that. I didn't really handle it well."

"Oh, you mean -- " She paused. It was hard for her even to say he didn't call her. She had waited for his call for weeks. Her whole family had known he was supposed to call her and didn't. Her parents kept asking her what she had done to offend him. "You mean you said you would call and didn't?"

"I said I would call?" He seemed surprised.

She blushed. "Yes."

"Oh, it's worse than I thought. I forgot exactly what I said."

She waited for him to go on, dying to know *why* he hadn't even considered calling. "It's okay," she said. "I guess I -- " She couldn't finish the sentence.

"I was immature about it, for sure," he jumped in. "I just didn't know what to tell you."

"You didn't have fun?" she asked, feeling silly.

"No," he smiled, "I did. I just had other priorities at the time."

She was confused.

"You know. I really wanted a ... hmm ... experienced girlfriend."

This reason for not wanting to date her had never occurred to her somehow.

"I know our parents were unhappy. They loved to talk about us... together. It was a lot of pressure, didn't you think?" he asked.

"Oh, yes, that's true. And I guess I was pretty shy."

"Of course, but it was my problem. I wanted to try to be more grown up. Anyway, what I really wanted to say is that I'm sorry for avoiding you after that. I'm not so immature anymore, Cat. I swear."

On their third meeting, he held her hand as they walked around The Village, crowded with people celebrating another Yankee's World Series win. When he dropped her off that night, he gave her a feathery kiss.

It was spring and nights were humid. They saw each other two or three times a week. He teased her about being afraid of her ten-year-old students. They talked a lot about the past: his dating history and her lack of one. She wanted to know about every girlfriend, especially the ones from high school, and what he'd done with them.

Everything came out. Her devastation over what had happened between them. Her anxieties about sex. How her parents had said they wouldn't pay her tuition if they found out she wasn't "behaving." But by the end of every date, they'd be laughing.

He'd walk her home late at night and give her this look, accompanied by words like, 'What am I going to do with you?' Then he'd forcibly unfold his arms from around her, and with a very serious look say, "I better go."

One night, he didn't go, dallying at her doorway. So, she offered to introduce him to her cat. He accepted. All her roommates were home and she had to try to make introductions while they looked him over. She wanted to be alone with him, but that meant inviting him to her closet-sized bedroom. She decided simply to start to walk in the direction of her room and see if he followed.

She pointed to a place for him to sit on her bed. There was no room for other seating. She sat down next to him and started babbling nervously about the stuff in her room,

"I don't have a lot of things … just a lot of school books and cat toys. I have a picture of my brother's wedding."

Her cat was hiding and wasn't available for an introduction. With a smile, he kissed her, running the knuckles of his fingers over her cheeks. "Are you sure you want to do this?"

She nodded, closing her eyes.

After that, they spent a lot of time at his place ordering in and lounging in his bigger bed. It was almost a year and a half later that they moved back to Connecticut and had a small wedding in her parents' backyard under a white canopy. That day was probably the first time her parents had ever seemed truly proud of her -- they always adored Robert.

Story-time over, Samantha got up and headed for the basement. While folding two loads of whites, she thought of what a nice story it was when the Anton part was omitted. In her mom's wedding pictures she didn't look pregnant, she looked like a taller version of the flower girls.

Chapter 10:

A week after an uneventful Valentine's Day, Samantha sat by herself on the bus returning from the match with Williams Prep. Leaning against the window, watching cars whizzing by from her high perch, she thought of how she'd discouraged her parents from coming to games, particularly away games. She now wondered if she might benefit from more of a cheering section. Perhaps cheerleaders were actually necessary. She had tried so hard that day, but they lost badly after their starting goalkeeper got a red card for handling the ball outside of the penalty box and interrupting a goal-scoring opportunity.

She heard someone in the back of the bus holler something about "Soccer-girl." It was probably Trevor or Brian. Her finger stroked her clammy cheeks as she strained to hear. All the guys sat in the rear with the cheerleaders. If she turned, she'd be able to catch a glimpse of Nicolette sitting on Delaney's lap. The coaches had long since given up on policing the older kids. She didn't want to attract attention, yet most of the noise from the girls around her had quieted, and she could almost make out voices behind her, so she twisted her neck, and immediately met Delaney's eyes. His face turned from blank to displeased, and he broke eye contact.

She righted herself, wishing she hadn't tried to look. Reaching into her soccer bag, she pulled out some blue bubble gum but before she had a chance to unwrap it, she saw Delaney in the aisle, staggering as the bus lurched over back-road bumps.

Her chest heaved as he stopped at her row and, with a gliding movement, sat down next to her. Wordlessly, he proceeded to slide his butt forward and prop his knees on back of the seat in front of them. She counted five deep breaths, waiting to hear the reason for this extraordinary move.

She heard 'Soccer-girl' come from the back of the bus again. Then, he turned to look at her and made a soft clicking sound with his mouth. There was another pause as he seemed to be trying to get his tongue to form some words. Finally he nodded his head twice and said, "Hi," then with a slight smile, "You guys lost again, huh?"

She nodded. The feeling of being close to him was exhilarating. He smelled like crushed grass and his knees were scraped up with streaky mud stains. She got lost inspecting the milky hair rounding his ear, waiting for him to speak again.

"Maybe you need to recruit some new players or something," he said, his voice trailing off a bit.

She opened her mouth to speak, then closed it again. Finally she got out, "Yeah, maybe."

"Anyway, I just thought I should tell you that -- " He picked at the plastic ribbing around the seat back in front of them. Speaking slowly, his voice extremely hesitant, he continued, "I thought I should tell you that I'm not really interested in you as more than a friend."

Wincing, she managed to nod her head in little jerky motions, the palm of her hand denting the plastic seat beneath her. That was it. It was over. She was never going to stare at him again, no matter how great the temptation.

"I just thought I should tell you that," he said with a forced smile. He got up very slowly, with graceful extension of his long legs, and casually walked to the back of the bus as they now zoomed along smooth highway road.

She prayed she wouldn't hear a burst of laughter from the back of the bus, and wasn't especially shocked when she didn't. It was impossible that she was hung up on a person who was cruel enough to come say something so hurtful as a means of entertaining his friends.

Indistinctly and out of context, she heard, "So, is she coming?" It sounded like Trevor's voice.

She felt reckless. She wanted to stand up at the toll booth exit ahead, bust out of there, and start jogging south with abandon. Otherwise, she'd have to control the rising tide of tears and self-pity. Here she was again, sinking yet another level deeper in Dante's circles of hell. Before that year, she rarely cried. She'd only cry over something serious like when she fell and skinned her knee at a waterfall, causing a scar, or when her cat Socrates died two years ago. Now she cried once a week, at least, over every little thing as well as a big thing like this. Feeling a crushing heaviness in her chest, her arms enveloped her duffle bag and she buried her face.

There were moments of staggering anguish, like when she thought about how her mom could attract two impressive men at one time while she only inspired the sentiment "get lost!" She was up late that night begging to be transferred to private school. Her dignity was wounded and most likely scarred for life.

But to her own amazement, Samantha held her head up at school the next day. In home room she saw Delaney's name in a headline on the front page of the school paper, but she merely read the article and moved on to the comic section. She dreaded their first time crossing paths -- although not because she worried he would add his voice to the chorus of kids making fun of her. When he walked past her as she waited outside math class, he casually glanced her way, acting as if nothing had happened.

She felt relief. This crush was going to wither away, she assured herself. She would survive. She was going to get over him. She was going to concentrate on making friends, which she needed practice at.

She and Ally had to be able to find something to talk about beside Delaney. She was going to keep her attention on her schoolwork, so she could get into the Ivy League. In math, she would completely focus on her textbook, even if it meant re-reading passages she already understood. At lunch she wouldn't ask Ally so many follow-up questions when talking about *him*. Instead, she'd asked Ally about her new boyfriend's adventures in off-road motor biking.

After school with her parents, she was clearheaded, unlike the previous evening. Hunched over, she sat on the edge of a satin love seat in her parents' bedroom. When she had returned from school without tears, her parents had looked relieved and invited her to come chat in their room.

Catherine lay on the plump four-post bed, rubbing the corners of her eyes. "It's not that you can't feel hurt, Sam. I understand it must seem so unfair."

"Not to be unsympathetic," added her dad, "but I think you should look at things in a way that makes them easier for you. You barely knew each other, so there's not much here for you to get over."

Her mom perked up a bit. "I think it might be possible that he was trying to tell you where things stand, without intending to be mean. He wants to be your friend!"

Samantha looked at her mom's silver vanity with ornate frames displaying group shots of her and her sisters. The familiar romantic décor of her parents' bedroom felt oppressive.

"You're much more than a potential date for some boy, or, uh, young man," said Robert. "How old is he?"

Stephanie peeked in from the doorway with a blinking-eyed grin. "Maybe he only likes blondes, so you didn't have a chance from the start."

"Yeah, maybe he's shallow like you." Samantha smirked, adding glumly, "Actually, you might be right … something like that anyway."

"Who knows? Maybe he's intimidated by your genius IQ."

"I don't have a *genius* IQ."

"Grandpa said so."

Samantha looked at Stephanie with an embarrassed grin, "Maybe Grandpa was talking about you."

"No, I'm the stupid one," said Stephanie as she pranced into the room, tossing her long legs onto the bed and bumping into her mom with a laugh. "Who knows? Maybe Delaney would like me."

"Steph," Robert began softly. "You're one of the most frighteningly quick-witted people I've ever met, and you're barely a teenager. And as for Delaney, there's an unwritten rule about never "liking" someone your sister likes."

Taking a shower, Samantha looked down at herself and noticed more of a curve from her waist to her hips than there used to be, but overall she wasn't impressed. There was nothing sexy about her body, even her pubic hair looked subtle, discreet. Lying on her bed, she couldn't manage the strength to rearrange her bedcovers for a real nap and just plopped on her back. When Plato joined her, she enthusiastically pet his fur. His happy chirping noises almost brought her to tears. She should have listened to Nicolette in the locker room. She was giving sound advice.

Finding an empty journal with water lilies by Monet on the cover, she took pen to paper.

Forgetting About D.T.

Step One: Sisters

Hanging out at the mall, without stopping at the sports store or bookstore, pleased Stephanie and Annabelle to no end and required only minor effort. Back at home, Samantha invited her sisters into her room to listen to downloaded music and talk about rock stars. All agreed how fascinating it was to try to interpret songs that one artist wrote about another.

They did not, however, agree on the merits of cheerleading. Samantha and Stephanie took on the roles of opposing counsels. Stephanie was determined to be voted most popular in high school, once she actually got to high school, and was convinced cheerleading was essential to achieving her goal. Gretchen, who tended to agree with Samantha, found the activity frivolous. Annabelle dug the dancing aspect of cheering.

Despite her aversion, Samantha tried to help Stephanie with the choreography of her original cheer routine. The cheer was in its early stages since her JV tryouts were more than a year and a half away. "I'm glad no one at school knows I have a cheerleader-wannabe for a sister. It would ruin my Soccer-girl reputation."

Step Two: Soccer

On Saturdays, she pulled her hair back, put on some sweats, and got her dad to drive her to the park to join in pick-up games.

"You here by yourself today, hun?" asked one of the men playing.

"No, my dad's over there sitting on a bench."

She scored a goal for Darcy at a home game with her parents in attendance. The opponent's keeper had been making saves all afternoon, but Samantha managed to slip one past her just as a light rain had slicked up the ball.

Step Three: Join clubs

After flipping through the clubs section of last year's yearbook, she decided to join Darcy's Habitat for Humanity Club.

"It's better than my normal completely selfish pastimes," she mumbled to her dad.

"Exactly," he laughed.

Putting down vinyl floors and painting walls and trim was somehow much more fulfilling than she'd expected. There were times when the foreperson wasn't so friendly with the high school students, but she always got restful sleep, uninterrupted by thoughts of Delaney.

Step Four: Indian Dance

She came across an advertisement in the newspaper for an Indian dance class, and a week later, she was standing in a mirrored dance studio with bare feet.

With an emphasis on arms, she used muscles that never came into play at soccer. Her wrists formed a sharp L-shape as she followed her classmates' lead, stomping her feet on the floor, then tapping her heal to the side.

She met a girl her age named Pritty, who was a serious student at a private school near Darcy. Cheerful and confidant, Pritty did not socialize with boys, except for male relatives. "When I'm old enough, my parents will go to India to find a *suitable* husband, then I'll get to meet him."

Chapter 11:

It was a rainy day and the windows overlooking the courtyard fogged up as a crowd of students stood waiting outside the auditorium for a drama club performance of scenes from *Julius Caesar*.

Samantha, positioned next to a tired-looking acquaintance from English, let her mind drift to thoughts of the self-improvements she'd been trying to accomplish. It concerned her that she still caught herself feeling jealous of people who received his attention. At that very moment, he was fifteen feet away from her, standing with Trevor and Brian, and she was straining her ears, wishing she could hear what he was saying. It was like shaking the knob on a locked door. It was senseless, ineffectual, futile.

Her introspection was interrupted by Nicolette's cotton-candy voice. Wearing her blue-and-white cheerleader uniform, the one with the single pleat offside in the front, and an eye-catching pearly gloss on her lips, she was, quite shockingly, speaking with a freshman, and more than that a boy who looked very young for his age. Bouncing in his sneakers and slapping the door jamb behind him, he asked Nicolette to go out with him Friday night.

"You've got to be shitting me," she replied. Her chest puffed out like someone posing for a photograph.

"But you're so hot," pleaded the freshman, with a curled lip exposing only one of his teeth.

"And you're trailer park trash," said Nicolette. Samantha didn't wear perfume but the females nearby apparently did. Her nostrils were irritated by an inundation of unnaturally intense flower aromas.

"You should see my dad's car," he persisted. "He lets me borrow it anytime."

"Does he let you borrow his sweater vests too?"

He swiveled in his corduroys. "Check it out, baby."

Nicolette tossed her head back with a whip of her fragile-looking neck, showing veins and pronounced strips of muscles. "I think I'm gonna hurl."

Delaney was still gabbing with the guys, seemingly oblivious. His butt, which Samantha knew well from having scrutinized him so many times on the playing field, was opposite her.

Nicolette gestured toward a pale freshman girl nearby, "Hey, maybe you should ask *her* out?"

"No way. She's fuckin' gross," the boy replied, looking to Nicolette for approval.

Samantha experienced an echo of the girl's beet red blush, fuming with condemnation. She felt compelled to intervene, like the time in psychology class when two boys started rating the girls in the class on a scale of one to ten, and she told them they were no prizes themselves, thereby drawing the teacher's attention and ending the evaluations. She couldn't just stand by and watch.

With pinching eyes, she looked at Nicolette and said, "You have so much going for you. Why do you feel the need to put other people down?"

Delaney, and the others with whom he was chatting, abruptly turned to look across at her. Samantha knew she was out of line. She knew she was provoking an enemy she couldn't defend against, but she did it anyway.

"What, Soccer-girl? Did you say something? She speaks!"

Samantha's heart was pounding like she was on stage making her debut in the play they were about to see. "I just don't understand why someone like you, who has lots of friends and lots to be happy about, has to be putting people down all the time."

By now, everyone in the crowd of students was mesmerized. Nicolette and Samantha stood opposite one another, offering themselves up for comparison.

Samantha had been studying herself in the mirror that morning while trying to cover up a red blemish with concealer. Perhaps her dad was right and she did have some of her mom's subtle features. Not that this seemed much of a draw to guys at school. Unadorned, she wore no jewelry. Her clothes didn't trace her curves, but rather made her look more square-ish than she was underneath. She wore no makeup to define her lips, although, as Stephanie said, her eyes were naturally defined by extra-long dark lashes. She hadn't put gel in her hair that morning to make it less wispy.

Nicolette was everything in the reverse. Made-up perfection.

"I don't know why you, a completely annoying slob who nobody likes, are always trying to get attention. It's like you think you're important or something!" She was almost hissing. "Why don't you get some makeup or something and then you might be able to get some dork to like you?" She motioned to the freshman boy who looked confused as to why he was no longer holding Nicolette's attention.

Strands of hair fell over her eyes, but Samantha didn't bother to push them back. And she didn't turn away.

"Everybody knows who you like," Nicolette laughed scornfully. "How's that working for ya? He doesn't even look at you, does he? I know he told you to fuck off."

Samantha felt an odd sense of pleasure. He was an asshole. He had told Nicolette about what he said to her on the bus. She was going to get over him. Be free of him. Her voice was crisp, clear, and brazen. "You may be pretty, but you're also *cold-hearted* and *vain* and *cruel*."

Nicolette looked like she wanted to throw a hissy fit. Samantha took the opportunity to walk away. Although she had been explicitly told by her teacher to wait, she left and headed downstairs to the girls bathroom. Skipping down the steps, she heard someone say something about "kicking her ass." It was the first time she ever cut a class.

The days after were a study in avoiding Nicolette. As she walked out of math, she was called an "ugly bitch," but she decided she got off easy as she raced out of sight. It was becoming a pattern for her. Spot Nicolette or another cheerleader, then get outta Dodge. She was not so intrepid as to step into the eye of the storm on a daily basis.

As she slammed three large textbooks onto her desk in Earth Science, the guy next to her barked to his neighbor, "Watch out! Don't mess with Soccer-girl!"

She didn't have any patience with freshman guys using her epithet, even if they all thought they had an invitation after the big fight. "My name is Samantha. Who are you?"

"Albert," he said, his expression friendlier. "I introduced myself the first day of class, and you've ignored me ever since."

"Oh, sorry," she grumbled, trying to locate a flyer on the wall to pretend to be distracted by. She couldn't find one. "Did you finish the problem set?"

"Yep, I actually got it done this time. What about you? Do you ever *not* finish the problem set?"

As class started she was praised by the teacher for her performance on a recent exam. She looked around, realizing her classmates all thought she was a kiss-up. A kiss-up who never bothered to talk to anyone.

The kid next to her was right. She never made an attempt to get to know him or others in her class. Her dad had told her to look for a guy off in the corner by himself with headphones on, someone not as busy as Delaney. But she hadn't taken his advice.

Later that week, when Trevor, looking rushed, almost collided with her in the alcove outside the principal's office, he laughed, "Uh oh, now you're gonna tell me I'm evil."

She smiled begrudgingly. "Maybe you are."

During the final weeks of the school year, Samantha's trigonometry class was again interrupted by the sex education seminar led by Mr. Franks -- who had recently been voted rookie of the year in the newspaper's survey of favorite teachers. After leading the class to the library, he introduced the topic of sexually transmitted diseases, telling the students they would be divided into pairs for a research project.

"Some of you will be asked to present your results to the class, so you'd better take the work seriously."

Pointing to a table built for two in the very front next to the stacks, Mr. Franks said, "Samantha, would you sit here?" As she did, he said, "Thank you."

Brian, wearing camouflage pants and a peace-logo T-shirt, was assigned to the table immediately behind her.

Nicolette, who was standing off to the side with Delaney, was told to sit at a table in the back of the room, almost as far away from Samantha as possible.

Delaney, now standing by himself, waited for his seat assignment. He was perfectly still except for his right hand tapping a notebook against the front of his thigh. Mr. Franks called out, "Mr. Troy, please take a seat next to Ms. Montclare."

Nicolette guffawed, choking on her laughter as she leaned back in her chair. She looked to Delaney for a reaction but he didn't glance her way.

Samantha wondered if perhaps Mr. Franks was partnering them in order to keep Delaney from wisecracking. During their last session, he'd gotten the whole class going by joking with Mr. Franks about whether it's vulgar to ask one's girlfriend "to take it in the ass." Just the idea that he was so comfortable with sex was more titillating than the crassest language.

Looking glum, he trudged over and sat down next to Samantha. As the remainder of the students were paired up, she and Delaney sat quietly.

The silence ate at her until, finally, she said softly, "Don't worry. I didn't want to work with you either."

He ran a fingernail down his cheek. "Really? I'm surprised." Complete and total sarcasm.

Brian leaned forward and interrupted, "Hey, Soccer-girl, *nerdiness* is kind of like an STD, right? It has the same effect."

Samantha, who heard Brian's comment clearly, ignored him. Looking at Delaney, she answered his question, "Yes, I don't think we'd work well as partners." Touching her stomach, she felt the snug fit of her shirt.

"Well, at least we're getting off on the right foot," he replied, no emotion in his voice. By now, Mr. Franks had begun to hand out a list of STDs, mentioning that the etymology of the word venereal could be traced back to Venus, the goddess of love. Delaney looked at the list handed to him. "So, what are we supposed to be doing here?"

Samantha, too distracted to start her work, turned to look at Brian, who was grinning, and asked, "What did you say?"

Delaney likewise turned to Brian. "She doesn't want to be my partner."

Brian laughed. Looking at Samantha, his eyes momentarily darted toward the list in front of him. "So, do you have any of these?" he asked with a wink.

"Actually," replied Samantha, "I'm certain I don't. However, each of you should make sure to look up all the diseases *you* have." As she said this, she glanced at Delaney.

Brian laughed at this, while Delaney looked piqued and exclaimed, "What?"

"We should split up the work," she said. "You look up the STDs you have, and I'll look up the rest."

Delaney looked at Brian, "What the hell is she talking about?"

"I don't know," he laughed. "Maybe she's pissed at me for asking her a stupid question."

Delaney stole a glance at Samantha. "Then why is she acting bitchy to *me*?"

Their voices were low, and the rest of the class was beginning to work and talk amongst themselves, so they didn't draw much attention.

"There are plenty of reasons to be mad at you," said Samantha, overlooking his language. Bitchy didn't feel nearly as bad as bitch.

The piercing blue eyes, which had haunted her for so many months, causing so much frustration, were now inches from her face. She tried to return his gaze with as much indifference as she could muster. Still, her internal barometer was screaming. The faintly irritated expression of his irises was surrounded by clear white. His hairline was speckled with 30 shades of blonde. His lips were so full they wrinkled at the center.

"Like what?" he scoffed, looking incredulous. Brian was talking to his own partner now, making more corny jokes. Delaney's face changed as if he'd had a sudden revelation. "I have nothing to do with your little tiff with Nicolette."

"No?" she exclaimed. "If you had nothing to do with our *tiff*, why did you tell her about what you said to me on the bus that day?"

"I absolutely did not do that. Despite appearances, I didn't say *anything* to her. You can believe me, or not. I don't care."

Straightening her back, she couldn't help herself. "And just because I might have talked to you and asked you a question once or twice, you assumed I wanted to ask you out or something. That's so narcissistic!"

His face showed open amazement, nothing suppressed or cool or understated like normal. "Seriously? You really wanna go there?"

She barely registered his words. "So you did *nothing* … *none* of the Soccer-girl stuff?" She felt weightless as she spoke. "You're completely guilt free."

"Am I supposed to apologize for what I said to you on the team bus? I don't like to leave people hanging, but if I misinterpreted you in some way, I'm sorry." Scooting his chair forward as he reached for his notebook, he added, "Would you mind if we actually did some work?"

"So you regularly have to blow people off like that? It must be such a burden for you."

"Yes, it is, actually," he said flatly.

"I guess I'm lucky. I don't really have that problem so much."

"Is this going somewhere?"

She forced a squinting smile. "You don't have to worry about me anymore. I got the message loud and clear. Sorry to bother you."

"You're not a bother," he said in a monotone. "Let's just work on this stuff." He got up from his seat. "I'll search online."

As class members were called on to make presentations, Samantha was asked to add something to a discussion of herpes. Mr. Franks gave her an encouraging smile as she offered a quote from the Center for Disease Control, barely stumbling on the word genitals. Asked by Mr. Franks about the fact that some people consider herpes a nuisance disease, she answered,

"A woman giving birth vaginally can infect her child causing birth defects or even death."

Delaney was not asked to speak.

After the presentations, Mr. Franks talked about preventing venereal disease, which was basically the abstinence-or-condoms talk. When a librarian showed up with a requested TV monitor, Mr. Franks asked the class to wait quietly while they set up for a video.

Brian was talking to the girl whom he'd been partnered with, and Samantha heard him say in a jovial tone of voice, "The best way to avoid STDs is to keep away from skanky girls."

Samantha turned toward Brian and noticed Delaney had turned also.

"That's hypocritical, considering you two are definitely a couple of skanky guys," Samantha asserted with a confident smirk.

"Huh?" said Delaney.

"You think I'm skanky, Soccer-girl?" asked Brian.

"Yes, much skankier than any girl I know."

"Fuck! That hurts! That really hurts. I guess I've got no chance with Soccer-girl?"

"No, probably not," said Delaney with the oddest thoughtful look.

That Sunday Ally called her house at around 8:30 pm. She had offered to do a little reconnaissance work and had a report.

"Well, I asked Mairin to ask him about you, but to do it really sly. What he said wasn't really bad, actually. Just that he doesn't really know you that well, but that you seem to have a tendency to go postal."

"Postal?"

"Yeah, you know, like a postal worker who flips out over having to do the same tedious job over and over and comes to work and starts shooting up the place."

"Fantastic."

"Really, if you think about it, he didn't really say anything that bad, just that you're high-strung. I could have told you that. You look like you're gonna burst every time you walk past Nicolette." And then with a snicker, Ally added, "And guess what else Mairin told me about him."

Samantha felt okay about the report. She had feared the u-word: ugly.

"She and Suzanne were hanging around watching TV, and we just started talking because I was planning to ask her what he thinks about you and some commercial for condoms came on TV and we all started laughing. Then Mairin told us Delaney -- "

Samantha jerked the phone away from her ear. When she returned the receiver to her face, she heard "Can you believe she told me that?"

"That's unbelievable," said Samantha.

Chapter 12:

Summer for Samantha meant sudden calm after heavily weighted final exams, projects and papers. She'd either go to somebody's pool or lounge on a hammock in the backyard, enjoying the breezes and alternating between throw-away reading and Thomas Hardy, which made her cry. This summer she was looking forward to no Delaney and no Nicolette. But first the family trip to visit Anton in Italy.

He greeted them at Leonardo da Vinci Airport. Walking up to Catherine, Anton kissed her on the cheek and held her until she let him go with a somewhat bewildered look on her face. He shook Robert's hand, then ceremoniously kissed the girls on the cheek one-by-one. Samantha, laden with two carry-on bags, was not bothered by the kiss. He didn't smell like strong cologne, his skin was shaven, only a little rough, and his lips were not wet. Gretchen blushed and swayed; he was not a relative but a virtual stranger.

Anton's palatial home had heavy drapes with millefleur designs, six-foot fireplaces in every room, speckled marble pillars along the staircases and ancient-looking furniture, which Samantha couldn't imagine feeling comfortable in. She and her sisters were shown to a cavernous room next to their parents with a hilltop view of Rome's cityscape. While Samantha unpacked ten days worth of clothes, her sisters created a wind tunnel effect by opening all the floor-to-ceiling windows as well as the iron lattice door that led onto a shallow terrace. They barely had time to determine the mechanics of the shutters pocketed around each window before being called downstairs for pastries and tea. Anton met them in an airy sitting room with a lacquered grand piano.

"You must invite all your friends to stay here," exclaimed Annabelle, excitedly. "Do they ever break anything?"

Without giving him time to respond, Stephanie asked, "How did you meet mom and dad?"

"Yeah. How are you friends with them?" Annabelle added, sitting up taller in her cushioned chair. "They've never even been to Italy. They went to London for their honeymoon."

Anton was quiet, looking like he was mentally preparing answers to their questions.

"It's probably better to start off by thanking Signore de' Medici for inviting us," said Robert.

After many questions, most answered by Robert, it was explained to Samantha's sisters that Anton had met their dad in New York City while looking for someone to design an office building. Not happy with the designs at the Manhattan Architectural Show, Anton had stopped at the NYU booth to question the students about their study of classical architecture and immediately alienated most of them. The students called in diplomatic Robert to talk with him, and the two spent a half hour discussing modern-day versions of neoclassical style. Later they met up at the bar where Anton asked Robert to an afterhours party, telling him to bring his girlfriend.

From early in the morning until dinner, Anton was at his office on Via Vittorio Veneto. The girls kept busy with a private tour guide named Vera, a perky Australian in her twenties, who led them around the Vatican, the Roman Forum, the Coliseum, the Spanish Steps, and the Trevi Fountain.

The sisters kept Vera occupied with a million questions about the portraits, landscapes, and mythological scenes exhibited. Stephanie, for once, was the most well informed. Their grandparents had encouraged her interest in art by giving her coffee-table-type books on Michelangelo, DaVinci, Raphael, and Bernini. And Annabelle had scores of tangential questions, such as "How do goddesses give birth?"

Vera, an art history student, was committed to her charge. When Samantha and her sisters became daunted by the endless rooms full of sculptures and paintings, she helped them choose which pieces to zero in on, making the museum excursions illuminative rather than overwhelming. She livened things up with gossipy stories about the personal exploits of the artists who created the landmark public fountains. Descriptions of the sewage system of ancient Rome with its floating carcasses discouraged them from over-solemnizing places like the Temple of the Virgins -- "Hey, that's our temple!" exclaimed Stephanie.

Samantha soon ran out of appropriate clothing for the restaurants Anton chose for them each evening. But this problem was solved by their pre-arranged shopping spree: Gucci, Prada, Valentino, Armani and Fendi were the more illustrious stops.

With the help of sales associates, who had apparently been instructed to let them purchase whatever they liked, they tried on hundreds of skirts, tops, pants, dresses, and even some shorts. Catherine curbed the enthusiasm by setting limits. Samantha had expected to find un-wearable short skirts that showed her underwear when she sat down and transparent tops like in magazines and on catwalks. But not all the clothes were too short or see-through, and the natural fabrics felt luxurious like Anton's sheets. Their construction reminded her of the handmade dress she wore for her cousin's wedding. These garments couldn't be classed with the teen outfits at the mall.

Her body looked different in these clothes. Her wider hips didn't seem out of proportion like when she tried on the narrow pants at the teen section of department stores. Her waist wasn't swimming in fabric like when she bought tees at Target. The smaller-sized tops fit her chest without being too tight.

Setting aside her new clothes for evening excursions, Samantha dressed for afternoons of touring in shorts, sleeveless tank tops, and flat sandals. She would have loved to be accosted with a "Ciao Bella!" by one of the young men zipping around on scooters, as her pretty tour guide said she often was. The ego boost would have done wonders, although she would have been too embarrassed to say anything in reply, despite having picked up a few Italian phrases. As it was, she watched lovers stroll and thought about what Delaney might look like leaning against the Ponte Sisto.

At their daily dinners, Anton asked questions about their day and offered his knowledge of the city. Annabelle and Stephanie had many pert anecdotes to relate about unseasoned tourist like the one who asked Vera, "Does the Pope have any grandchildren?" Even Gretchen felt comfortable enough to talk. She was interested in the relationship between the ancient Roman republic and the modern-day Italian government. Samantha spoke just enough to not be considered too quiet and found that she could get used to leisurely dinner conversation.

Anton shied away from any sort of admonishments or advice-giving like during his visit to their home in Connecticut. Catherine was on a calm emotional plain and avoided entanglements with Anton. She and he were unerringly congenial with each other.

"If you have plans," said Catherine, " or someone else you need to see or something you need to do, I hope you don't feel like you have to be with us every night … we'll find our way around."

"I cleared my calendar," Anton replied, running his fingers along the length of the thick-stemmed silverware at the side of his plate.

"Do you still spend a lot of time working in Manhattan?"

His eyes paused on her face for a moment before he said softly, "I do."

Robert asked, "You still have an apartment there?"

"I, yes, I keep it up," said Anton, nodding his head with a taut jerk, "but I usually stay at the Waldorf."

Samantha's breath caught. Her sisters were not yet familiar with her paternity situation. She had told her dad she wasn't ready for them to know. The subject was avoided when they were around, which was all the time. *Thank goodness.*

On their final day Vera cancelled her plans with the girls, leaving them alone in the house while their parents were out at a spa. Stephanie started opening ten-foot paneled doors and went exploring. In Anton's Gothic study, she found a photo on the desk of a woman in a thong on the deck of a boat, as well as "boring" books cased in shelves that peaked at the top like a cathedral, and a stash of "regular movies" including a romance called *The Lover.* "Let's watch this!"

Samantha threatened to tell on her when their parents got back.

Annabelle, fresh from the shower, watched the looks on her sisters' faces as she burst into Anton's bedchamber. There, by smoky frescoed walls, she tested the springs on his bed, which had a boxy wooden canopy carved in relief. Samantha became desperate. When the housekeeper entered the room, covering her mouth in stupefaction, Samantha called Anton's assistant on the phone.

In a quarter of an hour, Anton showed up, looking calm, and asked where Vera was, having been informed that Catherine and Robert were visiting a spa. He didn't get an answer.

Gretchen had long since retreated to the girls' room. Stephanie stood intrepidly in the center of the floor with a smirk on her face and a hand on her hip while Samantha disappeared into a corner next to a claw-footed table with a Greek-key design just like Vera had shown them at the museum.

Annabelle was attempting summersaults on the bed, sending shammed pillows onto the floor. "Watch this!"

Anton stood motionless with his arms crossed.

"We found pictures of your girlfriend," smiled Stephanie. "In the *library*." She sounded like she was playing CLUE.

Anton's attention turned from Annabelle to Stephanie.

Stephanie eyes flickered toward her little sister, who was now roaring, "Hey mambo, mambo Italiano." She asked, with a grin, "Are you scared of her? She might start opening drawers."

"No, but I am scared of *you*."

Out in the gallery Anton retained a poker face as he asked Samantha's sisters what they'd like to do for the afternoon. It was soon settled that they'd go to a subtitled movie with the housekeeper. Samantha ran to her room to get money for snacks and on the way back met Anton at the top of the stairs. As she approached him, he laughed, "Not one of you is like your mother, no?"

Samantha was surprised by his question and more so by his laugh. It changed his entire face for an instant, then was gone without a trace. As he walked her down several flights to the car garage, he told her the chauffer's full name and explained how to make a phone call from the limo if need be. Samantha decided she was happy to say the least amount possible around him.

As they found their seats in the first class section of the plane returning to JFK, Gretchen, who always sat next to Samantha so she could hold her hand during any turbulence, told their mom over and over again what a wonderful host Anton was,

"Although I wish we'd been able to meet some of his family ... since they live so close by. Is he divorced? He doesn't have any kids, right?"

With a twitch of her lower eyelid, Catherine shook her head, no.

Chapter 13:

Samantha started her sophomore year with a new wardrobe and highlights in her hair from the Mediterranean sun. Sneakers were gone for everyday wear. She was taller, almost 5' 8", with fuller breasts, although she put off buying new bras as long as possible.

When she met up with Ally at their neighboring lockers, Ally was effusive, "You look hot!" Samantha smiled cautiously, asking Ally about her newest boyfriend, a drama club geek who sounded more interesting than the motorcycle fanatic. After checking their schedules, they found that they didn't have the same lunch period. This was a major disappointment.

Passing half-empty rectangular tables at lunch, Samantha was keenly aware that she was the unlucky bum who didn't have anyone to sit with. She discreetly placed her backpack at a table with two girls from her AP Biology class. Greeting them with a simple "Hi," she felt a flash of paranoia about intruding, especially when they didn't say much.

Delaney and his friends had taken over the senior table at the far end of the cafeteria and seemed to be talking all at once, but she couldn't get a clear read on his face.

She had her period and bad cramps. No pharmaceuticals, not even headache drugs, were allowed at school unless administered by the nurse who required a lengthy permission slip. It seemed wrong that she was biologically able to get pregnant since the age of thirteen, and yet according to society and state laws she wasn't old enough for sex or kids until many years later. Her ovaries were encouraging illegal activity.

She had math with Delaney again. This time it was last-period Calculus with notorious Mr. Beaters, who complimented females when they wore floral-print dresses, joked about James Bond character names, and pooh-poohed alimony settlements. Fortunately, Nicolette wasn't in the class although Meghan, her cheerleader friend and rival, was. Delaney sat next to her.

Samantha accepted a seat in the empty front row and kept her gaze on Mr. Beaters' weathered nose. The class was going to be difficult, at least that's what Mr. Beaters had told her after quizzing her on how she was taking the class as a sophomore. She expected to have plenty to occupy her mind other than Delaney Troy. With a deep breath she told herself to add an addendum to her "Forgetting about D.T." journal on studying Ancient Roman Art.

As practice for the fall soccer season kicked off under the tutelage of a new female assistant coach, Samantha was blossoming into an attacking midfielder. Her job was to organize the midfield, contributing to the offense by setting up the forwards. Coach Simmons joked about changing her jersey number to 10, a traditional designation of greatness. She could tell this was condescending, but she felt flattered nonetheless.

Games were exhilarating, even when she was marked by the opposition's best defenders. Bouncing from hip to hip, she could let off steam and be aggressive, without getting in trouble, except for a foul call once in a while. It was still a losing team, but it was worth something to be looked to for leadership. Once or twice, she caught Delaney on the adjacent field turn away from one of Simmons's lectures and watch the girls' team.

In the locker room, Samantha's assigned locker was one aisle from Nicolette's. At times, when chatter quieted to a hum, she heard the cheerleaders calling her a loser or speculating on how she must have "begged Mommy and Daddy to take her to the big sale."

One day, after 5th period, she took a back hallway -- the main halls were heavily populated with cheerleaders -- and headed for the stairs near the gym's equipment room. As she entered the stairwell she came upon Delaney as he skipped down the last three steps and landed a couple feet in front of her. He was in a cotton gym uniform, with wet patches on the chest. Their eyes met, but she didn't hold his gaze more than half a second.

"Hey," he said, sounding out of breath. "What's up, Soccer-girl?"

She barely looked up but managed a croaked-voice 'Hi' as he passed her.

When she reached the upper landing, she grabbed the railing to steady herself and felt pleased with the idea they could be civil.

As if required to justify her presence in Calculus I, Samantha was called on at least twice per class. Afterwards, she'd trudge to her locker, mentally fatigued from the pressure of being prepared with the correct derivative at any given moment. Then, to catch the bus home, she'd head upstairs to wait for the final bell near the front doors. Sometimes she'd stop to talk to Ally, but often she'd lean against the wall and zone out while people around her chatted in groups.

While she stood holding a library book against her chest, someone approached her and, with some finesse, snatched the book right out of her arms. The title was *Human Sexuality* and, in it, she had bookmarked a chapter on *Homosexuality and Bisexuality*.

It was Delaney.

"What are you reading?" he asked. Without invitation, he opened the book to the page with the bookmark.

She blushed deeply. Her mind leapt to the memory of being told she dressed like a dyke, and she hurriedly offered, "I have a relative who might be bisexual, and I'm trying to figure out how he could have, sort of, experimented with, uh, sort of, being with a man at one point in his life, and then be married and straight now."

After a pause, he said with a flinch, "I guess some people aren't strict about those sorts of things -- either a guy or girl will do."

She nodded, collecting her thoughts. *Why is he talking to me?* He didn't seem like he was trying to taunt her. "Yeah, they're attracted to individuals instead of members of one gender exclusively."

He stepped a little closer, looking pensive and then smiled a little.

She had nothing to risk and jumped at the chance to shock him, "Do you think you could date a guy?"

"I don't think I could get it up with a guy." His voice was steady.

She blushed and searched her mind for something to say.

He relieved her with, "Although … since I'm such a skank, you never know what I might do."

She couldn't believe he was referring to her comment … from months ago. "You do date a lot of people … all at once."

"How do you know who I date?"

"Uh, for some reason, it's common knowledge around here."

He was quiet for a moment. "The only reason to date one person is if you can only find one person willing to go out with you."

"That's sooo…unromantic."

"Yes, but what's romance got to do with it? Why wouldn't I date as many girls as I can when I'm young enough to get away with it?"

"Wow, that's an interesting theory I've never heard before."

"Uh, I don't think so. Your dad said it in Franks's class: dating in high school is a joke, so go out with a bunch of different people." They'd had a parents day for the final session of sex ed. class with Mr. Franks; Robert had been one of only a few parents who showed up, and Samantha had left with him to catch a ride home.

"Uh, yeah." She was astonished that he remembered and referred to something her dad had said, and it was unfathomable that he was actually using her father's words to argue *against* her. "I guess that's what he said, but I just never heard it expressed the way you put it. I don't agree with him if that's what he meant." She looked up into his stunning blue eyes, which caused her hands to shake a little. "I think dating one person would be better because you can have real emotional … intimacy. Even though he scoffed at the idea of a serious relationship in high school, I'm fairly sure my dad was assuming kids date only one person at a time."

He wasn't backing away, just calmly waiting to hear what she had to say.

She continued, "He even went out with my mom once in high school. It's kind of funny. My sisters and I always make fun of him because he didn't call her after that one date, and she's still mad at him about it."

He smiled openly. It was like a new person standing in front of her. He'd never really smiled at her like that, except maybe that time, ages ago, when she apologized for kicking the soccer ball at his head. Back before Soccer-girl had become public enemy #1. She wasn't sure whether to go on, but he interrupted her unease with, "They must have gone out on a second date at some point ... I mean, to end up with more than one kid."

"Yeah, they got together after college."

"Girls are into dating one person. It's a possessive thing."

"What? Some guys want to be monogamous. Some guys are romantic. And ... it's not right to say that someone's opinions are determined by their sex."

"What guys do you know who wouldn't jump at the chance to fuck more than one girl?"

She had to look away for a moment. "I don't know very many people's private motivations, but ..." Absorbed by the debate, she itched to continue, but the final bell began ringing, and he smiled and walked away.

Needless to say, this opened up a whole new can of worms. She started thinking about him again. Starting from scratch, she wanted to figure him out correctly this time. Sure, everything he said she disagreed with, but the swagger with which he said it was irresistible. He was smarter than anyone gave him credit for, brilliant compared to some of his friends. And, he seemed so open-minded about ... sexual things. She wondered what he would say about her un-immaculate conception.

Scouting for him in the halls and at lunch, it was like she was a hunter and he was her prey. Loitering outside his English teacher's room made her late for class. She couldn't resist any bit of information Ally had to offer. She was masturbating in the bathtub thinking of him while listening to a song about a girl washing in her lover's old bath water. It was a pop song but the notion was so romantically 19th century. She told herself to cut it out. She told herself she was setting herself up for more disappointment, rekindling her interest in a two-timing, cheerleader-dating jock because of a little conversation. But her feelings took on their own life.

There was a rumor floating around school about a male teacher having sex with one of his female students. Samantha mentioned this to her parents. But since there weren't any specifics, there was nothing they could think to do about it. To appease themselves, they talked to Samantha about how appealing older men can be.

"Don't worry," she told them. "I'm not in danger of dating anyone, of any age, in the foreseeable future. You should give this speech to one of Anton's girlfriends."

At school, Ally fanned the flames of the brewing gossip,

"Everyone thinks the pervert is Mr. Fellows." He was Samantha's hard-edged A.P. Biology teacher who screamed at minor infractions like talking in line. "They say he might get canned."

Samantha didn't know what to make of this. She'd never seen Mr. Fellows act weird, toward anyone, and had nothing to accuse him of except giving loads of homework.

"It was so funny, Suzanne said that it couldn't be Mr. Franks because, if it was, she would have done him by now." Ally laughed as she tugged at the open shoulder of her ballet-neck tee. "Besides, he's got a really good-looking wife."

"And nobody with a good-looking spouse ever cheats."

Ally didn't seem to get the joke. She was checking out a guy in cowboy boots who'd just transferred to Darcy from Oklahoma.

"I don't think it's Mr. Franks," Samantha said, when Ally's attention returned, "He seems genuinely cool."

"I guess we'll find out next Friday at the Charity Dance. Mr. Fellows usually chaperones, so if he's not there then maybe he's the one."

Samantha grinned. "I don't think that's enough evidence to convict."

"I heard Delaney is trying to talk Nicole out of going to the dance. He's sick of them."

"I didn't tell you, but I had this strange conversation with him."

"In the library?"

"No, not that. Just last week. Before the final bell. He walked up to me and took this book out of my hand. I didn't even know it was him until after he'd already grabbed it."

"Cool. Samantha, I've been telling you this. You've gotta go for it."

"Go for it?" Samantha contorted her face. Ally had never told her to "go for it."

"If you want him, come to the party at the lake Saturday night. He'll probably be there."

"You know I don't do well at parties. My dad will kill me if I drink, and that's all anybody does." Since her freshman-year jaunt to the '90s Dance, followed by crashing a party with Ally and her friends drunk on peach schnapps, Samantha had bowed out of going to late night gatherings.

"What? You're not listening. You should go after him. He's a total player. He likes to hook up with a new girl every night. If he knows you'd let him bone you, he'll go out with you."

"What?" Not only did she not believe he would be willing to have sex with her on the fly, after telling her he wasn't interested in her that way, but she would never offer herself up like that.

"Do you want him or not? You've been drooling over him since like the beginning of freshman year. If you want him, go after him. Now is your chance. He must be interested in you if he talked to you."

"No, you don't know the bizarre things we talked about. He was probably just interested in the book or something. And, what about you? You say you like him, so why don't you ask him out?"

"He knows I'd give it up. He's not game," said Ally, seemingly unmoved by this fact.

"But, Ally, he told me he's not interested in me."

"Maybe if he knew you'd go all the way."

"But I wouldn't go all the way. I'd definitely want to have a boyfriend for a *long* time first before I'd even think about --"

"Are you willing to take a lie detector test?"

Samantha laughed, kicking at the legs of a chair next to hers.

"You could at least make out with him. Come to the party, please! A couple guys will probably get into a fight and push each other in the lake. It'll be fun. "

Samantha decided Ally must be having trouble finding someone to ride along with her.

Chapter 14:

She couldn't be talked into a high school party, but she did get her parents to drive her to the Charity Dance, where all of Darcy's sports teams collected donations for the local food bank.

Mr. Fellows was there, but no one was sure what that meant. The gym was lit with flashing disco lights stationed at all corners of the room. Samantha strained her eyes to find Delaney. When she located him standing with Nicolette, she recognized his light-blue jeans, almost white at the pockets, and ribbed shirt. They were her favorites. He looked tall, a thick black belt cutting him in the middle. His arms were particularly beautiful in the light, his golden skin contrasting with the dark color of his shirt.

Samantha danced to hip-hop with Ally and her peach-schnapps-loving friends, glad she wasn't getting a ride home with them as she watched them hike up their skirts like can-can dancers. Looking down at herself, Samantha concentrated on her hips, yet she kept her arm movements to a minimum, in line with the other girls. It was easier to get lost in the music when they played songs she hadn't heard on the radio a thousand times already.

Getting punch, she was able to scan the room for Delaney again. When she saw him looking somewhat in her direction, she turned away. Summoning the nerve to search again, she spied him dancing suggestively with Nicolette and felt ill about her recurring obsession. Jealousy whipped her back into reality. She had to continue to try to forget about him. She decided she would start … the next day. Tomorrow, when she caught herself thinking about him, she would snap a rubber band against her wrist.

After a split second pause, the sound system began pounding the opening cords of the varsity cheerleaders' victory dance. Samantha looked and saw only a few people dancing, none of whom was a cheerleader.

Ally ran over and dragged her onto the floor. "Come on!" Ally shouted as she began imitating the cheerleaders' moves.

Samantha knew all the steps after having sat through numerous sideline performances and then practicing the routine at home with her wannabe sisters. Nonetheless, she, at first, went through the motions only half-heartedly. But, eventually, the comedy of the situation sucked her in. She felt transported to her parents' living room. There, she had no inhibitions about making dramatic arm gestures of a kind never seen at school dances.

Disregarding the fact that she was probably pissing off the cheerleaders, she set about putting a satirical spin on their choreography. Exaggerating their strutting. Punching at the ceiling. Twirling until she stumbled from dizziness. The parody was aided by the song's lyrics. "Are you sexy, girl?" asked a male vocalist. "Yeah, I'm sexy," answered a female.

As the song ended, Ally and others were pointing at Samantha, who knew the most steps and had taken the lead with her fluid dancing style. She smiled shamelessly as she held her stomach and laughed. Turning, she noticed Nicolette standing on the edge of the dance floor with an irritated expression on her face. Samantha walked off the floor in the opposite direction and didn't look back.

Ally and her friends collected at the refreshment table, speculating on the effect of their escapade. After a couple minutes of listening to their jibes at Nicolette and the other cheerleaders, Samantha wondered off into her own mindscape, not paying attention to the conversation.

She imagined the courtyard and statues at the Medici Palazzo in Florence. Had Anton's ancestors held dances at the palace, locked behind the gates while the common folk peered in at them? Maybe they had flowers in their hair and spun ribbons around a maypole. She thought of Anton and her mom, their awkward détente during the trip. She still couldn't imagine them kissing. Then, she looked to her left. Delaney was next to her.

His face was dimly lit yet she could see he had full possession of her face. "Interesting dancing."

There was a new look in his eyes. Annoyance? No, she'd witnessed that before. He looked half-insane. His eyes were too noticeable, too piercing.

"You've changed your mind about going out for cheerleading?" He didn't smile.

Dumbfounded, she tried to decide if this was a serious question. "No, I just see the routine a lot at games. My sister, she's in 8th grade, wants to try out for JV next year and asks me to show her whatever steps I can remember."

He didn't reply but stared as her, expressionless.

Samantha waited. As seconds expired, she looked behind her (Ally was missing). Then she looked behind him (his friends were nowhere in sight). He was quiet and motionless, his eyes fixed … on nothing … on the wall opposite them.

Finally, he looked at her. "What did you do over the summer?"

"I… I went to Rome and Florence with my family. It was really nice." She wanted so bad to say something clever, but absolutely nothing passed through her brain except warnings about being sweaty from dancing.

He nodded, still looking solemn.

There was another excruciating pause.

"What about you?" she asked.

"Nothing. Went nowhere, except the beach."

"I was free the rest of the summer, which was really nice." *Nice?* Why couldn't she think of anything to say that wasn't banal?

"Are you busy tomorrow night?"

For an instant, she thought Ally put him up to this. She held her mouth open for a second, then after seeing he was waiting for an answer, not brimming with laughter, she said simply, "No."

"Do you want to go to a movie?"

He was still frowning. Sounded indifferent. She didn't know what to say, but heard herself blurt out, "Sure."

"Okay, I'll call you," he said with the slightest smile, and then took his right hand out of his pocket and gestured goodbye.

Was he joking? Was it retaliation for her making fun of the cheerleaders? She couldn't believe he would play with her like that. Yet, it was also unbelievable that he'd come ask her out. And how was he going to call her? He didn't have her phone number.

Did he want to be friends? Did he like her? She couldn't get her mind to process such an idea. She wished she had talked to him more to see what was really going on. She supposed that if he did call her tomorrow, she would have a chance to ask him some questions. But could that really happen? Impossible! What in the world was she going to tell her parents? She immediately decided not to say anything to anyone until he actually called.

The rest of the night was a daze. When she finally crawled into bed, she started thinking about sex. Did he want to have sex with her? She tried to imagine it, but she was overwhelmed with pangs and throbbing all over her body. Did he think she would have sex with him? Did he expect that? Was he going to make a pass at her? What in the world would she do? The words 'be careful what you wish for' suddenly streamed across her consciousness.

The next day was long. She had no one to talk to about her anxiety because she didn't want her parents and sisters to know of her shame if he didn't call. The phone finally rang around 4 pm. Her mom answered, asked the caller to wait a minute, and called upstairs to Samantha who had heard the phone ring and was standing at her doorway watching from the open upstairs hallway.

Her heart pounding, she picked up the receiver in her room. "Hello?"

"Hi," he said in a limp voice.

"Hi, I was worried you didn't know my number."

"It's online. DarcyHigh.com."

She laughed awkwardly. "Ah, yeah, that's right."

"It also has your address, but I don't know where it is."

She gave directions.

"Okay, I'll be there at like 7:30. When do you have to be home by?"

"Uh, 11:30, I think. What about you? Do you have a curfew?"

"Only when I make one up."

She hesitated. "Why would you make one up?"

"When I pretend."

"Huh?"

He chuckled. "Never mind."

She scratched her lower lip with a fingernail. "But really, why would you pretend?" She realized she sounded a tad overly excited.

"Never mind. I hate talking on the phone. I'd rather talk in person."

"Oh, okay."

"I'll see ya soon."

"Okay."

She hardly had enough time to tell her parents she was going out, listen to their never-ending admonishments, take a shower, wash her hair, get something to eat, pick out something to wear with Stephanie's help, and put on a little make-up.

She tried to get away with just telling her parents she was going out to the movies, but her mom immediately inferred,

"Are you going out with the boy who called?"

"Yeah, sort of."

"What's his name?" asked Robert, with a grin.

"Umm, you know him … the soccer player."

"Delaney?" His smile gone, he was clearly trying not to look stunned. Samantha nodded.

Both her mom and dad stood gaping at her for a several moments.

Finally, Robert asked, "What's his last name?"

"Troy."

"We don't really know him. Are you sure he's a good driver?"

"Uh, I guess." She felt sudden panic at the idea that they might not let her go. "All his parents' information is on the school website."

"If you think he's been drinking or you see him drinking, you have to call us to come get you, Samantha. We trust your judgment."

"Okay, I will. I promise."

"And you have to be home by 11:30."

"I know."

"Okay," he nodded. Samantha could tell his mind was racing.

"I have to get ready," she said softly.

But they kept her for half an hour. Both her mom and dad repeating after-school-special advice, which she'd heard from them before, about what could happen, about what could go wrong. Only now they spoke as if they were worried that it actually applied.

He arrived in the black mustang she'd seen him leaning on in the school parking lot after practice. It looked like a hand-me-down, eclipsed by the shiny Range Rovers and Audis the other kids drove. She had been waiting on the bench opposite the front door and jumped up the moment he pulled in, immediately walking out into his line of sight.

Feeling sick to her stomach, her hand swept across the front of her ruched top. Her hair was down, slightly wavy with some strands tucked behind her ears. She refused to try to blow-dry it straight as was the fashion. She didn't want to overdo it.

Delaney got out to open the passenger door for her with a smile of greeting that spread across his lips to the structure of his cheeks. *This really is a date.*

Pretending to look at the car's tidy interior, she eyed him as he crossed in front of the windshield then got back into the driver's seat. Every movement of his head and arms was a study in cool, James Dean cool. As he fumbled with the ignition and turned down the stereo, she was too rattled to turn her face in his direction, but instead looked back at the house to see if anyone was spying through the front windows.

He broke the silence. "So, did you learn anything from that book?"

"Not much," she chirped. They were now moving. Glancing at him, she took in afresh what a gorgeous person he was. Up close, Delaney glowed.

"Tell me," he said.

"I didn't find anything that helped me much." She didn't want to water down her vocabulary as she had a tendency to do. "I guess it said bisexuality has a lot to do with a lack of strict adherence to gender roles ... kinda like what you said."

His nose twitched a little as his bright eyes darted in her direction. "You sound like a dictionary."

She grinned sheepishly. "I didn't mean to." Her voice regressed to childlike. "I really didn't get much out of the book."

He concentrated on making a turn -- past an antique shop with the sign 'Best Selection. Stickley Furniture.' -- then asked, "So, when are you going to bring it up? You might as well get it out of the way."

"Bring what up?"

"The whole bus incident. You brought it up before."

She chuckled self-consciously. "Yeah, I guess I did want to ask you about that."

"Shoot!"

Her eyelids fluttered as she averted her face. "You know. You told me you weren't interested in me. Did you change your mind? Do you want to be friends now?"

"Friends? Not really. I have lots of friends."

"And you're so humble."

"No, not really."

"Why not?" She licked her lips.

"It's hard to say."

She shook her head, pleased to see him smiling, then fidgeted with her top, pulling it down over the top button of her jeans. "Umm, were you going to tell me something about what happened ... when you spoke to me on the bus?"

"What do you want to know?"

She told herself to calm down. "Well, you basically said you didn't like me, and then yesterday you said you wanted to go to the movies, so ... "

He glanced at her several times, like he was waiting for her to say more, but she held her ground.

"Yeah, well, I'm glad you asked. Although I don't have an explanation for you." Waiting at a stop light, he looked right at her. "I just couldn't resist hearing you try to ask me about it."

"What?" She squeezed her eyebrows together, frowning as he laughed. "That's not an answer."

"Too bad. It's the only one I'm going to give you."

"But you *told* me to ask."

"I knew you were going to anyway."

"But that's doesn't make sense."

"Deal with it." A little grin played at the corner of his mouth.

She felt her face burn, wanting to retaliate. "I have another question for you." She adjusted her seatbelt, swallowing hard. "Wasn't it strange to ask me to the movies while you were at the dance with Nicolette?"

He smiled wryly. "I have this strict rule: I won't talk to Nicolette about you. And, I won't talk to you about her. I want nothing to do with all that shit."

"Oh." She hesitated. "Do you apply this rule to all ... people, and not just to her and me?"

"I'd say so."

"What about when you told Mairin that I have a tendency to 'go postal?' In that case, weren't you talking to someone else about me?"

He looked surprised for a moment. "And who is your source for that juicy little tidbit of information? Oh, I know. Allison Geyger. For a second there, I thought you were involved in another spat over me."

She tried to catch her breath. *I can't believe he said that.* "I don't really know her ... Mairin, I mean."

"That's good," he said, with what sounded like relief.

She wanted to trip him up so badly. "So, because you can hide behind your not-talking-about-one-person-while-you're-with-another rule, it's okay to ask me to go to the movies while you're on a date with Nicolette."

"I was there with friends. Too bad most of your information about me is wrong."

Her facial muscles were sore from so much embarrassed smiling. "It's the curse of being popular, I guess ... people speculating about you."

"I have no interest in being popular. I'm grateful for my friends, but I don't want everyone else's attention."

"Like me. You thought I was watching you a lot and didn't like it."

"Weren't you?"

"I guess a little. I think you're a really good soccer player. I wish I played like you."

He laughed. "You're so full of shit."

"What do you mean? You don't know what I think."

"It's true, I'm not clear what you think now." His eyes lowered a touch. He almost looked conciliatory. "Although you definitely had this thing for me."

Recollecting the pain and embarrassment, she asked, "Why did you think that? Seriously, I'm really curious."

"Every time I turned around, you were there, looking at me."

"And I was so repulsive you had to go out of your way to tell me you weren't interested in me."

He grinned widely. "I see what you're doing. Trying to come through the back door in order to get me to answer *that question*. Very tricksie."

"No, please, I'm not trying to be sneaky. I really, really want to know. Please, Delaney." His name stuck on her tongue and almost didn't come out.

"Fuck!" He sounded exasperated. "What do you wanna know? Were you so repulsive?" His laugh brought her pure joy. "No, it wasn't that. Uh, probably I wanted to avoid all the drama with you and Nic and the Soccer-girl stuff, so I *ingeniously* decided to work some magic and nudge you in another direction. I could tell it wasn't really such a great approach from like the instant after I said it, but by then it was too late."

It was much more of an answer than she expected and took a while to digest. He wanted his friends to stop teasing her? He wanted to avoid drama between Nicolette and her? If that's so, what the hell was he doing asking her to the movies now?

What did he mean he wanted to nudge her in another direction? He wanted her to pay attention to some other guy? It had seemed he was barely aware she was around, let alone keeping track of her. He still hadn't explained his interest in her now.

Chapter 15:

At the multiplex they parked far away from the entrance because the lot was full. She had barely taken note of geography on the ride there, but she pretended to check out the staged greenery that spotted the grounds as they walked to the box office in silence. Neither spoke, and Delaney got two tickets.

As they sat down in the back row of the theater, he asked her if she wanted something to eat. She declined, and he sat back in his chair and rested his knees against the seat in front of him. There were only ten people total in the small screening room and no one else was sitting near the back.

"So, what's up with your soccer obsession?"

She smiled and looked down at her primly folded hands. "I don't have an obsession; I just like to get good at things I try. I have plenty of room for improvement, as you know."

He raised his head to see if the people up front were annoyed by their talking. "Did you even play before last year?"

"Not really. Just a little with my dad. How about you?" The movie was underway but they ignored this.

"I've played in leagues and clubs since I was pretty young."

"*That's* my problem. I should have started younger."

"Yeah, you play like a rookie … can't defend the ball to save your life."

"That's not true." Her cheeks swelled. "I've improved … "

He smiled as several strands of hair escaped from behind his ear and fell onto his cheek.

"It's not easy, you know, managing to be a loser both on and off the field."

"So you're gonna act all self-deprecating, are you? I thought you were the know-it-all math whiz."

"Yeah, well, math nerds aren't held in high esteem. Sometimes I wish I wasn't such an oddball at school. It must be nice to be looked up to like you and your friends."

"Give it a rest. Popularity is overrated. There's absolutely no benefit to having freshman girls call you and start giggling over the phone."

"Now I understand what you thought of me last year. I think you're ungrateful."

"What the hell are you talking about? You never called me, did you?"

He must get a lot of unsolicited calls, she thought. "No, but what I mean is you act like girls liking you is a nuisance."

He sighed, letting out a deep breath. "It is a lot of the time. You try to be honest and then you end up feeling like a prick. And you know what else, Samantha. You're way too concerned with social status for someone who prides herself in standing up to the bullies and putting an end to the *horrible scourge* that is cheerleading … all that shit you do."

She smiled. To hear him pronounce her actual given name felt better than scoring a game-winning goal. "I'll try to stop focusing on your social status and just treat you like Nicolette treats unpopular girls."

"Not Nicolette. I *don't* want to talk about her," he interrupted brusquely, then suddenly smirked, "Let's talk about you."

"What about me?"

He asked about her trip to Rome, and she talked a little about the museums and her sisters, without ever mentioning Anton. She asked him about the boys' soccer team and their position in the standings and what it was like to play in the finals last season -- "How do they decide tiebreakers?" He answered her questions, then, after a pause, asked,

"So you're a virgin?"

She doubled up, hiding her face in her lap as she tried to think of a comeback. Regaining an upright position, she said with mock seriousness, "Yeah, it's great. You should try it." She couldn't meet his eyes.

"Really?" He laughed. "I did try it, but I'm not sure I feel the same way."

"I've decided to wait 'til I'm old enough to join the varsity cheerleading squad and thereby become a real woman." She couldn't help laughing at her own joke.

"Come on, what is it? Are you religious? Did you take the virginity pledge? I couldn't believe that last year ... all those parents marching outside during homeroom with signs: 'My son took the purity pledge. You can trust him with your daughter.' Yeah, right, you can trust momma's boy to take your daughter out for a real nice time after he jerks off playing video games." He stretched his right leg out into the aisle. "But seriously, do you have a particular reason for wanting to be, uh, what's a politically-correct term ... 'cherry'?"

She ran her finger along the delicate skin of her eyelid, partially covering her face with her hand. "That's doesn't sound very politically correct to me, but ...Uh, I don't know. I haven't thought about .... I mean I haven't really…. I haven't had a lot of tempting offers." *Oh God.* She was trying to be honest, but it sounded all wrong.

Luckily, he didn't immediately jump all over the opening, just glanced at the screen. "I'll make sure to cover your eyes during the dirty parts." He reached over, his hand suspended in front of her face.

She studied him with something bordering on fascination. He had blonde hair between the first two joints of his elongated fingers.

"Didn't you learn anything from Mr. Franks' class?" she said. "Sex isn't dirty."

"Really?" He grinned suggestively. "Exactly what sort of tempting offer are you in the market for?"

She shook her head. "Don't ask me that," she pleaded softly.

Having barely followed the plot, they walked out of the theatre as the credits rolled and his hand brushed her arm, prickling her skin. As they reached his car, the lot had thinned out and there were no other vehicles nearby. She stood next to him, jittery, as he slid a key into the passenger-side door. She was waiting for him to start talking again, but he said nothing, his face a beautiful stone visage. He unlocked the door but didn't reach for the door handle. Instead, he turned toward her, his face tilted downward. He was staring at her. This can't be happening, she thought, her heart racing.

She closed her eyes, forcing herself not to lower her chin, resisting her shyness. She felt his hand grip the outside of her shoulder. Her lungs seized as his mouth touched hers … tentatively … like she was a skittish bunny who might hop away. Floating white spots appeared inside her eyelids. She gasped for air. He kissed her with more pressure, bending her head back, his lips moving against her. Her own lips were still but docile. Then he stopped.

As he let go of her, she lurched back a step, but he caught her hand. Her lips felt like they'd been shot up with Novocain. Looking toward the ground, she saw his legs pivot as he opened the car door. Her hand clamped onto the back of the passenger seat, and she tried to lower herself elegantly, but she couldn't, all her muscles were clenched.

After closing the door behind her, he walked around to the driver's side and got in, but didn't turn on the engine. She sat staring at the dashboard, trying not to hyperventilate. Out of the corner of her eye, she saw him look at her. With less hesitation than before, he reached for her, his fingertips tickling her cheek as he turned her to face him. His lips were almost pouty, the lower one redder than the top. His mouth not as set as usual. In the soft light of the sign from a nearby fast food restaurant, she noticed something murky and unreadable in the expression of his eyes. It was almost tender.

His hand moved to her neck, where she felt heat from his fingers, followed by a shiver. He pulled her closer to him and pressed his whole mouth against hers. In all the months of imagining it, she hadn't come close to how it would feel to be kissed by him. As the tip of his nose tapped her cheek, his hair fell onto her face. It smelled like coconut. Her useless hands trembled.

Puckering, she took a stab at kissing him back with jerky, fleeting jabs. In response, he opened his mouth and slid his wet lips over hers. She loosened her jaw, parting her lips, allowing him to move his tongue into her mouth. She heard a fire siren in the distance as he leaned forward, over the low center console. She let out an odd murmur, which she hoped wouldn't be mistaken for a protest. He stopped.

"Want to go in the back?"

She nodded, feeling so excited she couldn't speak.

He nimbly climbed into the backseat of the car, moved the driver's seat all the way forward, and gave her a hand as she followed.

Face-to-face on the bench-style back seat, she squeezed her eyes closed as he swept his hands over her arms, leaving a trail of goose bumps. He raised her chin and kissed her, his tongue moving slowly in and out of her mouth like slurping. He whispered instruction, "Stick your tongue out," and she felt a throbbing between her legs that terrified her. Yet she clumsily complied.

He caressed her side, his fingers lingering at the contour of her waist. Pulling back, he ran his hand over the front of her shirt, his fingers grazing her nipple over layers of fabric. She whimpered as he cupped her breast from below. Motionless, she felt him knead her denim-covered hips and thighs. Bristles of his hair combed her neck as he teased her tongue.

The spiky pain inside her abdomen wasn't like a cramp. She knew what it was about. No longer was she just imagining being with him while lying alone in her bed, it was actually happening. Every nerve in her body was registering her long-standing desire for him.

He kissed her cheeks and her forehead and stroked her hair as her heart thumped wildly. She wasn't surprised when she felt him tug at her top, but she wasn't sure what to do. She couldn't heartily tell him she wanted him to stop. She didn't. Her eyes watered as she tried to quell the overwhelming feeling of arousal and think rationally.

He apparently had second thoughts and reached his hand under her shirt. She gasped, her skin tightened, as he unfastened her bra in the back and slid his fingers under the fabric in front, petting her in a slothful, circular sweep. His palm skimmed her nipple as he moved his entire hand under her loosened bra and tugged and squeezed her whole breast. All the while his kiss was gentler.

When she blinked, she caught him intently watching her face. She could imagine her anguished expression. Without a word, he yanked her shirt up over her head. She shivered as cool air touched her sunburn-hot skin. He peeled the thin white straps from her shoulders and pulled down her bra, discarding it on the seat next to her.

Then he pulled back. Stopped kissing her. Completely disengaged. As she peeked from behind her lowered eyelashes, she saw him staring intently at her chest. She sank her nails into the seat. When she felt like she wouldn't last another second, she moved to cover herself. He gently pulled her arms away, whispering, "You're cute."

She couldn't begin to understand what he meant by that. She would never have thought of him using the word cute. She'd seen herself in the mirror a million times. She thought she looked somewhat … boring and non-descript. Moving his lips back onto her mouth, he started kneading her bare breasts, one at a time and then both. They felt chubbier in his hands.

And next. She'd never imagined him doing such a thing to her. He broke away from her lips, bent down, and put his month on her right nipple. His warm saliva felt tingly on her skin, which was now chilled. As he added pressure and sucked on her, she gave up maintaining an upright posture and leaned back. Her arm and leg muscles shuddered as he bent over her, his mouth chafing the now hypersensitive skin of her breast. She experienced something almost like a spiky orgasm.

When he started to unbutton her jeans, she stiffened. "I can't. I can't."

He put his mouth to her ear and rasped, "I wanna fuck you."

She felt what was definitely an orgasm. Wincing, she swallowed hard, trying not to completely lose it. "I … I don't think…" she whimpered.

"I have condoms," he said, less aggressively.

"I…" she felt a tear running down her cheek. She was torn. "Why? Why do you want to?" *Why do you suddenly like me?*

With overt phoniness, he said, "Because you're the prettiest and the …" But he interrupted himself, abruptly shifting to a serious tone, "That's like asking me why I want pleasure. I just do."

After a moment's reflection, she said dejectedly, "I can't."

"Okay," he replied calmly.

She panicked at the idea that he might take his hands off her, but he didn't. Instead, he nudged her onto her side and lay down next to her. Her face met his cotton shirt, their legs intertwined. Kissing her by her ear, his hand brushed her cheek as he weaved a lock of her hair between his fingers. He wrapped his arms around her chest and squeezed her so hard she couldn't draw breath. For a moment, all her anxiety vanished.

She desperately wanted to reach for his hair, feel the texture of it -- against her cheek, it almost felt like kitten fur -- but she couldn't rouse herself from her passivity and do it. It was so much easier to follow his lead than to act or make requests.

Adjusting, he kissed her softly on the lips, and she wallowed in the pleasure of it. There was nothing detached or haughty about the way he touched her. It was so different from his manner at school. Minutes passed and his hand crept down the front of her jeans. She knew the fabric was soaked. "Can I touch you?" he asked.

She felt calmer and nodded yes. Unzipping her, he slid his hand under her underwear, his boney knuckles jabbing her belly. She wheezed when his warm fingers reached her pubic hair, then, as he probed farther, she reflexively sat up halfway. Opening her eyes for an instant, she saw him smiling at her convulsions.

Her opened pants had shifted down, cinching her uncomfortably across the hip, so she tugged at them. As if offering assistance, he pulled them all the way down. Then, she let him do the same with her underwear.

The shock of being naked was compounded by his question, "Can I turn you over?"

She gulped, and nodded. In an instant, she was face down against the seat cushion, her knees on the floor of the car. The flesh of her cheek stuck to the leather as she exhaled moist air.

He caressed her bottom, gently prying between her legs, touching her. She knew she should say something if she wanted him to stop, but she said nothing. Lying prostrate, she admitted to herself that she wanted it. She craved more of him -- not like she craved ice cream on a hot day, but like she craved sunshine, oxygen, human contact.

Hearing him fumbling with his jeans, she assessed the situation. Her legs were slightly apart. Hopefully that was all she had to do, and she could just lie there. Maybe it was wrong, but she didn't want control. She couldn't trust him -- he was presumably still with Nicolette and Mairin -- but there was ecstasy in the idea that he was initiating this contact with her. He seemed to want her. Her infatuation was no longer one-sided. She prayed he was getting that condom he mentioned,

"You said … you have a condom."

"Yes."

She thought about what her mom had said about pain. She didn't care. She wanted the pain. Anything to dampen the excruciating longing. He started to caress her again and she let out a sigh.

He whispered, "I won't hurt you."

Lifting her face, she bobbed her head in reply, happy her face was hidden from his view, which made her feel less embarrassed about being so exposed elsewhere. She felt something flat touch her between her legs. Her muscles contracted as something like a blunt object pushed inside her, causing a razor-sharp sting. He held completely still.

She gasped for breath, and then began humming with agitation. The bristly hair of his thighs scratched her freshly-shaven legs. Hovering above her, he started to move in and out, gradually venturing further inside her, producing a squishing sound, like when toes press into wet sand. An irritating mix of frustration and desire made her twitch. It was not as satisfying as she had hoped. She felt over-stimulated.

"Are you alright?" he asked.

Her face burned as she realized that she had made some loud unintelligible noises. She nodded her head in short rapid motions.

"It's okay. Make as much noise as you want. I like it."

She wanted him to start moving again and began rocking. Overwhelmed with throbbing, she wanted him to rub her already raw skin, anything to stifle the pulsing inside her. She wanted more pain.

Short diving motions hastened to pounding as her knees dug into the car's turf-like floor. Before long she felt an orgasm coming. She couldn't wait for it to happen and whined, making strange sounds she didn't know she was capable of. Then her pelvic muscles clenched, followed by a feeling that was something like pleasure, or at least all discomfort gone momentarily. He didn't stop right away, thrusting faster until she felt him shake.

She squeaked when he pulled out of her. Her throat felt dry and hoarse as her mind began to process the fact that she had made an enormous amount of noise. She felt vinegar sourness in her mouth and grabbed her clothes. Averting her face, she heard him zipping up his jeans, then felt him petting the top of her head.

"Are you alright?" he asked.

She nodded.

"What's wrong?"

She shook her head, clamping her mouth shut.

He reached around to kiss her cheek and said, "You're okay. It's just a little blood."

She nodded. She hadn't notice any blood, although she had expected it.

He reached for her mouth, pulling her to him, and kissing her softly. His finger dabbed her cheek. "Did I hurt you?"

She shook her head. "No."

"Are you sure?"

Her voice was staccato. "I.. I'm ... feeling ... shy... right now."

He smiled, "Okay," then turned to look at the clock. "I've got to take you home now or you'll be late."

She nodded, holding his glossy stare for an instant. He looked so peaceful, the opposite of difficult. Not the gruff striker he was at school. Opening the door, he helped her into the front seat.

He turned on the radio and they didn't talk during the ride to her house, although he rested his hand on her thigh when the driving allowed. In shock over what happened, she stared out the window at the buildings lit by evenly spaced lampposts. The lust. The sex. The yelling. After months of staring at him, she had barely opened her eyes.

The progression from kissing to touching to sex had seemed the most natural thing in the world, nothing extreme or reckless about it. Yet as she reflected on the totality of the situation, her assent made less sense.

When they got to her house, it was 11:30. He turned to her, straightened her hair a bit, and gave her a quick kiss. She reached for the door handle and said goodnight.

There was a moment of silence before he blurted, "Oh yeah," as if he'd forgotten something. "I wanted to ask you. If the weather is okay, do you want to play soccer in the park next Sunday?"

"Okay," she said, a smile melting away the tension scrunching her eyelids. "That would be nice."

"I'll call you."

Chapter 16:

Inside she went to her room and from there into the bathroom she shared with Stephanie. After peeing, she saw a ribbon of bright red blood in the toilet water. She peaked at her underwear: it was too much; she set it aside, not wanting to deal with it. In the shower, she very gently washed herself, feeling grownup.

As she dried off, she felt a little sore but not scared or sad, just exhausted and preternaturally calm. Climbing into bed, she looked at the dusty Victorian dollhouse in the corner of her room. She had planned to pack it up or give it away. She clicked off her candelabra bedside light and fell into a dreamless sleep.

The next day she got out of bed at eleven, pulled on some lounge pants, and headed downstairs to make an appearance. Her sisters were already done with brunch, but her parents were waiting for her. Before they could get out their first question, she confessed, "I had sex with him." The spoken truth startled her.

"What?" Her mom practically screamed, then emphatically sealed her mouth closed, covering it with her hand.

Her dad jumped up and was at her side in an instant. "Are you okay? Did he pressure you?" Grasping her chin, he gently lifted it, asking with an oddly shaky voice, "Just tell me it was your choice. Because if it wasn't …" For a split second he looked like the sort of dad who might wield a shotgun.

She slowly turned her face away from him, unable to look him in the eye. She thought of the way he used to look at her when she was Annabelle's age and greeted him at the front door. On bare feet, she'd jumped for his neck with her arms wide open, and he'd tried to give her a hug despite being loaded down with scrolls and paperwork. She had a photograph in her room of herself, as a toddler, seated on his shoe, legs wrapped around his ankle, clinging to him as he walked across the living room.

"You don't look traumatized. But if I'm wrong, tell us now." He didn't sound angry, but there was definitely something troubling in his eyes.

"No, no. It wasn't like that," she said, shaking her head with a steely motion.

Her mom's lips were pressed into a tight, thin line as she took Samantha by the arm and brought her over to sit down next to her. "So, it wasn't a horrible experience … or … anything like that?"

Samantha felt blood drain from her face as she saw her mom glance at her abdomen. "Uh, no, I wouldn't say that. I…uh…"

Her father sat down. He seemed tense. His face looked unusually red, so unlike his normal serene coloring. "I'm confused. You two really don't know each other well. I don't think --"

"Are you ashamed of me?" she interrupted.

"No," Robert exhaled.

"Of course not," said Catherine.

"It's perhaps not the most well-thought-out decision you ever made," said Robert, looking like he couldn't stand up even if he wanted to. "It could be something you come to regret ... I mean, you seem to have rushed into this. There are risks. Not just medical but psychological."

"Yeah, I know ..." Her voice trailed off. There was silence for a minute as she reached for some fresh pineapple, scooping it into a bowl.

"We'd prefer if you waited until you were older," he said, turning the stem of his coffee cup from right-handed to left and then back again. "There are so many persuasive arguments against this, but you've heard them all, and it has to be your decision. We can't hover over your shoulders for the rest of your life and decide these things for you. But you absolutely must be safe. You used a condom?"

"Yes," she squinted, pretending to look over the table set with Kona coffee, fruit, and macadamia nuts, which her grandparents sent back from a trip to Hawaii.

"So, it wasn't ... bad?" Catherine asked gently, the pitch of her voice rising. "I mean, it wasn't an awful experience? Just tell me. Please."

Robert looked at Catherine, and then shook his head, breaking into a strained mug of incredulity. "Catherine, I can't believe you just asked that. Maybe you two should wait until I'm not around."

Catherine dabbed at her eyes. "Are you sure there isn't anything you need me to do for you? Is there anything you need?"

Samantha was wrenched by the panicky look on her mom's face. "No. I'm okay."

At school on Monday, Samantha was on a mission, determined to put herself in a situation where she could say at least one word to Delaney. She worried he'd return to his normal in-school persona, which was nothing like the fervor of his hands, his mouth, and his body on their date. The image of him hanging out with her at school was almost as mind boggling as the idea of him making a public announcement: I had sex with Samantha Montclare. Closing her locker door with a crash, then spinning the combination lock, she warned herself she ought to expect to come across him with Nicolette or Mairin.

At lunch, he remained with his friends at the senior table the entire period. She felt a gust of hope when she saw him coming toward her in the crowded hall afterwards. Opening and closing her mouth, she stopped as they were about to pass, but he just smiled and they both walked on. The smile was a droll smirk that made her thrill with excitement, but she wanted more.

He said nothing to her during Calculus when she turned to glance at him twice before class started. Her mind strayed to thoughts of what she had done with him. It was such an intimate experience to have with someone, who, despite their few probing conversations, was a stranger to her in so many ways.

She wouldn't be able to offer up his middle name if someone quizzed her. She couldn't say what kind of underwear he wore. She had no idea whether he had a pet, or even where he lived. She envisioned walking up to him and pulling back the neck of her shirt to reveal the black-and-blue lip mark on her shoulder. "You did this!" Somehow the thought made her smile.

She tried to tell herself everything was okay. His not talking to her wasn't really much of a surprise. It was just sex, which he had all the time. She was just another girl he was having sex with. No, she couldn't accept this. She couldn't allow herself to be just another girl.

Yet, as she shifted uncomfortably in her seat, pretending to listen to Mr. Beaters, she was experiencing twinges between her legs. Despite his silence, she was thinking about having sex with him again. He gave her a brazen, smoldering grin as they shuffled out of math class,

"Hey kid."

She paused with anticipation, feeling like an eager courtesan trying to supplicate the prince. After a slight gesture of goodbye with his right hand, he turned and joined his friends waiting outside.

On Friday, the lunch table where she normally sat with the girls from her biology class was full. She wasn't hungry. She thought of leaving, walking out to the quad for air, but then, impulsively, decided to confront him. She strolled down the center aisle toward the senior tables.

Delaney was sitting at the end of a ten-seat table, between Brynn and Trevor. Nicolette was there, wearing a pink halter dress, looking like a hotel heiress who does nothing but party, sue people, throw up, and spend money.

As Samantha approached Trevor's side of the table, Nicolette said with a sneer, "Now what the hell does she want?"

Delaney looked up. He actually had the nerve to look annoyed, his eyelids swelled and his mouth clenched tight.

Feeling likewise annoyed, Samantha said in a soft voice, "I need to talk to you, if you don't mind."

Gripping the table's edge in front of him, he pushed himself to his feet like an elderly man using a cane, and then led her to a vacant corner with a careless stride. "It's not a good time to talk."

"I was wondering if you still wanted to play soccer Sunday." She was suddenly feeling less gutsy, disconcerted by his blue eyes which pointed at her with laser sharpness. She so wanted him to smile at her.

"I told you I'd call. There's no need to remind me."

She heard someone say 'Soccer-girl.' Delaney's whole table was looking at them. "Why can't I talk to you now?"

"I'm kinda hanging out with friends right now."

"You mean Nicolette? I wanted to talk to you about that."

"No, I don't want to talk to you about her."

She nodded her head in agreement, unable to speak.

"I'll call ya later," he said, giving her a parting grin.

That was it. He walked away, returning to his friends.

She heard Trevor ask, "What's the deal with you and Soccer-girl? Now you're disappearing into corners together?" Each step demanded focus and muscle coordination as she headed for the cafeteria exit.

Outside in the hall, she dropped her book bag and kicked it into the wall. After what had happened between them, he was actually doing this to her. Maybe it was a little odd to approach him while he was sitting with Nicolette, but she deserved more respect. He at least should have found an opportunity to make small talk. She wished she could discuss things with her parents, but she knew her dad just wouldn't be able to understand why she wanted to see him again if she described his behavior at school.

Delaney stood with one foot braced in front of the other as he shook Robert's hand, the sinews in his arm prodding the thin skin on the underside of his wrist. They were the same height, just as she'd thought.

"Hello, it's nice to officially meet you," said Robert, white knuckled. There was an unusual hardness in his voice, like he was doing all he could to peaceably let her go. He had insisted on being introduced and followed her out the door when Delaney arrived to pick her up.

"Drive carefully," Robert said to them both as he walked back toward the house. Carved pumpkins of the grim reaper and ominous moons, courtesy of Gretchen and Annabelle, outlined the path to the front door.

Sitting next to Delaney as the engine started to rumble, the idea that he might kiss her made her unable to express her hurt over the way he had treated her since their last date. She salivated at the smell of the wintergreen gum he was chewing, tempted with thoughts of touching the denim cloaking his thigh. Yet she knew it was as likely that she'd reach over and sensually touch him as it was that she'd ask him to bend her over the back seat again. She was passive; he was aggressive.

He asked where in the park she played soccer, and she gave directions. "Who do you play with?"

"There are a bunch of older guys who play every weekend over the summer, and I played with them. I got the chance to try every position."

He smiled. "Did they hit on you?"

"No, it wasn't like that. They were really nice."

"I bet they were."

"No. Really. I was just some kid who wanted to play with them."

He laughed, and she saw the wheels in his head spinning. "So, you want me to play soccer with you and these old dudes?"

"No, I just thought you and I could play, and you could teach me some stuff."

"Okay, we can definitely *play* and I'll definitely *teach* you some stuff."

Pretending not to notice the suggestiveness in his voice, she started talking about the weaknesses of her game and ways she thought he could help her improve, prattling on in a demure voice.

"And what do I get out of this little soccer tutorial?"

She smiled sweetly. "The joy of helping someone."

When they got to the park, Samantha tried genuinely to play soccer but everything ended up a farce. He laughed at her attempts to score from midfield and taunted her with his control of the ball, running circles around her. She couldn't help but snicker at her attempts at heading; the wet ball missed her hairline by several inches and sloshed against her eyebrows. She felt ridiculous when he powered the ball past her, despite the impediment of loose jeans that fell low on his torso. His inane backwards dribbling was supplemented by crass commentary. "Come on, give it to me, Soccer-girl."

Hoping to inspire his competitive side, she challenged him to a one-on-one match. But he started tackling her like a football player -- American football player. Soon she was laughing so hard she collapsed on her back, struggling for breath like an infant inhaling for the first time. He fell on top of her, flattening her with what felt like six feet of muscled bones and no soft flesh.

The contest never got off the ground. But she got to see him move, up close, and manhandle him. When he gave her ludicrous instructions or pretended to direct her legs like he was teaching her to walk, she punched him, or kicked him with the top of her shoe. She couldn't stop smiling.

They were laughing and arguing as they returned the ball to his car. He suggested they take a walk, then, as if he had a destination in mind, guided her to an isolated spot next to the edge of the Long Island Sound. Near some heavy brush, he prompted her to sit on the grass. Once sitting, he immediately grabbed her. Although momentarily taken off guard, she responded to his forceful kiss. It felt surreal. She was frighteningly relaxed and acquiescent as her eyes scanned to see if there was anyone in the area. It seemed deserted.

Chapter 17:

Leaning over her, his tongue in her mouth, he slid his hand under her shirt, his fingers pressing into the flesh around her belly button. He pulled down her loose sweatpants. She couldn't believe what was happening. Again. She had to get him to talk about things. She couldn't go on being physical with him without telling him what she needed from him. As her mind wandered, she closed her eyes and sensed him pull back for a minute.

"Uh, do you have a--?"

"Yes, I have a condom," he whispered back.

In an instant, he was on top of her, face-to-face, spreading her bent knees apart. He nipped her lip and pushed inside of her.

"Aw."

Resting his hand over her mouth, he pushed farther inside her, calming her with a gentle, pacifying kiss on the edge of her cheek. Feeling absolutely no control over the noises she made, his hand hid her blushing face and muted her moans. She liked the feeling of him holding her in place.

Her eyes tightly closed, she arched her neck as he sucked on her skin, moving in and out of her with short, precise motions. His hair swept across her face as he kissed and groped her with urgency.

She thought he couldn't possibly jerk his hips against her any harder. Then he did just that, her bare bottom crushed against the ground where he'd laid his jacket.

Her only recourse was to make gurgling noises in her throat. She imagined herself begging him to be gentle, imploring him to slow down. The thought of pleading, of being overwhelmed, was an elixir. The heat of his panting breath touched her ear as he slowed for a moment. Then he sped up again. She felt her pelvic muscles spasm as a calm feeling swept over her. It was so much more pleasurable than last time.

His arms buckled and he dropped on top of her and lay still for half a minute. When he moved off, she was too embarrassed to open her eyes fully, but she heard him pull up his jeans without hurry. He helped her blindly find her pants.

Smelling wood and salt water, she opened her eyes and saw a sated look on his face. Then he moved so close to her his features looked blurry like a mirage. She didn't see a condom anywhere and wondered how he disposed of it. She was trusting that he used one, without visually confirming it, much too frightened of the idea of looking at his body.

Helping her up, he said, "I saw a place to eat on the way in."

As they walked to the edge of the park and crossed the street to the restaurant, he didn't hold her hand. Walking upright, instead of lying on her back, helped her feel ready to meet his eyes. They found a place under an umbrella at a plastic table with plastic chairs. It was a balmy day for October and the place was crowded.

After they decided what to order, he said, "So, what's up? You wanted to talk to me about something Friday?" He had finally called her Friday night after the fiasco at lunch but insisted that he didn't want to talk things over on the phone. She decided that the power of his physical presence made him prefer to hash things out in person.

"Oh, yeah." She blushed, glancing over at the trees circling the park. "It's about you dating other people."

"What's the point in talking about that?" Despite his grin, he looked like he wanted to run from the topic.

With a little-girl voice, she said, "But I don't think I can go out with you if you keep seeing other people."

"Uh. *Okay.*" He hesitated, sitting back. "But I can't let any girl control what I do when I'm not with her. That's totally out of the question."

"It's not about control." Her finger traced the edge of the table. She felt invigorated by the soccer and the sex, but she didn't want to overreact. "I know you don't know me that well, but … I'd like to get to know you better, and I just don't see how I can do that if --"

"You can't have any say over who I talk to … who I hang out with. That's impossible. Sorry." He was trying to maintain a smile. She could tell he was cautious because of what they'd just been doing. But his tone was firm. "When we're together, like now, I'm just with you … not thinking about anyone else … not paying attention to anyone else. But otherwise, I do whatever I want, with whomever I want, and no one tells me what I can and can't do."

"But -- "

"It's about being independent."

She wondered if he'd had this sort of conversation before. With Nicolette perhaps? "Uh, yeah, well … I understand where you're coming from. It's just that I can't …" Her voice was trembling with ardency. "I can't date someone under those circumstances."

"It's up to you," he said, strands of hair forming a parenthesis on his cheek. "I'll probably call you."

"But don't you think you might be missing out on getting to know someone who can't accept … your terms?" She cringed, feeling like she was repeating herself.

"I don't feel like I'm missing out on someone who wants to tie me down."

"But, take my mom and dad, for instance. They've been faithful to each other for 16 years." She faltered for a moment, trying to keep her voice steady as she skirted the threesome part of their history. "They would never have gotten together if my dad insisted on seeing other women while they were dating. My mom never would have gone for that, or at the very least, she never would have been able to get close to him, and then they might never have gotten married."

He laughed. This time a bit scornfully. "Yeah, okay. You sure do like to talk about your family. Tell me this story again when I'm thirty." He shook his head skeptically. "You do realize that we've been out together, like, twice and you're talking to me about marriage. You really are crazy, aren't you? The rumors are true."

She blushed, "I didn't mean to talk about … marriage. I just meant that they wouldn't have fallen in love if --"

"Fine, you want to talk about love and marriage? I'll tell you what I think." He leaned forward, his elbows on the table. "Marriage is complete bullshit. It traps people in an impossible situation that almost always ends badly. If I ever got married, I'd probably end up cheating like my dad, so I don't plan to *ever* get married, unless I'm completely desperate to get laid." He paused, reaching for a glass of water but not picking it up. "Your romantic fantasies are completely foreign to me."

"Your parents aren't together?"

"Oh God, I don't want to talk about my parents. I'm sorry I brought it up. Back to you. I think you're living in a make-believe world where people fall in love in high school."

"No, I was just using my parents as an example. I didn't mean to say I want to fall in love in high school … I just meant that I'd like to get to know someone well, not just casually, and I can't do that if they're having sex with other people. Can't you understand that at all?"

"I don't know." His eyes were mesmerizing in their expressiveness. Pain, empathy, and conceit passing through them all at once. "I'm not sure what one thing has to do with the other. All I can say is … it's up to you. If I call you and you don't want to go out with me, just tell me."

"If you call me …"

"I plan to."

"Okay," she mumbled.

By this point there was food in front of them. She saw him watching her as she pretended to concentrate on eating.

After a few minutes, he asked, "How'd you get that scratch on your arm? That's not from me, right?"

She blanched, raising her arm to see what he was referring to, worried that he had in fact left another mark on her and had noticed this time. She exhaled, "No, that's from my cat, Plato. He doesn't like it when I give him too many kisses."

"Kisses?"

"Uh, yeah, on the top of his head."

He leaned his chair onto its back two legs, overtly sizing her up. "I can't believe I had your ass sprawled out on the ground a half hour ago."

Her eyes lowered. "So now I know why you're interested in me," she said, a tad miffed.

He smiled. "You have a sweet face … even if it is false advertising."

149

She felt a jolt, loving the compliment even if mitigated. "Seriously?" To hear such a thing from someone as beautiful as him.

Soon she was in his car, wondering if she'd ever be alone with him again. She couldn't help but admire the way he'd spoken frankly and taken her request seriously.

"I don't mean to ditch you or anything," he said. "But I'm supposed to meet my brother soon, so I have to take you home."

"That's okay." She grinned politely. "What's your brother's name? He's older?"

"Uh, yes, he's older. And his name is worse than mine."

"You don't like your name?"

"It's very unusual. But anyway, his name is Gunther."

She smiled, thinking his parents were creative. "Is your name a family name?"

"No, I think it's from some romance novel my mom was reading when she was pregnant with me. She pronounced it wrong."

"Really?" Samantha laughed. "What's the correct pronunciation?"

"I think you can figure it out, Miss Smartypants."

She pretended to think hard, then spit out the more common alterative. "Duh-lane-ee?"

"I think so. No one's totally sure. You'd have to contact the author."

"Who's the author? What's the book?"

"You ask too many questions," he grinned slyly.

She twisted her hands in silence for a moment. "Do you have any other brothers or sisters?"

"No. Just a half-sister and half-brother but I never see them."

"Why not?"

"None of your business, Soccer-girl." He was still smiling.

"Sorry," she smirked. "How old is your brother? Or am I not allowed to ask?"

"He's 23."

"What does he do?"

"He works at a bar, and he's in a band."

"Cool! A rock band?"

When they arrived at her house, he looked as if he wasn't sure if she wanted to be kissed, so he placed his hand on the side of her head and stroked her hair with his fingertips.

Chapter 18:

She had so much to talk to her parents about, but she held off on most of it, just telling them that she had a good time at the park. On Wednesday night, she was caught off guard by a call from Delaney. He cut to the chase and asked her if she wanted to go out to dinner at a southwest place on Friday night, and she immediately said yes.

What was she doing agreeing to go out with him again? He'd definitely want to have sex again. She just couldn't. Yet seeing him in the hall the next day, with his typical in-school conceited air about him, made her wary of initiating another conversation on the touchy subject.

On Friday there was a pep rally. Delaney sat with his guy friends, smiling as the veteran coaches gave self-aggrandizing speeches. Not wanting to watch Nicolette, Meghan, and Brynn grind to hip hop, Samantha directed her eyes at anything but the scene unfolding in front of her. During the principal's remarks on school spirit, she scooted to her right, managing to obstruct her view of the cheerleaders who stood off to the side of the podium.

Heading for the gym exit, on the heels of her English teacher, she turned for one last look in Delaney's direction and was detained by the sight of Nicolette skipping up to him. Throwing her arms around his neck, she stood on tippie toes with her butt jutting out, the fabric of her cheerleading skirt barely concealing the apex of her legs. He gave her a quick kiss. The vending machine behind them circled their joined bodies with the bold primary colors of its full-screen advertisement.

As her classmates tried to navigate around her, Samantha was frozen in place, partially blocking the exit. She'd never seen him kiss Nicolette at school before. It was a bold-faced reminder that he was not hers. She thought of the first day she'd noticed him, watching him sing to Mairin. *He was taken then. He's taken now. What am I doing?*

She knew she couldn't have sex with him anymore. She needed to tell him this before their dinner date that night. He probably would not want to go out with her as "just friends," and she knew she was incapable of turning him down if he asked for more.

She decided she must talk to him at school. He had never invited her to call him or offered her his phone number. He always had to be in control, exclusive, like a trendy restaurant where you can't get a reservation.

She found him in the hall after lunch, talking with Mairin and another girl, both dressed in all black.

"I need to talk," she said simply, her eyelids blinking rapidly.

He shook his head, looking surprised that she dared to interrupt him again while he was *with another girl*, breaking his no overlap rule. A smirk formed on the left side of his mouth, "Now?"

Mairin just laughed. "Sure Soccer-girl, he's all yours."

Now Mairin was using her nickname?

He led her out of traffic, to the far side of the hallway near a set of double doors leading to a little-used staircase. She was sweaty, experiencing a dreadful churning in her stomach. "There's something about tonight. I mean, we might not be able to go out because … uh …"

"Okay," he replied, without a trace of emotion in his voice or any sign of regret on his face. "That's fine." She anxiously waited for him to ask a question, but he seemed ready to end the conversation at that.

"It's not that I wouldn't like to," she stammered, "but I can't date someone, unless it's exclusive."

He nodded woodenly, his eyes haughty and distant.

"I guess that's it … that's all I needed to tell you." As she spoke, her emotions took over. She'd twice had sex with this guy she'd been lusting after for a year. The last thing on earth she wanted to do was give him up, but she had to. She felt the skin of her forehead contort as tears slid down the curve of her cheek.

Delaney's eyes bulged for an instant, then a hardness washed over his face, his jaw set. With a sudden movement, he spun on his heel and opened the door to the empty stairwell, leading her onto the upper landing. There, he turned toward her, his mouth taking on an unpleasant twist. "What is it?"

"It's just not possible for me…" She sniffed. "It's just not possible for me to have any pride and dignity if …" From the look on his face, he didn't seem to want her to go on. "I can't be a self-respecting person and date someone who's dating other people … who's having sex with other people."

"Yeah, I got that part." His voice was all coldness.

"It's just really hard for me." She dabbed at the wet eyelashes stuck together at the corner of her eye, waiting, hoping he might say something else, maybe something nice about her, but he was silent. Almost a minute passed. Her eyes were still threatening to spill over.

Finally, he began as if speaking to himself, not looking at her face, "I knew this would happen. I knew I should never have touched you." He rolled his eyes to the ceiling and then found her face. "Now I'm going to be hearing from your dad, right? About how I took advantage of you."

"Has that happened to you before?" she blurted out.

He frowned deeply and didn't answer.

Then, in a surprisingly calm voice she avowed, "No, you're not going to hear from my parents. You didn't take advantage of me. I would never let anyone believe that. I have no regrets about what happened between us. It was completely my choice. I didn't do anything I didn't want to."

There was genuine surprise on his face as his long, heavy lashes twitched.

Two girls entered the stairwell, interrupting them. She averted her face as they stopped and stared.

"Do you mind?" he asked them.

The interlopers quickly headed down the stairs.

Having regained some composure, she said, "I'm just sad because I think we could be really good together." She strained to grin.

There was a long pause as he rubbed his face and roughly pushed back the strands of hair that fell onto his face, seeming irritated by them.

"You never know," she began, with unnatural hauteur. "One day I might turn out to be someone you wish you could be with." She grinned awkwardly.

He didn't laugh, just furrowed his brow. "You know, I could go along with this and fool around with you, for a month or so, and then end it. But then you'd definitely say I used you."

"No," she replied straight away. "If in a month you want to end it, I want to know immediately, not spend another day with someone who feels obligated." She stood taller. "I'm sorry for crying like this, but the last year has been really hard for me. A lot of other stuff happened."

He looked at her, gravely, and shook his head. "I don't know what the fuck to do. I really, really don't want to be at the end of anyone's leash."

"Maybe if I looked like Nicolette you'd be crying like me," she said, trying to smile as if it were a joke, but also sniffling.

"You know, for a minute there, you were sounding really mature."

"Sorry," she said dryly, mixing sarcasm and contrition.

"I don't know why you think everything about me has something to do with Nicolette. She's one of the best friends I've ever had, but I must be somewhat into you, or else why would I be standing here listening to all this?"

She quaked, locking her arms against her sides as if holding herself together.

"I wanted to see you again," he said defiantly, "but the whole 'going steady' thing is a fucking racket devised by manipulative girls."

"Yeah, well, who's sounding immature now?"

"I'm just trying to imagine how much you're going to freak out if I go along with this for a month and then end it."

"I'm not a hopeless sap. Even if I may seem like one after crying like this." She swallowed the last remnants of her tears. "I can handle being dumped by you. I've handled everything else you've done."

He seemed wrapped up in thought. The bell started ringing and students were pushing through the double doors. He didn't move. "Okay," he said softly, "meet me after school."

As they walked to his assigned parking spot, she did not turn to peruse his friends' faces, but out of the corner of her eye she saw some heads turn in their direction. It made her feel awkward, not proud. She'd overheard him offering girls rides before, so maybe that's what they'd think.

Glad to be moving and off school grounds, she scrutinized his soft-elbow driving posture, then gingerly mentioned that she'd forgotten about her cousin's baby shower that evening. "My dad will insist I not miss it. I just remembered last period. I really can't skip it."

"Shocking."

"What?"

"Nothing."

"Are you mad at me for canceling?"

He glanced at her, his protruding shoulder blades tense. "You've been tailing me for months, people telling me I should get a restraining order, and now I'm giving in … like some kind of…" His voice became too low for her to make out.

"Like some kind of what?" She was trying to stay calm and appreciate the huge step he was taking.

"I don't like the idea of not being the boss of my own fucking life." His tone of voice was less caustic than his words. "Not to mention I know you think I'm gonna ditch some of my friends, which I'm *not* going to do."

Trying not to feel injured, she focused on a dog sticking its head out the window of the car driving alongside them. "You *are* in charge of your own life. Maybe *you*, of your own volition, decided that you want to get to know one person for a while." She forced a grin, hoping for one in return.

His body seemed to relax a little. "And what if I want to get laid tonight?"

"How often do you … get laid?"

He didn't respond, but she noticed he was not frowning so intensely, a smile budding at the corners of his lips.

So badly did she want to touch the hair falling across his eye that her right hand had to restrain her left. Perhaps she wanted to yank it too. "Well … maybe you could try dreaming about me."

He let out a huffing sound, and then checked the rear-view mirror as he took the road toward her house. "Do you dream about me?"

"Yeah, I guess," she said, followed by a chuckle of embarrassment.

"What position am I fucking you in?"

She blushed, her fingers touching her suddenly dry lips.

After she didn't answer, he reached out and touched her narrow forearm, the frailest-looking part of her body. She studied the juxtaposition between his large hand and her smaller one with darker skin tone.

"I'm supposed to go over a friend's house tomorrow," he said. "And Sunday afternoon I'm going to help my brother with something. Are you free after 5 on Sunday?"

"Yeah, 'til 10 on a school night."

He turned into the paved lane in front of her house. After coming to a stop, he reached over and pulled her toward him. His lips were mouth-watering as he pressed against her nervous grin, making hushed, wet sounds. She felt a scrape of stubble and cautiously reached for the downy hair tickling her cheek.

Giggling greeted her as she shoved open the front door. "We saw him kissing you!" Even Gretchen was in on the merriment.

Chapter 19:

The next day, Catherine and Robert recovered from the baby shower with alone time in their room -- Samantha and her sisters understood the implicit 'Do not disturb.' Catherine had been upset by the end of the evening after several digs from her mom, including one about how she didn't buy her daughters "ladylike dresses."

The worst argument her parents ever had was three or four years back after a party hosted by Catherine's parents. Robert had spent "too much time" and been "too friendly" when conversing with one of his old girlfriends. Samantha's grandparents, unmoved by their daughter's pleas, had knowingly invited Robert's ex, saying, "She's such a nice girl and she sings in the church choir."

Samantha had been steamed at her mom for all the yelling when they got home. Her dad was just being polite. Why did it matter that he'd taken her to all the senior dances? That was years ago.

Yet when she thought about it now, she wondered if her dad had had sex with his ex, a possibility that had not occurred to her at that time. Maybe her mom had a more private reason for wanting him to avoid this

161

woman. While *he* certainly wasn't the jealous type -- he didn't mind visiting Anton and only seemed proud of his wife and daughters around him-- Samantha could now understand the sting of jealousy.

On Sunday Delaney greeted her with a straight face as she jogged over to let herself into his car. He mentioned nothing about where they were going.

She mumbled, "I hope it's okay, but I tried to call you yesterday -- using the number on caller id. The woman I spoke to -- maybe your mom -- said you couldn't talk."

He jerked his head in her direction. "That was you?"

She nodded. "You thought I was someone else?"

"I don't want to talk about it." His voice was calm and even.

Arriving at an avocado-green ranch style house built into a hill, they entered through a side door. There, past a garage filled with boxes, was a dimly lit room with a worn sofa and a TV. To the right were high windows at level with a grassy backyard. To the left was an opened door leading to a bedroom. It was like an in-law apartment separated from the rest of the house by a closed door at the top of a carpeted staircase.

Strewn about were schoolbooks covered with thick-stock Darcy book covers advertising local pizza parlors. There were dozens of music magazines, including Rolling Stone, Spin and Blender. Empty videogame cases were piled on a side table.

Without pause, he led her to his bedroom just off the sitting area. It didn't have much to personalize it. Bare walls and lots of empty floor space, nothing out in the open except for some ski tags and ticket stubs on top of a chest of drawers. A small plaque shaped like the state of Connecticut was leaning against the wall:

Delaney Troy
Most Valuable Player
State Championship Series

Glancing at a mattress and box spring set up on a low platform, she stood wondering where to sit while he walked over to a stereo on the floor and put on an indie record.

Returning to where she stood, his fingers gripped under her jaw as he started grinding against her lips. She went limp as he grappled with her clothes; she heard snaps as stitches ripped in her shirt neck. He then took off his own shirt and pushed her onto the bed. When she saw him touch the top button of his jeans, she closed her eyes. Almost immediately, he was on top of her and pushed inside causing her to yelp.

With reckless jolts, their pelvic bones clapped and she adjusted her hips. His hands grabbed her breasts, and then abruptly moved to her bottom. Arching her back, she let loose, screeching as he drove inside her. The loud music drowned out the noise.

Tangled in white sheets and a fleece comforter, she felt the pads of his toes brush against her as he got up. Then, she heard him pull on his clothes. When all was quiet, her eyes finally opened to find him looking at her. He gestured toward the bathroom door, offering her use of it with a motion of his chin. Then he walked out the bedroom door, without a word.

In his bathroom, she washed up while restraining her snooping inclination. There was nothing peculiar out in the open, just toothpaste, shampoo and white towels. Was he going to start talking when he got back, now that the sex part was over?

He returned carrying two bottles of soda and a white porcelain dish crowded with four sandwich halves, one partially eaten. He set the plate next to her,

"Hope you don't mind sharing a plate. I hate doing dishes."

"Yeah, me too," she replied with a grin.

He smiled back, his eyes shiny.

"You're a great cook," she laughed. It was the most delicious turkey and cheese ever.

He got out his math book and she sat next to him, pretending to look over the problem set but far too distracted.

After finishing, he looked at her, "So, you do all math assignments in your head?"

She hadn't written a thing. "No, my head's hurting a little."

He reached for her temples, and her mind skittered as his fingers made circles on her skin. She relaxed, slumping back, her neck exposed. She let out a whimper as he bent down to kiss her.

Turning her over onto her stomach, he pulled at her clothes while massaging her back and bottom with enough pressure that she felt it in her muscles. Then he kneeled behind her. She noticed him reaching for something in the drawer of the bedside table, but looked away.

It stung, but he moved slowly as she groaned softly. He reached around to kiss her, without pulling out of her or halting his hips. She loved the feeling of his body straining against the cushioning of her backside.

His slow movements turned unbridled, and he asked, "Do you like that?" and, after the shortest pause, thrusting again, "I said, do you like that?"

"Uh huh," she complied, squinting at the idea that he might use coarser language. He didn't.

He fell down next to her with a sound of exhaustion. She peeked at him. His hand resting on top of his head, he looked like Michelangelo's statue of a dying slave. She stealthily pulled on her clothes and went to the bathroom.

When she returned, he was flipping through CDs, so she sat on the floor next to the bed with her legs crossed, trying not to feel out of her depth. He turned to look at her, smiling as an overplayed dance song came on the radio,

"I bet you listen to boppy crap like this, don't you?"

"So you're a music critic?"

"I know crap when I hear it."

"It's an okay song. People need something to dance to."

He grinned. "I've seen what you call dancing."

She shook her head, lowering her eyelashes. "No, that wasn't serious."

Cranking up the volume, he jumped to his feet and with a bursting smile began impersonating the belly dancer in the music video. His shirt was off, giving him a perfect opportunity to mimic her moves. He raised his arms in the air, with flamenco-dancer flamboyance, and twisted, rolling his stomach muscles.

She tried not to act completely overcome with mirth, but, really, it was hysterical.

His jeans sagging low, she got her first chance to scrutinize his upper body without self-consciousness. She liked that he didn't look like he lifted weights or attempted any sort of vainglory bodybuilding. He was lean, willowy, and flexible.

There was a strip of blonde hair from his belly button down, which was stunningly erotic. His tan skin was smooth and even toned except for a faded scar below his ribs, which looked like it was probably from a bicycle fall. While in the bathroom, she had noticed a few red blotches on her body. Why didn't he have any? Oh, because she didn't reciprocate the touching and kissing. His underarms had long blonde hair. She felt shy about focusing on his nipples but noticed there was some hair on his upper chest.

As the song ended, he laughed heartily at himself and got a drink from one of the soda bottles.

Unsure what to say, she chuckled nervously with a shaky grin.

"We have one thing in common," he said, taking a seat on the floor across from her. "We both do dance parodies."

"Yeah."

He changed the music and they both listened until a thought made her frown and shake with anticipation,

"So, I might be wrong, but I get the impression you don't want kids at school to know about us."

He looked like he might refuse to answer.

"If we're only going out for a month or so, really, what's the point?" He sounded as if he was at least partly joking about the expiration date.

"Oh."

He took a deep breath. "I'd rather keep things private between us. I don't feel like trying to explain things to my friends. You don't get along with most of the girls I hang out with and trying to force you all to mingle is not the sort of scene I'm into, if you know what I mean. You're not exactly buddy-buddy with the guys I know either. Nobody hangs out with sophomores much. It's just odd."

Studying the ripples of skin gathered on his stomach as he leaned forward, she asked, "Were you talking with Nicolette last night ... before I called? Is she okay?"

His face said nothing.

"At the baby shower, this junior named Martha was going on and on about how you and Nicolette are the perfect couple."

"You have weird friends."

"She's not a friend, more like a distant cousin."

"If Nicolette's so perfect for me, why didn't she manage to rope me into the boyfriend trap?" He looked away with a shake of his head. "I don't give a shit whether people at school think Nicolette and I are an item. And, as for you, I'd rather spend time with you alone. Why is that anybody's business?"

"Could you at least say hi to me at school?"

"Fuck that, you don't want me to say hi. You want me to get into long conversations like this, which is impossible at school."

"Or on the phone," she added wryly.

He got up to fool with the stereo buttons again. Putting in another CD, he said, "This is my brother's band."

She listened as he played with the empty jewel case.

It was head-banger rock. She wondered if his brother was the singer. The voice was low and grainy like his.

"What do your parents think about his career choice?"

"They're thrilled. Just as you'd expect."

She laughed. "Neither of them are musicians?"

"No."

"When did your parents separate?"

He glanced at her like he was perturbed, and for a moment she regretted her question, then his face turned frank. "When I was 6 or 7. It was probably for the best. All they did was scream at each other."

"You remember them fighting?"

"Yeah."

She waited for more of an answer, but when he didn't give one, she decided not to push the issue. "How old are your *half* brother and sister?"

"She's about 8 and he's about 10."

She was about to ask their names when he added,

"The funny thing is. She once went out with a friend of my brother's and apparently she was a total slut." The 'she' he was referring to was obviously not the little sister.

"People say that about lots of women. It's not right, I think. Someone might say that about me, for instance. I mean, considering the last couple weeks."

"No, you're a real screamer and all," he grinned, "but she's nothing like you. A major hypocrite. Conservative Catholic, all that shit. Gunther and I are heathen influences on her little angels. Dad had to convert to Catholicism and marry her in a Catholic church because she's so damn precious. And the fact is, she dated Gunther's friend and was a complete whore."

"How can he do that if he's divorced? I mean, the Catholic marriage."

"Yeah, that's the thing. Not only did she, the devout Catholic, start fucking him when he was still married to Mom, but she insisted he get an annulment. My brother and I became … illegitimate…born outside of wedlock. It's so ridiculous it's funny." He smiled malevolently.

"What? I can't believe that!" She wanted to say the most self-righteous, moralistic things about his dad's conduct, but stopped herself. After some reflection, she composed, "He should have been thinking about getting remarried in a way that didn't hurt you and your brother."

"Anyway, that's my big sob story. It makes all the girls wanna give it up," he said, sounding like he was mocking himself.

Something told her he hadn't actually told this story often. "I should be more grateful for my parents," she said. "I get sort of down on my mom sometimes, for various reasons … last night for moping around. She was angry at my dad for not standing up to my grandmom about something she said at the baby shower."

The corner of his mouth inched up with amusement, and she felt encouraged to go on.

"It came up when they were talking about *me*. My cousin Martha said something stupid. I can't remember, telling everyone to call me 'Soccer-girl' or something. I told her that making fun of me for playing soccer was about as uncreative as you could get." As she said this, she realized she was probably telling the story wrong, leaving things out and changing the order of events a bit. But she didn't care about accuracy; she was trying to make a point. "And then my grandmom was, like, 'My word, Samantha. Don't be so sensitive. You should try to get along with kids at school. Your mom didn't have many friends in high school' and so on. It's horrible, but I'm so glad my mom's parents aren't the ones who live next door."

He was smiling, like he thought her conversation was either lame or childishly tame. "What's up with your parents and high school? I don't think I've ever heard my parents, or anyone over thirty, say a word about high school."

"They grew up around here and went to Darcy."

"No way. You should look 'em up in the yearbook."

She nodded enthusiastically. "Yeah, I've seen the pictures. My mom looks, like, ten years old. My parents have known each other since they were little kids. Both sets of grandparents live around here. They're all friends. My grandparents know everyone in Darcy. At the shower, my granddad said he knows Nicolette's dad; he said he knew something about your dad too… that he's in family law."

"You've been asking around about my dad?"

"No. *No!* Martha mentioned your name. She's involved in planning Junior Prom and she said something about last year's prom with you and Nicolette. I wasn't really involved in the conversation directly."

"Did you mention I'm fucking you?" he grinned.

She felt her cheeks burn and picked at her toenail, wishing she wasn't so obvious when embarrassed. "No, I only told my parents about that. They found it very interesting."

"Like hell you did," he said flatly.

"Yes, I did," she smiled. "After our first date."

"Yeah right. If you told your parents you gave it up on the first date, then I'm your soccer instructor for life." His smile made her belly tingle.

"They asked me if I liked it," she smiled boastfully.

"Bullshit!"

"No, it's true. My mom did."

He looked as if he was starting to believe her. "You didn't!"

She smiled.

"Jesus, what the hell are you doing? Are you trying to get me killed or something?"

"No. Don't worry; they'd never hurt you. They're completely harmless."

"I guess your dad did seem pretty easy going when he came to Franks' class." He was quiet for a moment and then exclaimed, "What the hell! They asked you if you liked it?"

"They wanted to make sure it was something I wanted to do."

"They weren't screaming at you?"

"No."

"Your parents are totally out there. My parents think I'm an innocent baby compared to Gun. All the while they're fucking everything that moves."

She itched to ask what exactly he meant by this very disturbing claim, but stuck to, "They really think you're innocent? With all the girls you've dated?"

"Wait a minute! You told them that and they let you go out with me again. They let me come to your house and pick you up." He looked like he was about to spring to his feet. "How old are you? Sixteen, right?"

She smiled at his eagerness. "They probably think I'm sort of young, especially my mom because she was a lot older, but they said it's my decision. It's not like they don't give me advice and stuff like that." She loved the way he looked at her with his sharp, expressive eyes, and the way his face changed when he broke into a smile. "How old are *you*?" she asked.

"I'll be 19 in a few months." He paused. "I wasn't held back. I started kindergarten late. Mom says I was hyperactive."

She giggled, imagining him as a toddler running around the house, bouncing off the walls like Plato did when he was a kitten. "Can I see a picture of you from when you were younger?"

"Yeah. Sometime. They're upstairs. But, wait a minute. I still don't totally understand. Are your parents hippies or something?"

"No, not really. They're very liberal though. And they were a little crazy when they were younger, in their 20s, but that's another story."

"You're totally unbelievable. Fucking unbelievable."

She smiled, feeling complimented.

Stretching her legs in his direction, she asked, "How often do you see your dad? Do you stay with him sometimes?"

His face lost its smolder. "She doesn't really like having us at her house or around her kids."

"And your dad goes along with that?"

"Yeah, he's an asshole. He's been cheating on her for years. Eventually, there will be a wife number three."

She was speechless. So much about him was clearer now.

Chapter 20:

Monday at school, Ally caught up with her,

"What the fuck's going on? I haven't talked to you in ages. Did Delaney call you or something? What happened?"

"Oh. Uh. Yeah."

"And?" Ally pulled at the trio of silver hoops perforating the outer rim of her ear.

"We went to the movies." Of course, that was several weeks ago.

"Really?" There was a hint of coolness in her otherwise enthused voice. "What happened?"

"Not much," she lied.

Samantha expected more questions, but Ally went quiet for half a minute and then started talking about her boyfriend taking her to a play Off Broadway for her birthday. There was a palpable change. *She's either a little jealous or understandably annoyed that I didn't volunteer more.* Samantha wanted to be more open but just wasn't sure how much to tell or where to start. She'd been so absurd before, gossiping about someone she thought she'd never get to know, but now it was real.

Friday night she struggled to pack an overnight bag for a long-scheduled sleepover at Pritty's house. She knew Pritty would shun her if she knew about what she'd been doing with Delaney -- not that she'd say anything about it. Dragging herself into the shower, she soaked in the hot spray and thought about what people would say of her, what her grandparents would say, what her former self would say about a girl who'd done what she'd done, twice in one day. She thought of all the statistics saying that because she had sex at her age she was less likely to finish college, more likely to be a victim of date rape, and more likely to mother a juvenile delinquent.

No, the statistics meant nothing to her. Having sex didn't cause any of these things. Statistics merely point out correlations that don't necessarily imply cause and effect. Chance and her own future actions would decide if these things happened to her.

She felt better the moment Pritty greeted her at the front door of her flat-roofed house that was big enough to be a small apartment building,

"Goody. Goody. I hoped you wouldn't be late. Bombay Dance Beat is coming on at 8."

She and Pritty danced for hours, watching the musical scenes from Bollywood movies with Pritty's parents and grandparents. The grandmother gave Samantha a box of sticky Indian sweets -- "Whatever you don't finish, take it home to your parents!" -- and asked tons of questions about her sisters, repeatedly telling her she was a "nice American girl."

Robert walked into her room as she was flipping through a sports catalog on her bed. "I don't think Delaney called this week, at least not according to Stephanie's charts and graphs on the subject." He'd been away on business for a day and half and was still in a suit.

She grinned. "Actually, we got together last night." She shrugged one shoulder. "I found out Trent Reznor's vocal performances are the best of all time."

"Does he still think he won't be able to keep his hands off other girls for more than a month?"

Her eyelids drooped.

"Regardless, there's something your mom needs to talk to you about." He stepped out the door to call downstairs to Catherine.

Her mom had made an appointment with her gynecologist. She wanted Samantha to go for an examination and get a prescription for birth control pills.

Samantha felt the exhilaration over Delaney drain from her body. It was alright for him to touch her because she lusted for it, but the idea of having someone else touch her seemed like a violation.

"It'll be alright," Catherine pleaded. "It's just that you need to be very careful. You're very young. But don't worry. I'll go with you."

"But, what about condoms?" Samantha's toes dug into the dense wool carpet as Catherine moved next to her on the edge of the bed.

Her dad closed the bedroom door, his hand resting on the handle. "You have to continue to use condoms. Carry them yourself in case he doesn't. I know it's embarrassing to talk about this stuff with him, but you have to."

Samantha nodded, admitting to herself that she hadn't visually confirmed that Delaney used condoms. She mumbled to her mom, "But you don't use two kinds of birth control, do you?"

Catherine blushed a pinker shade. "Uh, no, but if I got pregnant, it would be okay. It wouldn't be okay for you, Sam."

"But why weren't you more concerned...back then...when you got pregnant with me?"

"Oh my god, I was very worried. And, you're right. It wasn't smart. I'm not sure how I messed up. I don't remember skipping any pills, but I did get sick that month and maybe I vomited a couple pills." Taking deep breaths, Catherine looked like she was reliving some black moments. "It could have turned out very badly for me…and for you."

"But didn't Anton ever worry about you having a baby, and then suing his family, his precious company?" The talks with her parents about Anton were less frequent, but they still had them. "What about what you said about his so-called duty to marry into the right Catholic family and produce de Medici heirs? Wouldn't he be scared about having a baby with *you?*"

"Uh." Her mom looked dumbfounded, as if these thoughts had never occurred to her. Samantha almost felt guilty for intentionally wanting to rile her.

"He certainly knew your mom wasn't tricking him into something," said Robert, walking over to Catherine.

Catherine crossed her hands over her stomach.

"What about an abortion?" Samantha looked at her dad accusatorily. "Anton never suggested it…to anyone?"

"Samantha, I realize you're frustrated, but are you using this as an excuse to go on the attack?"

Since the Italy trip, she'd been swinging back and forth between finding reasons to dislike Anton and trying to formulate a less negative stance toward him, overlooking the things he sorely lacked. Samantha's mouth formed a pout, and her dad relented a bit in tone,

"I suppose it is hard to understand his feelings and intentions back then, especially when he seems so solemn now." He sat down next to Samantha, nothing solemn about him, an easy grin on his face.

Samantha looked at him with crinkly eyes.

"When we were all together, he ended up at fundraisers at Catherine's school, eating clumps of spaghetti. She sent him on errands to the drug store, refusing to let him send out one of his assistants. I don't think he'd ever shopped before.

"One time he spent an entire evening listening to Cat talk about a student who talked backed in class. He had this distressed look on his face, like he was struggling to think of something to say. He'd fire someone who challenged him. I could tell he wanted to comfort her, and clearly it was a novel sensation for him."

"But what was his reaction … ," Samantha glanced at her mom, "… to finding out you were having me?"

Catherine grinned a moment, then looked serious again. "Anton didn't say very much, but he didn't seem upset. He just said we'd be good parents … that Rob and I were meant to be together… he was happy for us. He never said a thing about abortion." She rubbed her index finger across her eyebrow. "The next day he told us he was going to Florence and that we could stay in the apartment as long as we'd like. He left."

She closed her eyes for a minute as her fingers pinched the fabric of her cotton skirt, raising it, then letting it fall onto her knees. "Much later, that's when I started to really think about what had happened. We couldn't help but feel some sort of sadness because he was completely gone from our life. When we called him, he seemed so … distant."

"To be fair to him," said Robert, "he most likely thought we were struggling newlyweds … dazed first-time parents. He stayed away for me, Sam … not because Catherine was emotional but because of me … and you. He didn't want to do anything to come between your mom and me, or me and you, as father and daughter. When I think about it now, I believe it's better for him to have some contact with you. *You* might very well be an important influence on *his* life."

She exhaled. "Maybe I can influence him to bring one of the Botticellis to Connecticut."

School was in an uproar. Even the teachers were huddling in corners whispering. A forty-something art teacher, who used to teach at Darcy but was now at neighboring Forest High, was seen at the mall with his arm around a student of his. Lots of kids at Darcy knew her, and everyone was speculating about what they were doing together.

Ally had lots to say on the subject. "I heard he's been texting other girls too, maybe even a girl from Darcy." She poked Samantha's shoulder. "It's not you. You're only screwing Delaney."

"What?" Samantha exclaimed. She dropped the homework folder she was carrying.

"And you haven't bothered to tell me *anything*." She looked to the left, then to the ceiling, then blinked, followed by a repeat of this series. "I know Mairin, remember? She got this really bizarre call from Delaney talking about hanging out as friends, and then you're suddenly going out with him. You must have put out."

"Uh."

"Oh yeah, play dumb. That's okay. Maybe you'll eventually let me in on the details."

"There aren't any. We just went to a movie; we didn't have sex or anything."

"Yeah, right."

Happily, one of Ally's schnapps-loving friends interrupted them.

At her grandparents' church for the November Choir Benefit, Samantha's eyes were only half open as she watched the choir perform Lacrimosa in their shiny blue robes with stoles draped around their necks. The night before, Delaney had claimed there was something he wanted to see on TV. On Saturday night? They went to a drug store where he bought condoms while she pretended to look at magazines.

The minute they got inside his house, he grabbed her by the waist and pressed her up against the wall. She had to admit it. She was turned on by his roughness.

She preferred focusing on him and what he wanted. That way, she didn't have to take on much responsibility. Like that little slap on her bottom that gave her chills, he did it *to* her.

Throbbing between her legs, she sat up, glancing at the people around her sitting in pews, amazed at her own irreverence.

Chapter 21:

At lunch on Monday, hunched over a tuna sandwich and milk, she was forlorn. She thought she'd gotten used to having no communication with him at school, except when he stopped her in the hall to ask when to pick her up for a date. She had told herself it was okay; this allowed her to concentrate on schoolwork and take advantage of lunch and other free time to get homework out of the way. But just then, it seemed unacceptable. She was just sitting by herself, wondering what he was saying to his friends in the senior section of the cafeteria. At her table, sophomores were chatting with each other, their bags strewn on the empty seats nearest them proclaiming 'no vacancy.'

She reached for a book. She'd been struggling with the battle scenes in *The Iliad*. As she opened to a passage where Achilles was lying in the arms of his dead companion, she heard someone call *his* name. She looked up to find Delaney standing nearby, talking to Jason from the soccer team. Jason was sitting amongst the common folk with an 11th grade girlfriend. After saying "See ya" to his friend, Delaney turned and looked in her direction. She tweaked the corners of her mouth upward.

Blinking with obvious reluctance, he parted a group of sophomores to get to her, magnetically gathering stares as he passed. As he pulled out the chair next to her, she looked around and noticed that he now had the attention of 1/3 of the room. His friends, however, were at the other end of the cafeteria.

"What's up?" he said, grabbing some grapes she'd laid out on top of her brown lunch bag.

"Not much" she answered. She could tell he knew he was being watched.

Reclining in his seat, the back of which was a foot too short for him, he purred almost inaudibly "Are you okay?" He smiled. "Did I hurt you on Saturday?"

"No," she shook her head, averting her face.

"That's right. You're made for it, aren't you?"

"Well, I guess everyone's made for it ... really. What do you mean?"

He smiled in a way that made her cheeks sting. "What are we eating?" he asked, as he proceeded to empty her lunch bag, which included a packet of leftover Halloween Skittles.

"You can have some, if you want."

"Yeah, I know."

She watched his neck muscles move as he swallowed, his head tilted back a little.

"I'm scared to call your house now," he said. He'd managed to make plans for their last few dates without calling her. She had assumed this was due to his aversion to phones.

"It's okay. Nobody will say anything to you, except, well, maybe my sisters. Annabelle and Stephanie will say almost anything."

"So, what are we doing Saturday ... besides *not* hanging out with your little sisters?"

"I don't know. What do you want to do?"

"You make it too easy. What do you think? That teacher from Forrest can't have all the fun."

She knew this was a joke but had to exclaim, "That's not funny. It's rape, you know."

"I'm eighteen, you're sixteen. Is that rape?"

"No," she said, stunned for a moment. "You're a teenager. He's a grown man."

"And you don't think I am?" He sat up, leaning closer to her. "Is it really rape if she went along with it? I don't think so."

"That's not right. It *is*. Statutory rape."

"But that's not the same thing as real rape."

"Even when he's a lot older?"

"Yes."

"Even when she's really young?" Samantha asked.

"How young are we talking about? I guess it depends on the girl. Some fourteen-year-olds go to concerts and get it on with the lead singer. Under a certain age it's a serious crime but not necessarily violent." He paused for a moment, looking like he was calculating something. "I mean, if she's a really young teenager, the guy should get in trouble. But it's not as bad as a rapist who leaves a girl half dead in a ditch somewhere."

"It's all pretty bad … although I still think sex with a girl who's, like, 14 years old is as serious a crime as forcing a woman to have sex … you could argue it's coercion in both cases because a child can't give consent."

His lips parted, a flash of teeth appeared. "Uh huh. So if I was sixteen and had sex with a 14-year-old, I'd be a rapist?"

"No, if you're a kid having sex with a kid, it's not rape. Statutory rape requires having power over someone, like a teacher's authority over a student, or an older man's over a young girl."

"I see. Remind me not to talk to you at school. You're too much of an earful." His smile turned warm as he got up to leave.

She noticed some lingering stares after he left, but it's not like he had touched her, only spoke softly.

On the bus ride home, she was stumped trying to decide for herself if a twenty-year-old man having sex with a fourteen-year-old girl who said she was participating willingly should be categorized as rape.

Samantha stood swinging her backpack at her side, wondering if she should tap Delaney on the back. He was standing in a misshapen circle with Brian, Trevor, and the cheerleaders, Brynn, Meghan and Nicolette. She inched toward him, but before she made much progress, Brian spotted her and called out, "Hey, guys! Did you hear? Delaney scored with Soccer-girl!"

She looked at him crossly as she walked up to the laughing group, and Brian seemed to relent a bit. "Come on, you know me. Can't I joke with you, Soccer-girl?"

"My name is Samantha," she said gently, feeling déjà vu. She'd corrected him before.

She looked at Delaney, digging her left hand into the flapped pocket of her pants. After lunch, he had asked if she wanted to do homework at his place after school. She said 'Yes!' even though she had several tests tomorrow. Delaney's face was expressionless as he nodded to her without breaking away from his friends.

Meghan, looking long and narrow in a mini-dress and knee-high socks with the word 'Couture' running down the side of her calf, turned to the others and said, "So he's bringing her everywhere now?"

Delaney's face turned grim, his jaw clamped.

"D, I thought you guys were on the down low," Trevor offered, flicking a smile at Meghan.

Although scared of the girls, Samantha scrunched up her face sarcastically at Trevor. He looked right back at her and exclaimed,

"Shit, she *is* a firecracker."

Delaney shook his head with an I'm-going-to-kill-you look. Samantha stepped backward and stared at the ground, deciding not to engage. Did he talk openly to his friends about sex the way she sometimes did with Ally? No, it couldn't be true.

Brynn, her voice several decibels lower than Meghan's but still snide, looked at Delaney, "How long before you figure out the whole virgin thing isn't all it's cracked up to be, Del?"

Samantha, her breathing increasing, watched for a reaction from Delaney, but Meghan quickly jumped in,

"The real question is, 'Who's Soccer-girl going to be stalking next?' I'm betting on Jason." Jason Patrician was the boys' team's amazing goalie.

In a full voice Delaney said, "Give it a rest, guys!"

Talk turned to soccer while Samantha scrambled to decide what to say if the girls came after her again. As for the guys, Samantha imagined kicking one of them in the jaw. They were tough guys; they could handle it.

Looking at Nicolette, Delaney asked, "Nic, who was that girl with Lila the other night? She goes to school in the city but comes back on weekends."

Nicolette gave him a look that said 'What the hell do I care?' and muttered, "Asshole," under her breath.

Brian addressed Delaney, "Is she the one whose boyfriend showed up that time and threatened to kick your ass?"

Trevor laughed and added, "And we were like, go ahead, take the douchebag down a notch."

Samantha's eyes bulged. His friends call him names like that?

Delaney lowered his eyelids, keeping them shut for a moment. "No, I told you I barely knew that girl at all -- but I think her name was Kyle."

"Yeah, well, I heard she's definitely prego ... You better make sure she doesn't finger you," said Brian.

"That would be impossible because, like I said, I've never been out with her."

Trevor interrupted, "Dude, you should consider ass fucking."

"At least I know the difference," Delaney shot back.

Samantha was quiet, watching them all laugh, except Delaney.

Nicolette pulled out her phone to show Brynn a photo.

"That's the guy from Prep, right?" asked Meghan, tapping the screen with her painted fingernail tips.

Delaney was watching them and, looking at Nicolette, asked, "Isn't there some cheerleaders' rule about not dating opposing players?"

"There aren't enough cool guys at our school." She paused. "He's not a fuckin' loser."

"Hey! Don't class us with him," said Trevor, waving his hand at Delaney.

"She does have a point, Del," Brian said affably, smiling at Samantha as if to see if she was listening. "Lately you seem whipped."

Delaney looked at Brian. "Yeah, fine, you're ballsier than me. But you were the one worried about losing to Eastern because you couldn't get anything past their keeper."

There were 'oohs!' and 'uh, ohs!' from his friends, but Brian seemed to acknowledge the point with a laugh.

Chapter 22:

She awoke under his fleece bedspread. It smelled like fabric softener and … her own body. Delaney was up, dressed in beat-up jeans and a white T-shirt. She watched as he pulled some gym clothes out of a Darcy Soccer bag and tossed them into a hamper in the closet. Then he started sorting through a pile of books on the floor.

Not seeing a clock anywhere, she asked, "How long have I been sleeping?"

He turned to look at her. "Not too long. I ordered pizza."

"Okay," she said, noticing the cordless phone on the floor. "I should probably call my mom to let her know when I'll be home."

"Sure. Whatever you want."

Inside his bathroom, after a moment's hesitation, she decided to help herself to the shower. Without getting her hair wet, she lathered up with his pine-scented soap, then imagined him using it as she rinsed thoroughly. She dried off on one of his white towels and hung the used terry cloth over a towel bar after making sure she hadn't left any stains on it.

As she pulled on her clothes, she looked in the mirror. Her hair looked rather wild, like the women in fashion magazines with stylized bed-head. She couldn't find a brush, so she combed through her hair with her fingers and then twisted it up and secured it with a barrette. She thought about walking out and declaring, "You know, Delaney, you're a bully in bed," then laughed at the thought of what he might say in reply. As she smiled into the mirror, she noticed all the normal seriousness vanish from her face.

Earlier, during the ride to his house, she had wondered whether they'd get totally naked this time and, if so, whether she could ask him to turn off the lights.

She had tried to slow things down a bit, calling out, "Wait!"

So he rolled over onto his back and propped her up so she was sitting on top of him. "Okay, you move," he said with a glaring grin.

"I can't," she replied, shifting tentatively. The ridiculing looks on his friends' faces were still fresh in her mind.

"Yes you can, " he said in a firm voice, his eyes cloudy yet commanding. "And I want you to."

Delaney was sitting on the bed reading a paperback of *American Poems*. A shadow formed along his jaw, his hair parted down the middle in a sloppy zigzag. His clothing slouched against his body in the most flattering yet understated way. He caught her staring and crawled over to her, moving his mouth to her ear. "I want you to blow me."

The idea sent shivers from her spine to pelvic muscles, but she frenziedly shook her head no. "Are you crazy?"

He laughed and backed away, resuming his reading. The silence felt uncomfortable, but at least he wasn't peeved about her firm no.

"Do you have any pictures from a homecoming or prom?"

"I don't think I trust your interest in seeing them," he said.

"I'm interested in your life."

His left eye shifted skeptically.

"What about pictures of you when you were younger? Can I see some of those?"

He stared blankly at his book for a moment, then marked the page. "I think there may be some upstairs. I'll get them. Wait here."

Clearly, she wasn't invited upstairs.

He returned with a navy-blue album. Opening to a fragile, yellowing page with a collage of baby pictures, she immediately recognized him. He was always beautiful. His cheeks looked doughy and pink. After staring as long as she dared, worried about seeming overly struck, she carefully turned the page to a kindergarten group photo. She had no trouble picking him out. He'd already acquired his defined cheekbones. His hair was shorter and windswept.

The next picture was of a smiling grade-school-aged Delaney with an older boy, who she assumed was Gunther. When she got to a picture with 'Darcy Middle School' printed on the bottom, she asked, "When was this? You look so young. And your hair's short."

"7th Grade."

"Hmm, sometimes it seems like I just got out of 7th grade."

"Don't remind me. You *did* just get out of 7th grade."

"Not really," she said softly and then looked up at him. "So much has happened in the last year; I'm not who I used to be." The album was finished; it was mostly school photos. "No prom pictures?" she laughed, pretending to look for them inside the back fold of the photo album.

"Give it up," he said, with his familiar wry smile.

His mom called from upstairs. "Get the door, Del." She sounded put upon, as usual. Samantha had yet to chat with her in person although she'd seen her once from a distance when leaving the house with Delaney. His mom had stood on the small front porch watching them but didn't call out.

He returned with a pizza box. Just as they were about sit down to eat at the low table in front of the basement sofa, the phone rang. He walked over to grab the handset off the bed. Although he barely said a word beyond hello, it was clear that the call was for him. She watched as he listened, the receiver between his shoulder and cheek. After some mumbled sentence she couldn't hear, he said in a pithy voice, "I gotta go."

"Who was that?" she asked, trying to sound causal.

"Nobody," he said flatly. After jumping onto the sofa, he looked at her, probably noticing the still curious look on her face. "Back off, Soccer-girl." His grin was brash and unapologetic.

"You've got so many rules. I'm not allowed to talk to you on the phone or ask whom *you're* talking to on the phone. I'm discouraged from walking up to you at school or stepping between you and your friends … Maybe I'm the one who's being controlled in this … *arrangement* we have."

"Oh yeah?" The glare of his eyes burned her. "I know the feeling."

She shrugged, a tinge of self-pity making her lungs expand sharply. "You've never officially given me your phone number, so I don't feel like I have an invitation to call here."

"Hit me up if you absolutely have to."

She knew she would accomplish nothing by pursuing the issue further. Yet, she thought of raising her voice, confronting him about making her feel like an intrusion in his life, an injury to his reputation as a player. With a few choice sentences, how easy it would be to make him break up with her.

To break up now rather than later would probably be less painful. His friends wouldn't be on her case so much. She might even get out of the OB/GYN visit, if only because her mom would take pity on her. Yet, as he stood there holding the TV remote as if it were a video game controller, she knew she didn't want to intentionally push him away.

Samantha was still cursing her willingness to give in, when it occurred to her that there was something else she wanted to challenge him about. "How often do you get into fights?"

"What?"

"Brian mentioned it. You were flirting with a girl and her boyfriend got angry?"

"I'm not sure *what* he was talking about. Maybe something from last year ... And for your information, Miss Perfect, I've never been in a fist fight."

"No?"

"I don't get into fights."

"No one ever tried to start something with you ... like Brian said?"

"When they do, I walk away."

He spoke with such certainty, absoluteness. So often she overheard guys at school talking about punching somebody, beating someone up, if only in jest. He openly eschewed that machismo. It was good to know he didn't have a violent side, just a domineering one.

Chapter 23:

Despite a nervous stomach, Samantha survived her OB/GYN visit, the paper robe, the pinching Pap test, and the awkward questions. After, she and her mom went to lunch at a Cantonese restaurant across the street from the medical center.

"I can just imagine the look on Stephanie's face when she gets wind of the threesome story, 'Wow, were orgies, like, trendy back then?'" Samantha sipped wonton soup with a scoop-like spoon.

Catherine grinned, her face so youthful in the soft light. "Well, Rob and I do want your sisters to know eventually ... when you're ready."

"Did Dad tell you what he said to me about Delaney, about how he's a rotten boyfriend?" Samantha looked down at the chives floating in her soup, smiling. "And, as you know, Dad's an expert on being a good boyfriend, like when he introduced you to Anton."

"Samantha," Catherine exclaimed, while shaking her head and closing her eyes for several seconds. "Your dad was the best boyfriend, the kindest, most loving and sympathetic person I've ever met."

Samantha nodded, wanting to agree.

Catherine unbuttoned and re-buttoned the jacket of the bamboo-colored suit which she often wore to work. "I don't mean to change the subject, but it got me thinking. I know you probably won't be real happy to hear this, but it occurred to me that Anton is, well, he's not very good at saying all the right things, but he's really been making an effort ... with you. Like never before. He just called about meeting in the city for dinner over the Christmas holiday."

"Yeah, he's fantastic if you ignore 50% of everything he says, and 99% of everything he did from the time I was born 'til last year."

"Sam!"

"Nevermind. Do we have to talk about him today?"

"No. We don't have to talk about anything you don't want to." Catherine glanced at her phone as a message lit up the screen, then turned it off. "I know we've gone over this before, but there is something else I ought to say. It's your body and your choice, but your dad and I were talking the other night. And we thought we should repeat that ... although we're not disappointed in you .... and we want you to have access to whatever you need ... we don't think it's the best idea for you to be having sex."

Samantha nodded her head in response, using chopsticks to pick up a dumpling from the oval dish delivered to the center of their table.

Gently, her mom continued, "Sex isn't like abusing drugs or drunk driving, but I'm just worried it's going to be really tough on you at some point."

"I know. I just ..." Samantha looked out the window onto the bustling street outside the restaurant with its artisan craft shops, clothing boutiques, and people double parked waiting for a metered spot to free up.

"I guess what I'm trying to say is that although we'll always support you, we don't want you to think that taking you to get birth control pills means we think it's a good idea for you to have sex with him." Catherine exhaled and waited for a reply.

Samantha straightened. "Before Delaney, I never even wanted to kiss someone. Maybe once in a while I thought about kissing a movie star, but that wasn't a real person. In the abstract, it doesn't make a lot of sense, but when I'm with him I feel, well, sort of ... he's just the most captivating person. Around him, I feel like *I'm* a more interesting person ... attractive too, I guess."

"You can't really know for sure whether he's as special as you think. Delaney could change. You could change."

"Don't worry. We're not making any commitments. We're so different, in very serious ways, and we both recognize this. He's not someone I can rely on. I know that *today*. I don't have to wait 'til I'm older to figure that out."

"Obviously, your dad and I want so much more for you than someone who continually insists he doesn't really want a girlfriend."

"Who knows? ... Getting the pills could be a big, embarrassing waste of time if he breaks up with me next week."

"Samantha, you know, you have to be okay if things don't work out with him. You can't let it knock you off track for other things you want to do with your life."

"When he breaks up with me, at least it won't be a surprise."

"Samantha, seriously, it's so important. You have to be able to move on no matter how wonderful he seems in some ways. You have too much to give. You're passionate and strong ... and so smart."

"I don't see why you always say I'm strong. I'm a complete wimp around him half the time, although I'm not even sure I want to change that."

"You're more confident than me, Sam. I'd be terrified of someone like Delaney. I get so jealous … like when the new intern from Rob's work called the house. It's just me. It's nothing he's done."

"Dad's not interested in anyone else."

"But I can't help thinking that he has a choice. He meets people all the time."

"Maybe, but if someone approached him, he'd turn them down! Dad is happy with *you*. I understand that more now than I ever did before."

Catherine smiled, looking as if being told this by Samantha was like learning something new. "Yes, I know. I don't mean to scare you, Sam. I'm just trying to be candid with you … like you're being with me."

Samantha looked at the couple sitting at the table next to them. From what she could hear, they were discussing 401k plans. Not a touch of emotion, stress, or worry in their voices. Her relationship with Delaney wasn't solid, but he could make her tingle from head to toe, exasperate her, make her question things. "Do you think Dad could have sex with someone just for the physical thrill of it, and the novelty of it, and then practically forget about it the next day, like it meant nothing? I know Delaney can."

"Uh, I guess … or at least he has in the past, I think … a long time ago."

"What if we lived in a different time -- Medieval Europe, The Antebellum South, Regency England -- when women had to put up with that sort of thing from a husband, would he be able to have a fling, one that didn't affect how he feels about you?"

"No matter what time we lived in, I'd do everything I could to convince him not to do something like that. But, yes, I think he'd be *capable* of it."

"I don't understand guys that way. Letting someone they don't even care about, at all, look at them naked … get physical with them."

Catherine ordered tea and, as the waiter walked away, looked at Samantha. "But, if Delaney wants to have flings like that, maybe you shouldn't be so comfortable getting undressed around him either."

"I don't have sex with him because I feel comfortable around him. I'm *un*comfortable around him most of the time. I've never even seen him naked because I'm too afraid to open my eyes when ..." She took a loud breath. "Maybe I like feeling off balance when it comes to him. I don't think I would change anything if I could."

"Oh, Samantha, sometimes it scares me the way you talk about him. But I shouldn't say that. No matter what happens, everything will be okay for you."

Chapter 24:

She got her period and marked an *X* next to 'Friday' on her desktop calendar. It was a few days early. Although she felt lucky it hadn't happened the day of her gynecological exam, she worried about broaching the subject with Delaney that night.

They'd planned to go to an opening night movie at the theater in the mall, but it sold out, so they decided to walk around a bit.

"This place is a mob scene," he said, as they started down the main corridor. On Friday nights, the mall was crowded with teenagers, mostly early teens, who cased the floors without doing much shopping. Delaney twisted to get out of the way of a girl who was walking backwards while talking to a trio of boys in skater T-shirts. "Too many kids."

"Every Saturday my sister has a meet up with her friends here. It's the social event of the week."

"I used to ... years ago ... way too old for it now."

"I've always felt too old for it."

He smiled. "Were you sick yesterday?"

"I had a doctor's appointment."

He nodded, looking her over from the tips of her black shoes to the hood of her cardigan, as if he wondered which part of her anatomy had been poked and prodded.

They stopped in front of a window display. It was a little boy's bedroom with a round soccer-ball rug and black-and-white soccer sheets. He reached out and jabbed her arm. "Is that what your room looks like?" As she smiled at him, he leaned in and gave her a light kiss, his hand lingering at the side of her waist. "Simmons is making us take the bus to the game, so I can't give you a ride to Hartford."

"Do you want to ride home with me?"

"And risk my life with you behind the wheel … " He watched her smiling sneer in response and then added, "There's some shit about a permission slip if you want to be driven home."

"I guess I might come by myself then, if you want me to."

He was thoughtful for a minute. "We're going out partying afterward. Mostly just guys. There'll be a lot of drinking."

"Okay, I'll just come to root for you." She was a little disappointed.

"Bring one of your little sophomore friends … just not that crazy punk chick who likes to crank call me."

She laughed dismissively. "Ally doesn't call you."

He turned his face toward the striped double doors of a candy shop.

"Does she?" she exclaimed.

His voice was barely audible as he leisurely shook his head.

They stopped for a moment near the glass elevators. Samantha noticed a group of girls looking at Delaney as they exited onto the second floor. "I was going to ask you about Christmas break. Will you be around?"

"I'm going skiing with my brother part of the time, but we can get together when I'm home."

"Okay," she smiled, suddenly more cheerful.

"Looking forward to your Norman Rockwell Christmas with the family?"

"Yeah, same old same old."

As they neared a lingerie store, he glanced at her crimson sweater. "I like that color for you. I was thinking of buying you something ... to go underneath it."

"Uh, thanks, but that would not be fun to explain to my parents." Something in the tone of his voice rekindled her anxiety about the no-sex issue. "I have my period," she blurted out, then she added with an awkward smile, "Sorry if it's really weird to mention that."

"No worries, I was just about to tell you my ass was itching this morning."

She chuckled with embarrassment. "Boys must think that's so gross, huh?"

"I'm not sure what *boys* think, but I can't say it bothers me much."

"You don't think it's gross?"

"Uh," he grinned. "I probably thought so when I was like 12, but now I'm like, whatever, it's not a big deal."

She nodded, feeling intrigued and alarmed at the same time.

He studied her face. "I remember when I was younger, my brother used to come home and tell me about his night -- he goes out with a lot of women although he's not really the most charming guy, sort of an anti-feminist type."

"What does he have against women?"

"He has prejudicial ideas about women ... but anyway, one night he came home, talking about how he'd had sex with this girl who was on the rag. I remember thinking he'd lost it ... gone totally insane ... worried my parents were going to have to commit him."

"Do you still think it's insane?" She was worried that he would answer in the negative.

"Not at all, babe," he said, in a silly voice, pulling her hips closer to him.

"Well, I don't know. I don't think…"

"Yeah, yeah, I understand."

She was pleased, once again, with his easy reaction but wanted to confirm that they had an understanding. "I'm not ready for something like that."

He nodded and asked with a salty smirk, "Yeah, well, I've been meaning to ask you about getting a blow job. I've noticed this strange coincidence. Ever since I've started going out with you, no one's gone down on me."

She was shocked that he mentioned this again … so soon. "Well, I don't think I want to do that until I'm married or something … and … I've heard you say things about that at school that were really hostile."

"What?" he stopped abruptly, looking flabbergasted.

"I heard you say things like 'Suck my dd…d-i-c-k' when you were mad at someone."

"When? I said that to a girl?"

"You were talking to Brian, I think …"

"Yeah, so what's the problem with that?"

"You talked about oral sex in such an aggressive way … that bothers me. If you like doing that … why do you talk about it like it's some sort of threat or something?"

"You're off in lala land again, Samantha, or … maybe this is from Franks' class. Is that what it is? You want to hear something less vulgar … like, uh, fellatio? Is that better?" They were now standing next to a seating area surrounding a large oval planter.

"No, but it's confusing how you use it to express your displeasure with someone. And it seems to me that it's a very sensitive, intimate thing. I'd want to be in love to do that with someone."

He nodded, then leaned forward, almost hovering over her. "Maybe this has something to do with your fear of looking at my dick." His voice cracked. "You like to be fucked but don't want to look at what's fucking you."

She turned her face away from him petulantly. Feeling a tear washing over her eye, she heard him laughing and turned to find him holding his stomach. His hand was raised to say 'give me a minute.' She slouched onto a bench, feeling stunned. As he joined her, he said, "Sorry." After a couple deep breaths and more chuckling, he added, "You're just so entertaining. I'm sorry."

She sat still, feeling sullen.

"I'm sorry. I couldn't resist." He studied her for a minute.

"Have you been laughing at me ... about ... you know?" she asked with a frown, her eyes focused on the speckled floor. "Your friends think it's funny?" she whispered.

"Come on, I'd never say anything to anybody about us fucking around. I never have, although I know my friends sometimes guess stuff." Smiling broadly, he added, "I just think it's a riot the way you like sex but are afraid to look at me. It's kind of quaint, actually."

"I suppose you're right ... I'm shy." She watched him, trying to enjoy the merriment on his face. "But I do think guys say 'suck my ... ' ... well, you know, and say it antagonistically and actually mean it as a reference to sex."

"I never say it to a girl unless I mean it as a literal come-on," he grinned, reached over and kissed her neck. She looked down at the white sheen of his hair, hoping he'd come up and kiss her mouth, but he backed off, studying her face.

She leaned forward and kissed his cheek, rubbing her face against the side of his and breathing in. As she reached up to touch his hair, she heard some giggling coming from behind the leaves of the giant palm in front of them. He gently pulled away from her and nodded in the direction of some girls whom she recognized from school.

"Let's get out of here," he said softly. "Unless you want to stay and start some gossip."

In minutes, they were in his car, parked by the side of the mall, a sign for **Darcy Town Center** overhead.

"So what do you use? Pads or tampons?" he asked as he slid his hand up her thigh.

"I can't," she said breathlessly, pushing his hand away.

"Come on," he whispered.

"No!" she said firmly, with a smile. She was *not* going to have sex with him.

"Samantha," he grinned. "Give me a chance."

"No," she laughed nervously.

"I have something I want to show you."

She laughed, and he cajoled her by repeating her name softly.

He reached for her hand while kissing her, gently placing it on his lap. She felt a pang of nervousness and her hand shook. She didn't want to pull away like she was repulsed by him.

When she got home, she imagined him finishing what her hand had started.

At Darcy High it was crunch time. Term papers were spit out at an alarming rate of up to ten pages a night. With final exams looming, class notes for AP biology were passed around like pirated downloads of a Jay Z concert. Projects assigned months ago, yet to be started, were embarked upon with what might be mistaken for the zeal of scientific curiosity. Samantha, who was "at the top of her class" according to her guidance counselor, was tucked away in her room each evening. For the first time, she had put off a lot of work until the end of semester. As much as Delaney, a B+ student.

Robert leafed through a draft of her English paper on the use of metaphor in *Jane Eyre*. "You aren't required to always get the best grades -- that's too much pressure -- but reasonable grades *are* required. I'm sure you'll have no problem, although there's clearly been a change in your work habits since ..."

She slumped against her chair cushion. "Don't worry. Deep down, I'm still the same obsessive-compulsive student all the other kids love to hate."

"Glad to hear we have a diagnosis." He wrapped his arms around her neck and kissed the top of her head.

Despite the overload, when Delaney rang, she wrapped up whatever couldn't be put off, threw on a nice top and drove to his house. She empathized with Jane Eyre leaving Mr. Rochester after discovering he was married, and kept his mentally ill wife in the attic, but couldn't help thinking that she herself might not have been able to leave.

Chapter 25:

The first day of winter break, Delaney left for Vermont with his brother. He wouldn't be back until January. Through all the normal holiday activities, such as shopping, visiting, and wrapping presents, Samantha looked forward to the solitude of bedtime, when she could think of Delaney without interruption. She tried to imagine her soccer hero skiing and wondered what he and the guys did while hanging out at the lodge. Probably not caroling or stringing popcorn.

Her dreams were dismal. In one, he called to say they were over. In another, he didn't call at all, not even "once or twice" as promised, and she frantically tried to reach him, only to be told by Gunther to stop calling or he'd report her for telephone harassment.

Before he left, she had asked, "Why don't you get a cell phone? Maybe you can ask for one for Christmas."

"I'd lose the damn thing before I let my dad call me every time he wants to yell. Why would I want to always be reachable?"

She wondered if he listened to the CD of Bhangra dance mixes she'd given him. Not wanting to go overboard, or make him feel bad if he didn't get her a gift, she'd burned some songs onto a disc and made a Christmas-wreath-shaped label for the case:

Merry Christmas. This is for practicing your belly dancing.

—Samantha

"What's up?" her dad asked, as she helped him unload the car for a present exchange at her grandparents' house.

"Nothing," she mumbled, balancing two overstuffed shopping bags on her hips. "I was thinking maybe I should get a cell phone … so people can call me when I'm not home."

"Meaning Delaney," he said as he closed the trunk. "You know we aren't crazy about the idea of you and your sisters getting phones unless they're only for emergencies."

Inside, Samantha planted herself on the hardwood floor next to a miniature sleigh decorated with mistletoe. Annabelle pranced around, hurrying Gretchen who was crawling under the sagging branches of the ornament-heavy spruce tree, locating gifts to be handed out.

As her cousins screamed over scooters and play kitchens, Samantha twisted her legs into various contortions, rotating position every five minutes. Soon her family was commenting on her lack of enthusiasm.

"All she cares about is her boyfriend," Annabelle explained.

"He's a god … who looks like David Beckham," added Stephanie.

"Boyfriend?" asked Uncle Stuart. "'Sam, is that true? Are you even legal?"

If there were no audience, she would have loved to talk to her dad's younger brother about Delaney. He was itinerate, traveling around the world, working freelance and never unpacking his suitcases. A serial monogamist, every time they saw him he had stories about his latest girlfriend.

"Legal?" exclaimed Grandmom Montclare. "What on earth on your talking about, dear?"

On January 2nd, she got up, took a shower, and dressed in a thin cashmere sweater. She calculated and recalculated the driving time from Vermont, waiting for him to call, yet by nightfall he still hadn't. It wasn't until 9:30 pm that she heard from him. He didn't have time to talk but called to say he wouldn't be getting back until the day before school started. His brother had run into some friends who invited them to stay at their place.

She mumbled non-words to her dad when he asked what was up. Behind the closed door to her room, she collapsed on the bed. Squeezing her comforter between her legs, she writhed about, then flipped on her back, breathless and feeling pitifully sad. Then she felt fear. He'd only called twice since he'd left.

The next morning at around 10, she called his new digs.

An unfamiliar male answered the phone. "Hello?"

"Hi, is Delaney home?"

"Just a minute."

Several minutes later, a groggy voice came across the line, "Yeah?"

"Hi, it's me," she said in a baby voice.

"Uh huh, it's you."

"Sleepy?"

He breathed loudly. "It's way too early."

"I just wanted to talk." She waited for him to answer, kicking at the bed skirt hiding the boxes of old notebooks under her bed.

"I gotta go back to bed. I'm beat, Sam. We'll hang out when I get back."

"Oh, okay. I guess I'll talk to you later."

She immediately dialed Ally, who asked her to come over.

They gossiped for nearly an hour on Ally's bed, eating junk food and lodging complaints about the guys in their lives.

"Why doesn't he want to talk to you on the phone?" asked Ally. "I'm sure I heard Mairin say he calls her."

Samantha finished chewing a piece of eggnog taffy, suddenly tired of it tumbling in her mouth. "Maybe it's about facial expressions and body language ... without them, you can misunderstand what someone's trying to convey."

"So, you're misunderstanding him when he cuts you off and says he's going back to bed?"

"No," said Samantha with a flinch, "but I think I'd misinterpret half the things he said if I wasn't able to watch his face to see if he's only kidding."

They settled down to a boring, argument-free episode of an MTV show, but the silence was interrupted when Ally's sister Suzanne opened the door without knocking. With her was Mairin.

The day before classes started, Delaney called. He was back in Connecticut, but wiped out from the long drive home, so he asked if she could drive herself to his house. She arrived twenty minutes later.

He came out to greet her in the driveway wearing an unzipped ski jacket, his snowy hair tucked behind wind-burned cheeks by a knit cap.

"Hey," he said dimly.

She forced herself to be polite. "How was your Christmas?"

"Okay," he said without enthusiasm.

"You were grumpy on the phone when I called, and you never called me back."

"I told you when I'd be home."

She followed him into his bedroom where he started pulling off her clothes. When they were both standing in their underwear, he kissed her, wrapping his arm around her lower back, pulling her up against his erection. She used to mistake the hardness for a belt buckle or the metal of his jean buttons, or maybe that was denial.

He positioned her on her hands and knees with her butt in the air. She steadied herself with braced arms as he moved in and out of her. There was too much friction. She thought about how she'd felt while he was away. "I want to turn over."

"I don't take requests." He was breathless. "Just lay there and take it."

She dove forward, disengaging from his body and landing face down on the bed. Turning to look at him, she cried, "You have to take requests; you have to listen when I say stop."

In a low voice, he said calmly, "I know. I'm not serious. When have I ever not listened to you? Never." Reclining next to her, he was quiet for a moment. "That's what gets you off, you know ... when you give up control."

She covered herself with his blanket. He didn't, his body left fully exposed. There was something so wrong about lying next to him without touching him. She barely looked down but with only a glance, could see he was aroused. Didn't it bother him to be so noticeable?

She reached for his arm, pulling his bicep as if she could move him without assistance. He willingly came to her. She put her mouth to his and he kissed her back, his hot breath filling her lungs.

When she attempted to find out about his trip, he was monosyllabic. So she tried some shock therapy. "I saw a video of you from after prom last year. You weren't wearing a tux though."

"What?"

"It was you and your friends hanging out at someone's house."

"Uh, where did you see it?"

"At Ally's. Mairin showed it to me."

His expression darkened. "Why would you watch that?"

"She just walked in the room and put it on. I guess I was curious."

"Nicolette and me sitting on a couch?"

"Yeah, do you remember someone taping you?"

"Sort of."

"Nicolette looked good in her crown." She wanted to sound upbeat and sincere.

"I wish I could figure out your interest in her."

"Everyone's interested in who's prom queen and you used to go out with her."

"Who knows? I might again."

"Why are you mad?" she said, almost whining. "I haven't seen you in so long. I missed you so much. And now you're mad at me ..."

"It wasn't the best two weeks for me. There were lots of girls there and I couldn't really hang out with any of them."

"Why?"

"We'd hook up -- and that wasn't allowed."

"And so ... you're rethinking *us*?"

He rolled his lips. "One of my least favorite things about you is your envy of Nicolette."

"I'm curious what you two liked about each other and seeing the video gave me a little bit of an idea, I guess."

"What was Mairin saying?"

"She just laughed at the two of you ... particularly what you were wearing."

"What was I wearing ... jeans?"

"Yeah, and Nicolette was in a silky nightgown." She crossed one hand over her chest, now covered with a bra and thin undershirt. "She has really nice breasts, huh?"

He raised one eyebrow. "I've never heard you say something like that before."

"I'm full of surprises," she said sarcastically, then her voice turned lackluster. "Over Christmas, we got together with my parents' friend from Italy. He was with the most beautiful woman; he said she was his assistant. Once before I saw him on TV with an actress."

"No shit?" he grinned. "Which one?"

She mentioned the name. "Don't tell me you like her because I can't handle that."

He shrugged off the news, seemingly unfazed.

"If you could be with someone like that, would you be willing to be faithful for the rest of your life?"

"Nah ... why would that change anything? The 'rest of your life' part is a nonstarter. For college I'm moving to the city ... going to NYU if my dad will pay for it. I'm gonna hit it with any girl I want ... go to concerts, clubs, parties ... try stuff I've never done."

She didn't want to believe that he intended to sound so insensitive, but self-pity welled up. "I guess you'll forget about me."

"I don't know. We'll see whether or not you're talking to me by then."

"Why wouldn't I?"

"I don't know. If I started going out with other people ..."

"You're thinking about doing that. That's why you didn't call? That's why you don't want me to talk about Nicolette?"

"I don't want to talk to you about her because it's a fucking pain in my ass."

"Sorry for being curious about you ... and Nicolette." She couldn't pretend to be okay; she reached for her pants. "The two of you together were always quite a sight. I guess being seen with me would be a letdown for you ... for everyone."

"*That's* what you want. You and me as this kickass couple at school." His piercing eyes dove into her. "What's the point of dating you if I have to go back to all that? I did that already ... with Nicolette ... as you continually remind me."

"Actually, if you really want to know..." She grabbed her socks. "I haven't thought much about Nicolette at all recently, except to feel a little guilty because she's probably insulted by you dating a geeky sophomore instead of her." She tugged on her shoes. "Maybe you don't understand why I'm curious about your past because you're not very interested in my life."

He looked anxious for an instant and then said softly, "I'm interested in your life."

"You really don't know much about me. You've never really talked with my parents or met my sisters, and you have no idea about my *real* family situation."

"I listen to you talk about your family all the time."

"Sorry to burden you."

"It's all good." His voice was deep and soft.

"When you break up with me, which it sounds like you're going to do -- some night right after having sex with me -- I don't want anyone to know about my secrets, so I can't tell you everything." She could feel the pulse beating in her throat, but felt no tears.

"I would never tell anyone something you told me in confidence. I'm not a gossip."

"We only gossip about you because we're interested in you. It's not persecution, Delaney. You'd appreciate it if you ever liked someone … who seemed out of reach."

"Tell me your secret," he said, his gaze soft and intent.

"You don't want to know." She felt her eye watering. "And you wouldn't believe me anyway."

"I believed your story about telling your parents we did it on our first date."

Her sweater was in her hand but she let it fall. "Tell me something about *you* … about your mom maybe?"

"What do you want to know?"

In her softest voice she said, "Maybe we could go upstairs. I mean, if your mom's not home, we wouldn't be bothering her."

There it was, on a mantel in the living room, next to a cluster of random collectibles. The picture of his mom she knew existed, the one where she looked like him, where she looked happy and smiling and glorious. "She's not so happy anymore, is she?"

"She basically decided her life was over when he left."

"But that was ten years ago, right?"

"Yeah."

"She didn't want him to leave? I mean, it wasn't a mutual separation?"

"He was packing and she came running in and told Gun and me that he was leaving us … all three of us. He said that wasn't true, but then Gun and I never got to stay long when we visited him … never overnight … I could only talk to him on the phone. Now, I'm like, whatever, I don't give a damn, why would I want to go over there and have to put up with his wife's snippy comments?"

"Oh," she said, regretting the pitch of their earlier conversation.

He stood by a tufted, floral-print chair like he was standing in a museum display; it was clear he never used the furniture. "She would cry and drive by his new house. Eventually, she started going out to bars, drinking and bringing guys home."

"That sounds so … bad." She looked around. There was a curio cabinet on the far wall. It was filled to capacity with figurines of small children: children holding security blankets, children carrying lunch pails, children playing hopscotch. None of the children were playing soccer, or flirting with girls, or banging on drums in a rock band. Maybe his mom wanted a daughter. "Aren't things any better now?"

"A bit. She has less luck with the guys, but she still drinks a lot. And she acts so pitiful around him, making scenes about stupid stuff like not getting invited to his birthday party."

"Please tell me some good things about your parents," she said gently, with a pleading tone of voice.

He squinted a grin. "He sends me money. He says he'll pay for any college I want to go to as long as I don't piss him off too much. And my mom, what's there to say? She's a mom; she does normal mom stuff."

She nodded.

"I've always relied on my friends, not my parents."

"And your brother, I guess."

"Yeah. It was great, hanging out with him, meeting older girls. I've seen him fuck up in every possible way with girls. I learned what *not* to do."

She smiled, "Like for example …"

"Lie and say you like a girl more than you actually do. Pretend you're not seeing other people when you actually are. I've never done that kind of shit. I watched it get him in so much trouble."

"Yeah, I'm glad you don't lie to me," she smirked. "I like being fully aware of the fact you're not as into me as I'm into you."

"I wasn't in the best mood earlier."

She nodded, following him into a small room with striped blue wallpaper. There were blocks on a shelf and a tub of Lego on the floor. "No soccer sheets?"

"Apparently, they wanted me to be an engineer or something. This is actually Gunther's room, but he moved downstairs and then I got it."

"Oh, so that's not your teddy bear?" she grinned.

He pulled her down onto the bed, nuzzling her neck. "Did I say anything too mean earlier?"

"Something about breaking up and going out with Nicolette again," she whispered, clinging to him.

"Being celibate bites."

Chapter 26:

Trevor was finishing up a story about some shenanigans over winter break. "Man, I wish you were there," he said to Delaney, as they stood together outside Calculus. Samantha saw that Trevor had spotted her, but he continued on, "Did you get laid over break?"

Delaney's jovial expression stilled as he shook his head, seemingly oblivious to Samantha's presence off to the side of the hallway. "There was one girl who managed to get nailed by every guy at the lodge. Apparently, she did *everything*."

Samantha stepped into their circle. "What are you guys talking about?" she asked with fake obliviousness.

Delaney turned to her, saying, "Hello," in a clear voice that surprised her. After all, he was with his friends.

"So, Gun was on you the whole time," Trevor asked Delaney, "telling everybody you have a kiddie girlfriend?"

Delaney's infectious smiled vanished. "That's all I heard out of him."

"I told you what Gun said to me," Brian added, looking at Trevor, "he was, like, 'Beauty queen's into it deep with a sophomore. I never would've believe he was that gay.'" Brian paused to laugh at Delaney and smile at Samantha. "And then he was, like, 'This girl at the place in Vermont was begging for it and he did nothing … went home to call his girlfriend.'"

"You guys are assholes," said Delaney.

Samantha took a step closer to Delaney and chirped, "Who's your girlfriend?"

Trevor and Brian laughed while Delaney squinted at her.

Over the weekend, out with Pritty for a movie, Samantha got teary-eyed during the final scene. After days of elaborate wedding festivities surrounding an arranged wedding, the young Indian couple was left all alone in their small house with nothing to say to each other. All was quiet as she chopped vegetables in the kitchen and he watched sports on TV. There was no sign of the flowers and streamers and firecrackers from the day before.

Pritty had a very different reaction to the ending; she thought it was happy. "After all, their parents are very pleased with them."

"By the way, I didn't tell you," said Samantha, "but I have a boyfriend now. His name is Delaney and he plays on the soccer team."

"That's so exciting! Fantastic!" said Pritty, her black eyebrows curling with hesitancy. "What do your parents say about it?"

They talked a bit about her mom and dad being "pretty much okay" with her dating, but Samantha noticed Pritty didn't ask any questions about Delaney. They both let the subject drop.

Although Delaney wasn't willing to chat on the phone, Anton started calling her. After speaking to Catherine or Robert, he'd ask for Samantha. For fifteen minutes or so, they'd discuss everyday sorts of things, like an article he'd read on a women's soccer league or a profile he'd seen of a Yale graduate doing real estate development in Rome. She offered to send him a link to the photographs she took in Rome, or rambled on about Stephanie's latest conniption over a missing hair accessory.

The vice principal sent out a letter to all Darcy High parents telling them that a former Darcy teacher was on suspension for having an unprofessional relationship with a student. "Following an investigation, we believe the teacher in question may have tried to contact several current Darcy students, and therefore we advise all parents to speak to their children about appropriate and inappropriate contact with academic professionals."

Then … somehow … Ally became the epicenter of the controversy.

She repeated, to anyone who would listen, a story about how she'd met the girl from Forrest High at her mom's gym and seen the racy e-mails sent to her by the suspended teacher. Guys at school, including Delaney's best friend Trevor, who'd never paid any attention to Ally before, were now flocking to her.

Samantha tried to ask her some serious questions -- "Why would she tell *you* all this stuff?" -- but got nowhere.

"Hey," said Samantha, as Ally sat down across from her at the lunch table. "What's up?"

"You tell me," Ally replied. With her was the girl who had pulled out the peach schnapps after the 90s Dance last year. They all had the same lunch period for the spring semester.

Samantha looked at Ally. "I got your message … something about Trevor."

"I'm so juiced," said Ally, as she scrunched up a plastic soda bottle. "He took me riding around in his Jeep. It was off the hook. Damn, I'm not going back to dating sophomores ever again."

"I still can't believe that," said the schnapps girl. "You and Trevor Thomas. That's hardcore."

"There's a party at his girlfriend Brynn's house Saturday," said Ally. "I'm thinking of going and flirting with him. I love to cause problems."

"That doesn't sound like a good idea," said Samantha. "I mean, if Trevor and Brynn are together."

"Yeah, yeah," said Ally dismissively. "You going to the Valentine's Dance with Delaney?"

"He said he probably won't be going."

"What the fuck! You gotta stand up to him. Just because he's a walking orgasm doesn't mean he can jerk you around." Ally had a new hairdo with thick blonde streaks that looked like stripes. "You should come to Brynn's party and keep an eye on him; he gets drunk and walks around hitting on everybody."

Samantha frowned deeply. "I've never seen him like that."

"I forgot to tell you. According to Mairin, Nicolette's been going around saying you blow him like every night."

"I don't think I want to hear about it."

"It's weird that you two are still friends," said the schnapps girl, looking at Ally. "I thought you were into him too."

"They're not serious," said Ally. "She's just his fuckbuddy. Right, Sam?"

"Yeah," Schnapps-girl interrupted, "her and half the girls in Connecticut."

"Well, actually he's my boyfriend," said Samantha.

Schnapps-girl snorted.

"What's so funny?" Samantha countered icily.

Ally interrupted, "So I was talking to Meghan --"

"You've been hanging out with Meghan too?" Samantha stammered.

"Yeah. Why not?"

"You're friends now?"

"No, we were just talking at a party. She told me she and Delaney are going to prom as friends."

Samantha felt faint.

Ally looked at her other friend. "You know Meghan, right?"

"She's no worse than anyone else," the schnapps girl replied. "It's not like I'd say I'm great friends with any girls at this school. It's too fucking competitive around here. There are like a million hot girls and two good-looking guys."

"So, Sam, are you coming to Brynn's party with me?" asked Ally. "I mean, if you're not going with Delaney."

"Ah, I don't think so," said Samantha, trying to catch her breath. "I'm pretty sure Brynn hasn't invited me. And I don't like parties."

"Wait a sec." Ally hopped up out of her seat. "I'll be right back."

Samantha watched as Ally marched over Delaney's table, helping herself to an empty chair next to Meghan, tension following in her wake. With a pert smiled, she opened her mouth to talk. *Oh, she wouldn't say anything about me, would she? What in the world is she doing?*

Delaney and Trevor were studying Ally. Trevor spoke, a smile on his face. Hopefully Ally was just using Brynn's party as an excuse to chat with Trevor. But it looked like Meghan and Nicolette were also talking.

When Ally returned, Samantha asked hastily, "What happened?"

"I asked Meghan to get both of us an invite to Brynn's party. She was like, 'Soccer-girl can ask for herself.' Then Nicolette said to me, 'I'm sure all the guys will want to hang out with you and Samantha … alone in the bathroom for about 4 ½ minutes!' She's such a bitch."

"Uh, I didn't realize you were going to try to get me an invitation to the party."

Ally laughed, glancing at her schnapps friend, who also looked amused. "I told them, 'I'm not coming unless Samantha can come with me.' Delaney was like, 'She sent you over here to ask about the party?' Fuck, he has the sexiest eyes."

"Uh, did he think you were serious?" asked Samantha.

"Don't worry. I told him off. I was like, 'Leave her alone; we're having a girls night out.' He just gave me this pissy look, and Meghan said, 'What are you talking about? He's been trying to get Soccer-girl to leave him alone for months.'"

Samantha blanched. "Uh, I don't think you should try to speak for me anymore, Ally."

Outside the lunchroom, Delaney caught up with her. "Why do you want to go to Brynn's party?"

"Maybe we shouldn't talk about this right now. I'm feeling taken in," said Samantha.

He shook his head. "You're so naive."

The bell rang and they headed to class in opposite directions.

That night she called Delaney at around six.

He didn't seem to want to talk, only answering her with 'Uh huh' and 'Yeah.'

When she tried to mention something Meghan had said to her in the hall after lunch, he interrupted, "I've heard it all before. I'm not responsible for what Meghan or anybody else does."

"Uh huh," she sighed.

He said nothing for a full minute. Samantha waited, embarrassed at their inability to have a normal phone conversation. Her sisters talked on the phone for hours with boys from school.

"Sometimes Trevor seems to be toying with people ... lately with Ally. What exactly is his relationship with Brynn?"

"I don't know. You'd have to ask them."

"Yeah, sure, Delaney, I'll walk up to Brynn and ask her if she and Trevor are just hooking up --"

"What else would they be doing together?" he snapped. "Stamp collecting?"

"What do you mean?"

"Nevermind." He was quiet again.

She was grave. "Meghan really dislikes me; I think she wants you. Maybe you're sending mixed messages."

"Humph."

Samantha sighed, holding back.

"Come on, Soccer-girl! Can't we just have fun?"

When they saw each other Friday night, neither said a word about Meghan or Ally. Samantha didn't ask about Brynn's party.

At a bowling alley with black lights and glow-in-the-dark pins, they ate nachos and bobbed to techno music in preppy bowling shoes. He didn't pay much attention to aim, throwing the ball as hard as he could, and she beat him soundly with gentle tosses. Leaping in the air, she celebrated her victory with shouts while he laughed boyishly, both of them drawing stares from the twenty-something players in neighboring lanes.

The day after his birthday, having not heard from him, she called his house. "What's up?"

"Not much," he said, blandly. "Sorry I didn't call."

"It's okay. It was your birthday. I understand. You were busy." She waited for a reply. "Did you have a good time?" Her voice was shaky.

"I'm exhausted ... and hung over."

"But it wasn't your 21st birthday."

"Right," he said flatly.

"Were you with your brother?"

"Yeah."

"Did you see your dad?"

"I had lunch over there."

She was quiet for a moment, drawing pentagons on a piece of scrap paper on her desk. "I was going to ask you if you wanted to go to the Valentine's Dance. I'd really like to go. I've never gone to a dance with a date or anything."

"I'm not really interested in another lame school dance. Let's go out and do something else."

"Oh, ok," she accepted. "So what else is new?"

"Just the usual. Talking on the phone's a drag. We'll talk when I see you."

"Well, I just wanted to tell you happy birthday. I got you a card. I thought I might be able to bring it to you today."

"I think I'm gonna just veg today."

"Okay." She waited, but when he didn't say anything else, she felt she should end the call. "I guess I'll talk to you later."

"Bye."

She immediately called Ally. "Hey, Ally, what's up?"

"Samantha! I was just about to call you. Did you know it was Del's birthday?"

"Yeah, he went out with his friends."

"He went out with Meghan."

"What do you mean?"

"Suzanne ran into him at a bar. The one where his brother works. Meghan was sitting on his lap and getting totally smashed."

Samantha felt a pang. "I thought he was out with his brother."

"Yeah, I think he was there too. And Trevor and Brian."

"Oh, okay, well, that's what he told me … I guess."

"Suzanne called me, so I drove over," Ally exclaimed. "I told the guy at the door I knew Delaney's brother, and I got in! Trevor and I ended up dancing."

"Really?" Samantha felt something bordering on humiliation. Earlier that day she'd been feeling sorry for Ally and her pleas for attention; now she was jealous of her for having been with Delaney on his birthday while she hadn't even been invited. "Can I call you back?"

"Uh, sure."

Chapter 27:

Ring. Ring. Ring. Ring. Ring. Hang up. Ring. Ring. Ring. Ring. "Yes?" asked an annoyed female voice.

"Hi, Mrs. Troy, it's Samantha. Is Delaney there?"

"Wait a minute," she replied, still sounding vexed.

Samantha heard an audible sigh and wondered why his mom disliked her. Suddenly she was paralyzed with fear. *What if he won't take my call? Would he do that?* She wouldn't be able to get through the night without talking this over with him.

"Yeah?" It was Delaney. Samantha felt a rush of relief.

"I'm sort of upset about something," she said, breathlessly. "Someone told me you were with Meghan last night, and I was just wondering why she could see you on your birthday and I couldn't." Before he could answer she added, in a tone sounding more and more flustered, "And it bothers me that you won't go to a dance with me although you went to several dances with Nicolette. Meghan's already telling people you're going to the Senior Prom with *her*. And they believe her because you haven't explicitly told people about us being a real couple. Is our relationship just about *sex*?"

"Relationship? What *relationship*?"

She waited for more of an answer as seconds ticked by. "That's all you have to say?"

"I don't care if someone told you I was banging Meghan last night. I don't answer to you."

Samantha felt tears welling up. "I know you don't … answer to me. But what about my feelings, Delaney?"

"What about your feelings? It's not my job to make you feel secure or popular or whatever."

"You don't care about how I feel? You don't care if I want to see you on your birthday? You don't care if I want to go to a dance with you?"

"At this moment, I couldn't give a damn."

"That's a really lovely thing to say."

"You're taking things between us way too seriously. We're not attached at the hip. I have more of a *relationship* with my friends than I do with you."

Tears streamed down her face, but she tried to keep from sobbing out loud. "Oh, okay, I didn't understand that. I was … mistaken about us. If that's the case, I don't think I want to see you anymore.

She heard a deep breath. "Fine."

She waited for him to hang up the phone, but there was just silence. After what seemed like an infinite pause, she softly hung up the phone without saying another word.

She crawled into bed, crying so uncontrollably she couldn't catch her breath. This is what Dad was talking about. Why had she ever had sex with someone so cold, someone who didn't care for her at all? She was delusional

Walking in the hall after class, it struck her that she didn't truly believe he wasn't worth having and that this might actually haunt her for the rest of her life. Pure terror made her go to the nurse. She lay on a cushioned bench for an hour but declined the nurse's offer to call her parents.

Back in class, she started sweating. *Why does he have this power over me? Why do I have these thought ... these feelings ... feelings that maybe I can't live without him?* She thought about calling him and groveling on the phone, begging him for forgiveness.

The fire alarm squealed for a scheduled drill. Samantha was breathing slowly and feeling dizzy as she walked outside and lined up with her class. Delaney and Trevor were a couple rows over, but she only subconsciously noted this.

Shivering without a jacket, she heard her name. Then she heard Trevor's distinctive laugh. She turned and saw Delaney and Trevor looking her way. Were they pointing at her?

She frowned, shifting from foot to foot and forcing herself to look straight ahead. But when she heard another laugh coming from the same direction, she lost it. How could he be happy when she was so ... ? Squeezing her face into the nastiest expression she could manage without a mirror, she turned and scowled at him. She wasn't sure what she was responding to, but she was ready to fight.

Delaney frowned, his eyebrows drawn, as he held her eyes for a moment before breaking away. Her look of fury drew the attention of some of the students in the row next to hers. She exhaled and focused on the gravel at her feet, remaining motionless and tense.

The fire drill was interminable. Everyone was getting restless. With peripheral vision, Samantha saw Meghan and another girl leave their assigned line and head toward Delaney and Trevor. They were smiling with satisfaction as Trevor greeted them. Delaney was still frowning implacably.

Samantha refocused on her feet. Counting to ten, she repeated to herself a mantra about how she'd get suspended if she went over there and slapped somebody. And if she was suspended, then she might …

A light tap on her shoulder startled her. As she turned around, she adjusted her frown to a pout. Delaney said nothing as they stood eye-to-eye, she with her head tilted back slightly and he with his hands in his pockets.

He shifted restlessly, awkwardly cocking his head to one side, but still did not speak. Turning his head, he looked off into the distance, then glanced at the students standing in front of and behind her in line.

Finally, in his softest voice, and with a vacant yet comely look on his face, he said, "I lost my temper."

"Yeah, well if that's what you think about me ..."

Still whispering, he said, "I don't remember exactly what I said, but I know I was angry. I didn't like being spied on and lectured. And I was already in a rotten mood that day -- the only thing my parents ever agree on is that I should be kissing their asses."

She hesitated, her fists clenched. "Oh, so you didn't *mean* what you said?"

"It just gets to be too much sometimes … so heavy. It's like I constantly have to tell you to simmer down. People are always on me about you. I can't even get away from it for one night. And why the fuck are we arguing about going to a dance?" They spoke quietly but still drew the attention of students standing nearby, most notably his friends. However, the girls nearest Samantha were otherwise occupied and didn't seem to be eavesdropping.

"I wasn't spying on you. I just heard from Ally, whose sister must have unintentionally gone to the same place as you, that you were with other girls on your birthday and I had thought you were only with boys. I wish you would have wanted to spend your birthday with me. But if we have no relationship, it doesn't really matter what I feel."

"I'm trying to apologize for saying that. I just don't have the same positive view of relationships you do. And the way you said it, all accusatory, didn't exactly warm me to the word."

She breathed in a stream of air and exhaled quickly. "I guess I don't know how to talk to you about my feelings. I didn't mean to pressure you or presume that we have some sort of relationship we don't. And I didn't mean to lecture you. I was just trying to express how I felt."

"Your feelings are hard to deal with sometimes."

She nodded gloomily, not trusting herself to speak.

She was startled as she felt his fingers on her face, brushing the loose hair falling over her cheek. As his finger traced the line of her brow, her eyelids fluttered.

He slowly leaned forward and kissed her protruding lips. She smiled ever so slightly, her knees shaky, and looked down and away from his friends.

"So, where do we go from here, jellybean?" he said.

"You tell me," she whimpered.

The teachers left their huddle and called the students to order, leading them back to class.

As she walked inside, warmth surging through her, she felt light and free. She hadn't been totally wrong about him. Despite the horrendous doubts she'd suffered through, waves of astonishment were not washing over her.

Chapter 28:

Samantha almost stepped up onto the bus after school when she spotted Delaney walking up the stairs at the side of the main building. He waved her over and she told the driver, "Oops, my mom's here to pick me up." She hated lying but as she headed over to meet him, she broke into a jog.

Inside his car, she leaned the side of her face against the headrest, looking at him. "Thanks for the ride."

He spread his knees wide. "Can you come back to my place?"

"Yeah, I guess." She gulped. "Can we talk? I have some questions … I really need to …"

"Hold off on the tough questions. I want to blow off some steam first."

She turned away, looking into the side view mirror to see how lousy her skin looked. Stress made her breakout. "Did you get together with anyone … while we were apart?"

"Don't bother asking me that. *You* broke up with me, remember? And I'd like some credit for the past …," he hesitated for a moment, "…four months. You told me not to do anything, and I didn't."

"Yeah, I didn't have sex with anyone else either … not counting the threesome Saturday night," she said, blinking.

Amusement flashed in his eyes.

Pulling out a pack of gum, she offered him a piece, then unwrapped one for herself. "I think I heard you say my name earlier, during the fire drill. Or maybe you were pointing, or waving?"

"I was trying to get your attention … call you over. I couldn't take much more of that ticked-off look on your face."

"Oh." She stopped chewing. "I heard somebody laughing. I thought you guys might be making fun of me."

"Yeah, Samantha, since you hung up on me, I've declared open season on you."

"No, but you haven't spoken to me either."

"Ditto."

"I thought you didn't like me at all … or, I couldn't figure out what you thought of me after those things you said."

"Yeah, I know. I was sort of pissed at you for a while."

Her stomach sank and she was quiet.

"I told you. This is all a bit much for me sometimes."

He left the door open to the bathroom, and she watched him cleaning himself, openly staring. He didn't treat his body with any sort of fastidiousness or delicacy, just splashed water with a distracted look on his face.

After nuking some leftovers, they crawled onto the couch watching TV. Leaning against him, their arms and legs entwined, she watched as he grinned like a little kid watching cartoons.

"Delaney, can I ask you any question I want ... absolutely anything ... and you won't get mad?"

He looked calm. "Shoot."

"What made you change your mind?"

"About what?"

"What made you want to get back together with me?"

In a staid voice, he answered, "Besides your tight pussy."

"Del!" She sat up to face him fully. "Did you worry about me after we argued?"

"You're, like, incapable of hiding your feelings. That's not good. And everyone was immediately saying we broke up, and it wasn't like I said anything to anyone."

"Did you want to come up to me, or call me or something?"

"I did, didn't I?"

"Yeah," she smiled. "I'm so glad you did. I don't know when I would have been able to. I didn't mean for you to get ... so upset. I'm not even sure how it happened."

"It's not like there's something I can't stand about you," he said with a confident blink of his eyes. "It's about being somebody's boyfriend ... following the rules ... being *checked up on.*"

She frowned. "Speaking of checking up on you, a couple days ago, I saw you talking to a couple of girls I'd never seen you with before. It made me think you were already over me."

"It's not hard for me to act like nothing's bothering me."

"But it was bothering you?"

"Yeah." He looked absorbed in thought. "I didn't like seeing you miserable."

She was too emotion-filled to speak. This was the kind of feeling she had wanted to hear about when she called him the day after his birthday.

After some quiet cuddling, brushing the blonde hair on his forearms in the wrong direction, she began, "I also wanted to ask you … was Meghan sitting on your lap when you went out with her and your friends for your birthday?"

"Yeah, she does that sometimes."

"Do you like the feeling of having her on your lap? Feeling her, uh, backside on you? I know you like to have sex like that."

He laughed, shaking his head. "It doesn't get me hard, if that's what you mean."

"What would you do if she told you she wanted to have sex with you?"

"When? Now?"

"Uh." His questions weren't reassuring. "Yeah. Now."

"I'd tell her I can't because I'm with you … now. But I didn't agree not to flirt."

She bent down at picked at her little toe, which Annabelle had decided to paint for her. "Delaney, what do you really think about us?"

"What do you mean?"

"You said I take things between us too seriously. How do you take them?"

"I don't know. I like things the way they are. The whole monogamy thing isn't so horrible when it's only for a limited time."

"Otherwise, it's horrible?"

"Otherwise, it's not me. It's unnatural to me."

"Do you think you'll always feel that way about … permanent, or, uh, committed relationships?"

"Right now I don't see that changing, but I guess it's possible."

She hesitated. "Do you think there's any way we might get back together after college?"

"I have no idea," he grinned, almost laughing. "Let's talk about it in four years."

"Do you think I'm taking things too *serious* right now? With these questions?"

"A little, but it's okay."

"Do you think there's any way you could ever have serious feelings for me?"

He took several deep breaths, his face a little flushed. "It's not about serious feelings; it's about who I am. I can't see being with only one person for the rest of my life. And I'm *not* going to be a cheater like my dad."

She inclined her head in compliance, leaning against him.

"Don't be upset, Sam. I didn't say anything negative about us."

"I want to tell you something. I don't know why, but I really want to tell you ... so bad."

"Okay," he said, sounding a little worried.

"It's not about ... us." With trembling fingers, she reached for the smoothness of his upper cheek. "But you have to promise to never tell anyone ... *ever!*"

"I promise," he said, wedging her between his legs, his hand tracing the curve of her pointy elbow.

"Remember when I told you about my relative who experimented with something that seemed sort of ... bisexual?"

He nodded, looking perplexed.

"That was my dad."

"What?" he shouted, his voice higher pitched than usual. "Holy shit."

"Remember the Italian guy I told you about. The friend of my parents who I saw over Christmas. We met him for dinner."

"Yeah, I remember you talking about some Italian guy with all the beautiful women."

"When I went to Italy last summer, he was our host ... the whole time. He planned the trip for us, we stayed at his houses, and we met him every night for dinner."

"Right."

"He knows my parents from before they were married."

"He and your dad were lovers?"

"No. No. No," she exclaimed, then added more calmly, "It's worse than that. My dad and my mom were dating for a while. They were talking about marriage. They'd been talking about it since before they even had sex, which wasn't until they'd been together a few months."

"*Okay*." He looked like he wasn't sure how she could be privy to this information -- or why she would share it with him.

"Anyway, then my dad met Anton -- that's the Italian guy's name -- and my dad introduced my mom to Anton."

"Uh huh." Now Delaney had a funny grin on his face.

"Then my dad told my mom that he wanted ... I'm not exactly sure what he said, but basically he wanted to watch my mom having sex with Anton. Or, maybe Anton wanted to watch my dad having sex with my mom. I never got all the details." Her cheeks burned all the way to her ears. "Eventually, they were living together, all sleeping in the same bed ... at least that's what I think happened. My mom told me they were both having sex with her ... maybe the same night ... maybe at the same time, but I can't picture it."

Delaney laughed. "I could show you a video."

"Delaney, *please!*" She didn't want to laugh. "Seriously. Mom and Dad said it was this, sort of, three-person relationship, but that still doesn't make much sense to me. And after about a year, she got pregnant with me. Anton is my biological parent. His family is this really famous Italian family. I'm half Italian."

"Yeah?" His eyes were dazzling with interest. "You kind of look like you could be part Italian."

She nodded, feeling dismal.

His grin slowly dissipated. "So, he brings model-types when he visits you?"

"Well, actually, I didn't meet the actress, just saw him on TV with her. I guess because he's so wealthy and never fell in love with anyone, he dates younger women. It bothered my mom a little that he brought his assistant to dinner. She gets all emotional around him, but my dad's not jealous at all. He says my mom couldn't have sex with someone for a year and not care about him. Both my mom and dad keep telling me how they care about Anton and how it's okay that I'm *connected* to him."

"Sounds farfetched." He regarded her somberly. "But maybe it's true. If he was pissed, he wouldn't be taking you and your mom to see this guy."

"I didn't know anything about it until last year. That's when I met Anton for the first time. I can't really stand him half of the time. I wish I just had my regular dad back." She couldn't go on. Her nose was running, and she held her fingers to her nostrils.

He hurdled over the couch to get her some tissues and, when he returned, wrapped his arms around her neck. She shivered as the warmth from his body pressed against her. They were quiet.

Sniffling, she began rocking impatiently, peering up at him. "They all knew he was my dad from the time I was born, but Anton agreed that my parents would be the best parents, so...."

Delaney smiled slightly, "So, in Franks' class on parents day, when your dad was talking about the girls he dated in high school, he was actually ..."

"He wasn't lying. He's not gay! It was more of a voyeurism thing." She paused. "Did he seem gay to you?"

He laughed. "No, he didn't seem gay. He seemed ... cool. Gutsy for showing up and not acting like the sweaty dude standing next to him. Maybe he was a little ..."

"What?" she almost yelled.

"He seemed very open. Willing to talk about anything. I guess your parents are a couple of free-love types. Make love, not war. It's all cool. Although, your mom, I haven't spoken to her for more than like a minute, but she didn't seem that kinky to me. I have a hard time picturing her doing two guys."

"I guess I don't have the perfect family you thought."

"No, well, maybe ... just because your dad tried wife sharing doesn't mean all your glowing descriptions of him must be false. My dad would want nothing to do with me if some other guy's name came up on a paternity test. He'd be in court the next day suing to get back his child support money."

"I wish you could see it. My dad acts really normal around Anton, the same way as he does around his other friends or his brother. I mean, I can't imagine. When I think of stuff like anal sex ... "

"Wait a minute! You've been thinking about anal sex?"

"No, I mean, not for me. But I remember you said stuff about it in Franks' class and ..."

"Why not you?" he smiled. "We should definitely do it."

"Del!"

"Your mom must be used to taking it in the back ... living with two gay guys, I mean."

"Shut up! You said he's not gay."

"No, *you* said he's not gay. I'd say he's bisexual but there's nothing wrong with that. I mean, he must like fucking women too. Your sisters don't look half-Italian. Your mom is the opposite of butch. So, it's plain he likes women too."

"Oh, *God*. Please stop grinning. *Please*."

"Why? Who cares? So they were all over each other with this ménage à trois thing. And they don't regret it -- they still like each other. It's just that they decided to give it up and breed. Your mom must be a real minx."

"No!"

"It's okay. Now I see where you get it from."

"Oh my God. Delaney! You're supposed to feel sorry for me."

"For what?"

"For everything."

"I guess it was hard learning you have a different father, but, otherwise, it's not a big deal. It's just sex. Let them have their fun. You like sex too, don't you?"

"Not with more than one person."

"I don't think I could see myself having sex with you and another girl at the same time. But there are some girls I could definitely imagine in a three-way."

"I hate this. It's just making you think I'm a pervert too."

"Don't worry. You're a monogamous pervert."

"Delaney!" Her mouth rippled with mirth. They fooled around on the sofa, grabbing each other with no obvious goal in mind, until she tackled him onto his back,

"You know. I've completely opened up to you ... told you my big secret. Now you have to open up to me ... tell me something you never thought you'd tell anyone."

"Uh, like what?"

"What girls could you imagine in a three-way? Tell me who you're talking about. Tell me about you and Nicolette. You and Mairin."

He was pensive. "Okay, but this is also confidential." He sat up. "The first time I met Mairin, she came up to me at a party -- I was there with Nicolette. She asked me to come over her house the next day. When I got there, she was, like, 'Okay, let me see what you got.' I felt like a piece of meat."

"But you didn't hate it."

"It was great, actually."

"So, what are you doing here with me?"

He leaned forward, his face inches from hers. "Don't worry, Guido, you're very sexy too … in your own tightly-wound, submissive girl sort of way."

"Guido?" She was unable to keep the laughter out of her voice.

Chapter 29:

"Good evening, Samantha."

His years at Oxford showed when he pronounced her name. He drew out the syllables like a Brit theatre critic astounded by the nerve of an American attempting Shakespeare in London. Did he dislike her name? He probably hadn't been consulted when her parents chose it.

"Thanks for the laptop." Last week she received a box containing a Mac book. During one of their previous phone calls, she mentioned typing at her desk. "It's really cool."

"I would like to speak to you about something important," he began, after acknowledging her thanks. "Your mom told me --"

"You want to talk about Mom?" She grinned to herself.

"Something else," he answered succinctly. "About you, actually. Your parents talk a lot about how tremendously intelligent you are, and I think there is something --"

"Uh, thanks." she said, cutting him off, but trying not to sound ungrateful. "I'm sure you're very smart as well."

He was silent for a moment. She thought she heard a helicopter in the background.

"Where are you?" she asked, still hopeful of pushing him off his chosen topic.

"I'm in Tokyo."

"By yourself?"

"Actually, there are millions of people in Tokyo."

"Ha ha."

"There is something critical that I need to speak with you about … if you will hear me out."

"Okay," she said, exhaling in defeat.

"You ought to have very high aspirations for yourself, Samantha."

"Uh, okay. I think I do."

"And, more to the point, you cannot settle for anyone who is not worthy of you."

"Uh, I'm not so sure that I want to think of myself as better than other people."

"But you are. In many ways. And you should not attach yourself to anyone when you are too young to realize this."

"Uh, I think I know what you're driving at, but …" She didn't want to be the one to bring up Delaney.

"You have personal qualities that will put you in the way of the most intelligent, successful and influential men."

Why does he have to talk like a cable news pundit? "Uh huh. So, this is the marry-the-rich-guy speech?"

"Not only rich, but, really, whatever you desire. Bottom line, you will not have to settle … as long as you do not do anything now that might hinder your prospects."

"Yeah, well, I don't want to be Miss Debutante. If I ever got married, it would be for the right reasons, not money, power, or anything else. *And*, I wouldn't date people half my age." This probably wasn't nice, but she wanted to shut him up.

"Okay. I do not mean to upset you, as I often do." His tone was apologetic but not at all fawning. "I wanted to say something positive: you are beautiful and intelligent. You have a great family, and you have wealth. All these things should allow you to have the best in life, including career and family."

She definitely hadn't shut him up. And for some reason, his words made her eyes water. Was it because he said she was beautiful? Why would that matter?

"According to the girls at your school, you are lucky to be with what's-his-name, but in the real world, the world outside your high school, he is the one who hit the jackpot. And you need to know that."

"I'll tell everybody you said so," she said dryly.

"Your mom can be a little … unworldly … at times. She might suggest to you that this young man is an amazing specimen. She has no experience; all men are a mystery to her, except your dad and he is not hiding much, so he is easy to figure out. She is not the one to ask for advice. Talk to your dad."

Samantha flushed. His knowledge of her parents made her head spin.

"The soccer player is going to end up working at a gas station, and you are going to associate with the highest rungs of society. This is the truth, regardless of whether your friends at school realize it."

Her hands started shaking, and not just from sudden realization that he was probably going to give her money. "I … well, I'm not sure what you mean. It's nice of you to send things to me and my sisters, but I don't think …," her thoughts shifted, "… and you definitely don't know Delaney. The fact that you make those kinds of assumptions about him shows you don't know him. Anyone with him is lucky."

"She will be lucky because he can give her babies? That is not enough. What else he can give is yet to be determined, and you do not know what he will be in five or ten years. He may be successful. He may not. You have to give yourself time to judge and not make hasty decisions. You will meet a lot of interesting people at Yale."

"Not that it's your business, but we have no plans to stay together … in the future." She heard the agitation in her own voice. "I guess he doesn't realize what a catch I am."

"My worry is that you will believe him and buy into the idea that it is enviable to be with him. You can find someone with all the qualities of this soccer player and more if you give yourself time.

"I do not mean to disparage your mom, but just the idea that you have attracted the interest of someone like him --"

"What did she say?"

"She told me she could barely stand to face him."

After a quick intake of breath, she sighed audibly.

"Have you ever considered that he may seem like God's gift to women because he is older and more experienced than the high school girls he impresses? There are dozens of nineteen-year-old men living on my piazza who could impress the girls at your school."

"Lucky for you."

He was silent for a moment. "Very funny, but, in all seriousness, there are thousands of men who could impress sixteen-year-old girls with their sexual prowess. He seems like the only man in the world because he is your first lover."

She was stunned. She refused to talk to him about sex. "Uh."

"I am not completely backward. In my family, girls who have sex when they are sixteen and unmarried are excommunicated. I understand things are different in your family. But you do need a dose of reality. When you are older, you will be able to have any man you want, and he will not be a high school soccer player."

"Yeah, uh, thanks for the compliments. But I gotta start my homework now, so…"

"Please, do not do anything that would cause you to be forever tied to him. And obviously I am not just referring to tattoos or coordinated college plans."

"I definitely won't," she said, annoyed at being thought irresponsible. "We all know what kind of problem *that* can cause. Hope mom didn't mess up your own plans for perfect primogeniture."

"I did not mean to suggest … Do not put words in my mouth. I have no regrets about you, Samantha."

The girls' soccer team was jumping in unison as parents and other spectators flowed onto the field. It was obvious, even from the parking lot where Delaney stood with Trevor, that the girls had won.

Samantha was with her parents when she caught his eye. Waving, she watched him hesitate and then change course and head back toward the field. She ran to meet him.

As she stopped, he took another step closer to her, hovering as their bodies grazed. "You think you can take me?" he said with a cocky grin, bumping her with his chest.

She smiled, pushing him as she spun around 360 degrees.

"So what happened? One of you bad boys actually scored?"

Samantha briefly summarized the final minutes of the game. She made an assist, a cross to the forward line, and her teammate lobbed the ball over the goalie's head. "My parents are here. I'm sure they'd like to say hi."

Delaney looked to where her parents were standing, less than twenty yards away and caught her mom's eye. Catherine gave him a shy wave, which he returned with a smile. Turning to Samantha, he said, "I gotta run, babycakes. Trevor is waiting for me. There's a party with the team."

Recently, Samantha had accompanied him to a party at Lila's house, feeling so excited about finally attending a social event with him. But the exhilaration she had expected never hit. Despite being bumped, stepped on, and having drinks spilled on her, she was yawning after twenty minutes of his friends sharing anecdotes she couldn't follow and talking trash about other seniors. The worst part was the relentless body snarking by the girls, of whom only Lila said hi to her. At curfew time, things were just getting started, and she had to leave. It was as bad as her first high school party with Ally and her schnapps-loving friends.

She reached around his waist, playing with his belt loops. "My mom asks when you're coming to dinner."

"I'm sure they're great and all, but I don't think so."

She tried to sound playful. "You don't want to get to know my family?"

"It's not my idea of a good time. I can only guess what your dad would like to say to me … with all you've told 'em."

"No, he just thinks you're trouble. That's all." She smiled, squeezing him. "Dad had this idea. He thinks the guys from your team should come and act as cheerleaders for our games."

"Tell him we don't have male cheerleaders at our school. The gay cheerleaders all go to Williams Prep."

Her lips twitched as she said with didacticism, "That's homophobic."

"Yeah, well, now you know why you don't want me talking to your dad."

"But you're not. You're not homophobic. Compared to most of the guys at Darcy, you're a progressive."

"Whatever you say."

Her tone softened. "It was so cool when you stayed to watch my match last time. Hopefully we're not so painful to watch anymore. Maybe you and Trevor could--"

"I will. Next week I'll be there."

Tucked in the backseat of her mom's car, her parents up front, she offered, "Sorry he didn't have time to stay and chat."

Robert turned to her. "Let's not pretend any of us actually believe that."

"Dad! He's worried because he knows all the things I've told you guys about him."

"And he has a guilty conscience."

"No, dad. He's just ..." She stopped.

"I think you probably give him way too much leeway. I've heard you make a lot of excuses for him."

"I don't think he's used to getting along with older people, definitely not parents."

Her mom, sitting sideways in the front passenger seat, smiled. "I guess we're the scary older people now. We wouldn't be much fun for him, Rob."

"No, Mom," Samantha intervened, "He's not ... he's said nice things about you. He said you're pretty, especially for someone with teenagers."

Catherine just stared wide-eyed at Samantha, her cheeks blossoming with color.

"Great, now he's got your mom on his side for life," Robert said to Samantha.

Way back, when Delaney first met Catherine, Samantha and he had unexpectedly run into her while strolling down Main Street in Darcy. Delaney had no idea who the bashful-looking woman standing in front of him was, even as she greeted him with a "Hi, Delaney" and stood with her blonde, mini-me children. After Samantha made an introduction, he looked surprised, his mouth dropping open for a moment as he sized her up. Clearly she wasn't what he expected. Then Samantha's sisters took over the conversation, telling him they wanted to be "Mrs. Troy" as he laughed and matched their first names, which he'd heard from Samantha, with his last. Samantha ended things as quickly as possible while trying to determine if there were a word for killing a sister, like fratricide means killing a brother.

Chapter 30:

A concert at Jones Beach with Gunther and his friends should have been easy to turn down. The first time Samantha had crossed paths with Gunther was during a short visit to the band house; he had turned to Delaney and said, "Yeah, Mom and Dad told me all about jailbait over here. You're such a pussy." But her thirst to spend time with Delaney was unquenchable. And Delaney had extracted an oath from his brother not to speak to her the entire night. There were several other girls going, including Gunther's current squeeze, so Delaney was convinced this wasn't an idle promise.

At the gate to the arena, Gunther and his pals discussed how to sneak liquor past security. After watching the line, they noticed the women weren't frisked as carefully, so they got past inspection by hiding their contraband up their dates' skirts.

The music was mostly instrumental including an unending drum solo that almost put Samantha to sleep in the dark haze of the amphitheater. She found herself frequently losing interest in what was happening on stage and focusing on Delaney and what he was consuming.

He drank and smoked rolled-up cigarettes with the others. Eventually she figured out it was marijuana. She was the only one who abstained although second-hand smoke and the rhythmic sounds made her feel a little dizzy as Delaney wound her hair around his pointer finger and acted more than usually cool, mellow and spaced out. She stared at his silly smiles and sly grins as he pulsed to the music, rubbing against her abdomen. He put his arms around her neck and leaned on her as she looked up at him. His eyes were almost closed, a sliver of dark pupil showing. His T-shirt felt cold and sweaty against her exposed skin as she pressed her lips to the erratic pulse of his neck.

After the concert, the group stumbled to the parking lot. With a sleepy smile, Samantha prepared to climb back into the van, then realized the group was pairing off. Some headed for the beach, and Delaney opened the back of the van and motioned for her to follow. Inside, they got into a sleeping bag. With a faraway look, he brought his lips to her mouth. She heard another couple lie down together on the middle seat.

Dazed, she kissed him back, shuffling his satin-smooth hair with both hands. He grabbed a bottle of toffee-colored alcohol and, after offering her some, drank from it. "I think you've had enough," she said. But, he tasted so good she couldn't let go of him. As he fumbled with his jeans, she told herself to resist temptation. "I can't. You're drunk."

"Yeah … yeah … yeah," he murmured with a grin. His speech was somewhat slurred. He kissed her and purred like an animal on the prowl. She couldn't help but grin with delight.

The other couple was making the seat squeak as he tried to pull off her jeans without much success, his usual suaveness gone. Samantha felt his liquored breath on her face, but her eyes were so close to his face that she had trouble focusing on his amusing mugs.

"Help me," he giggled. With her assistance, he managed to remove one of her pants legs and put on a condom, then immediately push inside her. It felt delicious but she didn't make a sound as she raised her pelvis and guided him further inside. He moved slowly, moaning in the back of his throat. He never vocalized so indiscreetly.

After what seemed like an hour, she was so aroused he was swimming inside her. She felt ready to climax and let out a few of her usual noises. As he moved over her, she hurried, "Please," wanting him to rub her in the right place.

"Your cunt is so soft," he warbled, continuing the rhythmic stroking.

The front doors opened.

"What's going on back there?" Gunther barked.

Delaney instantaneously sobered from his groovy stupor. "Shut up and turn on the radio."

Her body clenched as she heard several people talking and laughing. She was concentrating on his penis, which was pushed as deep inside her as it could go, against her cervix. She didn't try to make out what was said, but she did hear the turn of the ignition. Then she heard the radio. Soon they were on the road and she felt Delaney's body relax as he started to move to the jostling of the van.

Not at all like the subtleness of before, he began plunging swiftly. As an orgasm pierced her, a tear slid over to her ear. He didn't stop and slammed his pelvis against her sensitive, fleshy thighs until she felt a second orgasm, this time harsher, sharper, almost painful. He finished with a gruff thud as he fell on top of her. From there, he immediately fell asleep.

His warm chest expanded and contracted against her torso for the remainder of the ride home. His weight made her incapable of movement. Yet she felt secure and weightless in her manacled state.

"Do you think I'm a fool?" her dad asked.

She was home, in the front room, having trouble keeping her eyes open, shivering in the warm house, her cheeks twitching.

"I didn't smoke anything, but they were smoking around me."

"Bastard," he blurted out, looking away for a moment. "Is he scared I'm going to chew him out? He should be." Delaney had walked her to the door but no farther. The most he ever did was say a couple words to her parents and make faces at her giggling sisters.

"Dad!"

"If you get hurt, if you end up in a hospital, in a car crash ... I'll ..." He didn't finish, just grabbed her by the shoulders. "Samantha, *you* are responsible for this. *You* made the decision to be around someone drinking, smoking pot, and driving."

"I know I messed up, but, Dad, I think that maybe ... you don't understand ... you don't totally understand what's going on." Looking at her feet, she tried to keep from wobbling as he let go of her. "I think ... I think I might be falling in love with him."

"Love?" He threw up his hands. "Do you love shock trauma? Do you love head injuries?"

"I'm scared," she whined, her head throbbing.

A glimpse of his normal open countenance emerged. "Scared of what?"

"I'm scared of being in love with him," she mumbled, staring blankly at the front of his shirt.

"Samantha, I don't care if he's the second coming, you cannot risk your life to be with him." His face was tragic, his eyelids sinking, yet he sounded determined. "You're grounded. And if you don't find a way to convince us that this won't happen again, you're never seeing him again."

"No! You don't understand. Dad, I have to see him. He didn't do anything wrong. He didn't drive. His brother drove; he was sober." She didn't actually know that Gunther was sober, but he at least seemed much more so than Delaney.

"Fine, get him over here to tell your mom and me that while he was smoking pot his brother wasn't. I'd like to hear him try to tell me that."

"Dad! I told you ... What about what I said? You can't tell me not to see him. I couldn't tell you not to love mom."

"I'd rather have you alive and heartbroken than a dead Juliet." His mouth was creased at the edge. "If you want to see him again, get him over here. I have some things to say to him."

"Dad, I can't ask him to come over so you can yell at him."

"I've made up my mind. And I mean now, not next week. I mean tonight, or tomorrow as soon as he's sober."

"Tonight?"

"Yes. If he can't give us assurance that this won't happen again, then you're not seeing each other anymore."

"What? Dad! You can't decide *for me* whether I see him. *You* said that."

"That was when you hadn't behaved so irresponsibly. The truth is, until you're eighteen, I *can* say whether you see him." Although he was heated, he wasn't out of control. Once when she was 11, he'd lost his temper because she'd punched the boy next door but later apologized for yelling so much and lessened her punishment. But now he seemed grave. She ran to her mom.

Crawling into bed an hour later, she was cried out, unsuccessful in convincing her mom to intervene on her behalf and insist that her dad retract his demand. It was too late to call Delaney. She didn't want to wake up his mom. And, in any case, she wasn't sure what she could say to him to get him to come over.

The next morning she woke with a headache. Ally called but she said she didn't feel well. She spent a half hour in the bathroom with a stomach ache. She avoided her dad.

When she finally dialed Delaney's house, his mom answered the phone sounding less annoyed than usual. Maybe things were better with his mom; for once, they hadn't been arguing. Maybe he'd be willing to make the effort. Shaking, she waited for his voice.

"Uh, huh?"

"It's me," she sniffled. "My dad … my dad's mad at me."

"Yeah?"

"He says you have to come over and tell him that Gunther wasn't drunk when he drove us home."

"What?"

"I told him you guys were smoking and drinking and stuff, and he said that I'm grounded for letting someone drive me home drunk, and then I told him Gunther wasn't drunk, and then he said you have to come over and tell him Gunther wasn't drunk." She heard herself talking like her mom when placating.

"And why do I have to tell him that if you already did?"

"Uh, I think he wants to talk to you about drinking and stuff. He's worried about my safety. He says he's worried I'll end up in the hospital."

"Why would you tell him we were hammered?"

"He knew. I think my clothes smelled and I was stumbling around and acting all sleepy and weird."

"I never saw you take a hit."

"No, maybe it was second-hand smoke."

"You got high off second-hand smoke?"

"It's not funny. He's serious."

"Yeah, and I'm, like, gonna come over there and let him rip into me."

"Sorry, but he says I can't see you if you don't come over and talk to him ... *today*."

"Uh, huh, well, you're really the only one who can deal with your dad. There's not much I can do."

"But he's serious. I know him; I know he's serious. What if we can't go out again? That's what he says."

"Samantha, there's nothing I can do. My coming over to your house is not going to change his mind. It would probably make things worse."

"You won't come? If I tell you that it's the only way we'll be able to see each other again, you won't come?"

"I can't," he said, barely audible.

"Delaney! If you don't do something, I'm gonna be grounded for a month. What are you going to do ... forget about me?"

"I don't think we should talk if you're gonna flip out on me."

"Delaney, you can't see me again if you don't come over. Is that okay? Is that okay with you? It's not okay with me." She waited.

"I'll talk to him over the phone for a minute."

"I think he wants to talk to you in person. Del, you *know* it probably wasn't such a good idea for everyone to be smoking and drinking."

"Yeah, but what exactly is the point of confessing that to your dad."

"Maybe I should have driven."

"Uh, huh. Right." His breath was huffy. "Listen. If I want a lecture, I have my own dad. You have to figure things out for yourself."

"*I* want you to come over. I want to see you. I need you right now. My dad's really mad at me, and I want you to come be with me. It scares me when he's so angry with me. He's never so .... cold to me." She sobbed. "Maybe he wishes I wasn't the way I am ... I mean, the way I like you. Maybe he wishes he had a different daughter. I don't know. I'm not sure." Maybe she was exaggerating, but it was true that she'd had nightmares about being passed to her dad as a newborn and having him look down at her with disappointment on his face as he realized she was from Anton's gene pool.

"Yeah, that doesn't sound like a situation I want to get into."

"But Delaney, I'm asking you … I'm asking you to come over here and help me. I need you right now. Do you understand what I'm saying? I *need* you."

"There's nothing I can do to help, Samantha."

"That's it? You won't even try to save things between us. I don't get it. What about doing something that's hard because it'll help me?"

"Fine, I'm an asshole. I'm not going to argue with you."

"I just want you to come here, please. Please. I don't think you're an asshole. I like you a lot."

"I'm sorry."

She was stunned with pain. The phone went dead for half a minute. "I have to go now," she said.

"Okay, call me," he said softly.

She found her mom in the basement laundry room. "He won't come. I don't care what Dad says; I'm going to see him."

"Samantha, it'll be better when everybody calms down. Then, we'll be able to come up with a solution."

"Please talk to him."

Chapter 31:

Samantha was calm by dinnertime. Her dad wouldn't do this to her. He would relent. She'd tell Delaney to wait for her until she convinced her dad. Tomorrow at school she'd tell him.

They all retired to the great room, discussing yesterday's brunch when Grandmom Fisher had told Annabelle that she would never be a famous rock star. "What a foolish, silly notion!"

Stephanie turned on a TV show about face creams used by movie stars while Catherine encouraged Annabelle, "You can be anything you want to be, Annie."

"I'm going to put on shows for my friends when I'm not busy performing in stadiums," said Annabelle as she jumped up and ran to the front door. Samantha hadn't heard a knock, but she turned to see which neighborhood kid she was going to have to deal with.

Instead, she was confronted with Delaney's tall figure. She sprang to her feet. Breathless, she forced out, "Hi."

His face was rigid and his shirt clung to his chest in a way that reminded her of the night before. His hair was tousled and a bit greasy. His eyes looked tired and dark blue but still breathtaking. His cheeks seemed more depressed, which made him look older, and more attractive in a grown man sort of way.

Everyone was quiet, even her sisters. He stood motionless and then shrugged his shoulders. "You called?"

"Uh, yeah," she stammered, glancing at her parents. "Would you like something to drink?" As he shook his head no, she motioned to a seat next to hers.

The television was turned off and Robert asked her sisters to go upstairs to watch their show. They were hard to convince.

Delaney said nothing to Samantha, his eyes wandering to the open upstairs landing, where her sisters had retreated with their books, magazines and juice boxes.

"How often do you use marijuana?" Robert asked.

There was silence. Delaney was studying the strips of colors on canvas hanging from the tallest wall of the great room. Finally, he turned toward Samantha, then glanced over at Robert, "Are you talking to me?"

"Yes." Her dad's voice revealed a worrisome lack of desire to give Delaney a real chance

Delaney returned a defiant, that's-none-of-your-business stare.

"How often do you smoke pot?"

"I can't remember," said Delaney, with a flash of his eyes.

Robert shook his head, then took a deep breath. "Okay, can you remember how often you drink and drive?"

"Yes."

Robert waited for a full answer, looking angry.

"Maybe we should start over," interrupted Catherine, reaching for Robert's hand pleadingly. "Did you two have a nice time at the concert?"

"Yes, it was okay," said Samantha in a high, nervous voice.

"Your brother was driving," said Catherine, "Uh, is that right ... Delaney?"

He nodded. Samantha looked at him hoping for a glance in her direction, or better yet a smile.

Robert interrupted, his voice louder than normal. "You are operating under a false assumption,"

The expression on Delaney's face said what he was thinking: *I'm ready to be informed of my mistaken assumptions about drinking and smoking pot.*

"You think Sam is fortunate to be with you. But it's the other way around."

Samantha started to stutter, preparing a rebuttal, then she noticed Delaney grinning,

"I don't disagree with that," he said frankly.

She stilled.

Robert looked as if the words were a tad unexpected. "And it's better for her in the long run to be rid of someone who cares so little for her safety ... and who's never returned her regard as she deserves. We've all had enough of your arrogance and childishness."

"Dad!" She was desperate to draw his fire away from Delaney.

"We're going to be here for Samantha, and we're ready to support her in any way she needs ... no matter how hard it is. But it is over."

"And, what's the point in bringing me here?"

"I don't believe the story about your brother not smoking pot like the rest of you, so you don't need to repeat it. The fact that you and Sam got into a car with him and risked your lives is unacceptable."

"Uh, huh," said Delaney, raising his chin, his elbows propped on the arms of his chair. "Sam was the only one who hadn't had a drink, and it would have been more dangerous to have her try to drive a van than to let Gun drive. Have you seen her try to pull onto a highway?"

"Yes. You should have called a cab."

"We were basically asleep in the back and Gunther seemed fine after walking around for a while, so …"

Samantha glanced at him, relieved he was making an effort.

"If he was drinking, he wasn't fine, and *you* shouldn't have asked our child … You're over 18, you're legally an adult, correct? … You shouldn't have let our child, who was your guest, ride in a car with someone who'd been drinking."

"Okay," said Delaney calmly and quietly.

"Is that all you have to say?"

"Next time, we could get a hotel room but then she won't be home on time."

"At least that's not *necessarily* life threatening," Robert retorted.

Samantha was quiet, hopeful. But she wondered if her dad was referring to AIDS or something sinister on Delaney's part; she really needed to talk to him about Delaney's positive qualities more often. She'd been using her dad to vent.

Robert's eyes fixed on Delaney as if he were weighing options. "You never answered my question about whether you drink and drive."

"When I've been drinking, I crash at a friend's place. I don't drive."

"Always?"

"Yes."

"If, for the sake of argument, we were to change our minds and let you see her again, what sort of insurance could you give us that you and Samantha won't ride with someone who's intoxicated again?"

Delaney shrugged.

"I promise. It won't happen again," said Samantha earnestly.

"Yeah, I've heard that from you before. That's not good enough. We've talked about this a million times and still you did it."

"But, Dad, I know now that you ... I know that I would be grounded ... for a really long time and I wouldn't be allowed to go out. I believe that ... completely."

"If you do this again, worse than that will happen."

"What?" she exclaimed, cringing.

"No soccer. No summer vacation -- you'll stay with your grandparents. No driving."

"Okay. Okay. It won't happen. I'm not going to make this sort of mistake again. Say you believe me."

Delaney leaned forward, his eyes on her dad. "What sort of insurance do you want?"

"I'd like you to tell me."

There was silence for a minute.

Sounding confident and motherly, Catherine spoke, "So, Delaney, uh, Samantha told us that you have a basement apartment ... all to yourself. That must be nice to have so much ... privacy. Your mom must really trust you."

"I doubt it has to do with trust." Robert looked at Delaney. "Presumably you and your friends smoke down there ... among other things."

Samantha couldn't remember her dad ever being so antagonistic.

"At least I don't use it to invite cute guys over," Delaney sneered.

"What?" Robert exclaimed.

Catherine blushed with a half grin. Samantha kicked Delaney ... hard. The first real visit to her home and he was gay bashing?

"What exactly do you mean by that?" Robert looked to Samantha. Her face said all he needed to know, and she realized this instantaneously. "I hope you don't plan to repeat private confidences Samantha has shared you with."

"No, she just told me you're a switch-hitter and all. It's no big deal. Your secret's safe with me."

Robert exhaled loudly. "Let's get back to the issue at hand. We're looking for reassurances that you won't exercise such poor judgment again, not your opinion on my life."

Delaney nodded, the slightest smirk on his face. Samantha thought his face reminded her of how he looked when taunting a teacher.

Catherine smiled, nervously squeezing her lower lip with her fingers. "You're both so very young to be drinking at all. It would be such a tragedy if anything happened … to either of you. What if you were arrested for having drugs? Think of the loss, such a great loss … all the wonderful plans you have. I don't know what I would do. I would never get over it.

"You both have so much going for you. You shouldn't be risking your futures for a high … or whatever you get from drinking. I don't think you should drink at all … it's not just drinking and driving. You're both going to college and you're both athletes. Why would you jeopardize that?"

Samantha watched Delaney openly study her mom, presumably assessing whether she was for real.

"Since we're being completely honest here," Robert began, "I'd prefer if you and Samantha ended things."

"But, Dad --"

"Yes, I know. Let me finish." He looked at Delaney. "It would have been better for Samantha if you'd stuck to trying to one up your friends by seeing who can run through the most girls. I don't think she needed to grow up so fast and start spending time getting schooled in various sexual positions by a 19-year-old."

"Dad!"

"I'd like to know where you see all of this going, this thing between you and Samantha. Is this a serious relationship at this point?"

"I'm not into labeling things," said Delaney, glancing at Samantha.

"Just because you're teenagers doesn't mean you can't treat each other with respect. There's nothing weak about being faithful and committed to one person, but I don't think you believe that."

"I've already heard all Samantha's monogamy lessons, and I get refresher courses on a weekly basis."

"That's not true," cried Samantha, feeling hurt.

Delaney closed his eyes for a moment, then glanced at her. "I'd rather not talk about this ... now." His eyes returned to her parents.

Robert was looking at Catherine who smiled at him, looking peaceful. His expression was almost resigned. "I'd still like to hear your offer of insurance, as an adult, that the drinking and the drugs won't happen again. I think you should hand over something valuable, with the understanding that you'll lose it if you break your pledge."

Delaney looked facetious. "You want the title to my car?"

"That's a start." Robert's eyes narrowed on Samantha, then returned to Delaney. "Are you sure you don't want to take this opportunity to back out gracefully?

"Back out of what?"

"I guess that's a no."

"I could think of a much easier way to back out of this ... like if I'd stayed home."

Catherine smiled at the comment, and Delaney noticed, half-smiling back.

"Okay, you may hand over the signed title to Catherine to hold onto until some point in time that we no longer think it's necessary. And if you two drink and drive again, Catherine will donate your car to charity. And Samantha will never speak to you again ... until she's out of college and we're no longer supporting her. Understand?"

"Are you serious? My car?"

"You have to put up something you deem of value."

"You guys are nuts," Delaney said and then laughed as he glanced at Samantha. She gave him an encouraging smile although inside she was anxious.

"If you have another idea," said Robert, "we'd like to hear it."

Next to Samantha was an untouched glass of pink lemonade. She picked it up, sipped some, and then offered it to Delaney, who downed the rest of it. He looked at Robert with a resigned expression.

"I guess that's settled then," said Robert, "although Samantha is still grounded for the time being."

Her mind moving quickly, Samantha tried to determine how long she'd be grounded, given the circumstances.

After a minute of silence, Delaney looked at Catherine and said, "So, while I'm here, let me see one of those pictures of the Italian guy who dates actresses." He was clearly ready to run from the drunk driving lecture.

Catherine looked taken aback. "Anton?"

Robert frowned. "Sam, it would be really rough on you -- and your sisters -- if your friend here ever decides to tell someone what you told him."

"I know, but I trust him."

Catherine looked intrigued. "I have a picture but there isn't an actress in it."

Delaney rose fluidly from his chair, Catherine leading him toward the back of the house, with Robert and Samantha following. In the study, Catherine got out the photograph she'd shown Samantha. "That's Anton when we were together in New York."

Delaney studied the picture for a moment and then looked at Samantha. "Don't tell me I look like him."

"No, I mean… you don't look like a guy," he replied gently.

Samantha glanced at the photo. For the first time she noticed there was a cat photobombing the shot. He was standing on the shoulder of the sofa ready to spring into the air. He must be Mom's cat from when she first lived in Manhattan; he'd made it into Anton's condo.

Delaney turned to Catherine and said casually, "That's hardcore: you and two guys."

"Well," she blushed. "It was nothing to be impressed about."

Samantha noticed her dad holding back, watching passively.

Delaney smiled. "So, why didn't you wait until after you had Samantha to decide which one you wanted to marry?" As he said this, he glanced at Robert haughtily.

"No, no," she laughed. "I wanted to marry Rob. And I definitely wouldn't have been able to have a family life with Anton. It was strange though. Sometimes I feel like I was really bad for a year and then at the end of it I got this really great gift … Samantha."

"Mom, *please*," said Samantha, smiling widely.

Delaney grinned and, looking at Samantha, said, "I ought to get out of here."

"Don't you want to see my room?"

His eyes darted in Robert's direction for a moment. Samantha took his arm and led him towards the staircase.

He walked a straight line to her most prized possession and studied it. A framed detail of a Pompeii mosaic hung on the wall by her closet.

Crossing the room with a smirk, he bent over to look at a photo on her desk of her sisters dressed as candy canes. A figurine of hello kitty in a striped jersey with a soccer ball at her feet seemed to catch his eye and he picked it up.

"Gretchen gave that to me, for my birthday."

He turned to her, reaching for her cheeks and tilting her head back as he shook his head. "You and your crazy family."

She met him with puckered lips, applying pressure as they exchanged saliva. Her arms around him, her body molded to his as she got lost in the embrace.

Moving his mouth to her ear, he said, "Brain. That's all I have to say."

"Huh?"

"Go ahead and look online. Ask them on the Ivy League Message Board."

"No, tell me what it means."

"I want you to go down on me."

"Oh ... "

He grinned like a fox. "Remember our conversation that day at the mall. I think I've waited long enough."

"Eh." She pulled back a little, biting her pinky nail. "I don't know. When?"

"How long are you grounded for?"

"I'm hoping I can get it down to two weeks."

"Hmmm. There's prom night ... the afterparty on Nicole's dad's yacht."

"Uh ... Well ... Maybe. Is there a totally private room? With a lock?"

He returned to her ear, exhaling through his nose. "I don't just want it; I want it from *you*. I want to watch *your* mouth on me."

She lost her breath and leaned into him. That night she'd be fantasizing about oral sex. She was ready to go back on the promise she made to herself about waiting. "I'm such a slut."

He laughed.

"You agree?"

"I'm cool with you being a slut." He kissed her. "I'll see you at your game on Friday. And meet me in the quad before lunch tomorrow. We can hang out."

She beamed at his willingness to work around obstacles.

"Is that him again?" he asked, pointing to her computer screen. Her laptop was open and the screensaver was a slideshow of all her photographs. One of Anton in Italy was now showing.

"Oh, yeah, that's from over the summer."

It was outside a provincial-looking grocer, in late afternoon, the sun almost set. He was in a black suit, perfectly groomed, while an older woman selling vegetables stood in the background, dressed in a print housecoat with a scarf wrapped around her hair. "He looks a little like someone from *The Godfather*. Is he yours?"

"No, I don't have a godfather. I think my dad's brother Stuart is my guardian if anything ever happened to my parents."

"Really?"

"Yeah. I think." She frowned at the idea of Anton being somehow legally responsible for her. "Unless they change that."

"It seems like he would be your backup dad. If you lose one, you have a spare."

"I only have one dad," she said softly, squinting.

"If you worked it right, you could definitely get a Ferrari out of this."

Grinning, she noticed Delaney's height made her furniture look smaller, more suited for a child's room. "Stephanie's clamoring to go back to Florence, but I don't know. Lately, he's been calling me, trying to tell me I should marry European nobility."

"No shit?" His eyes were wide but he was still smiling. "I think I'm starting to like him."

"What?" She felt a chill. Delaney could never like Anton, and Anton would certainly not be pleasant to Delaney. Their meeting would be a day that would live in infamy. "No, I can't dump you for prince charming, not after you came over here tonight."

He grinned. "I hope you didn't talk shit about me."

"Well, actually, he brought it up. My mom said something to him. I tried to avoid it." She paused. "He can be so condescending."

He didn't look bothered, his elbows out to the side, hands buried in his pockets as he shrugged. "Look on the bright side. Someday when Stephanie's older, she could go to Italy, marry Anton and their kids will be the threesome offspring."

She felt a squeezing stiffness in her chest. "First of all, I would murder him. Second, that doesn't make any sense. Stephanie isn't half my mom and half my dad. She's her own person."

"Okay, I'm just joking around. I better go. Nice room. Very wholesome."

"Thanks," she said sarcastically.

"That's romantic, the curtain hanging over your bed. Now I can picture you there."

Chapter 32:

Tapping her heel, Samantha couldn't sit still at the final awards assembly. Walking up to the stage for the third time, she didn't look down at the certificate handed to her by Principal Townsend. She just wanted the school day to be over, so she could go over Delaney's house. Her mom didn't have a drawer full of awards, but she had someone who loved her back.

As Samantha sat in bed writing an English paper on Chaucer, Plato refused to keep her company because she kept getting up every fifteen minutes for a drink or bathroom break. A visit to Ally's house ended badly when she got a stomach ache after realizing her new cell phone was dead. It was a daily ritual, trying to decide how long to wait for his call before giving up and making the call herself.

Only time with him was fulfilling. Everything else felt like going through the motions. The minute he was available, she was there, driving over his house as soon as he called. The end was near.

Without telling anyone, he'd applied for an internship at *Turntable Magazine* in Manhattan. "I never thought I'd get it. I figured they'd have a shitload of applicants. You get to go to events with their concert reviewers."

His first assignment was to check out a band in lower Manhattan. He'd be leaving for NYC immediately after graduation, no break for a summer vacation.

As soon as they were alone, she found herself touching his hair or taking the initiative to kiss him. They'd quickly end up in his bed. As they lay together beneath the cool flowing air of the overhead AC duct, she was hit by the scary feeling of wanting to spend the rest of her life with him, accompanied by a painful cramp in her abdomen.

Trailing kisses under his chin, down his neck and onto his shoulder, she jumped on top of him for the third time that day. Reaching into his underwear, she squeezed his still firm yet spongy penis with a nervous giggle.

He opened his eyes and rasped, "How many times do you want me to fuck you in one day?"

Her eyes fell. "I don't know. Too many, I think."

"You're high maintenance."

She smiled for an instant and then wrinkled her forehead. "Delaney, you're not just a super attractive guy who lots of girls want to hook up with. You're a special … precious person. When you move away, remember that. You're a precious human being."

He broke into a broad, open smile, but, after studying her face, his eyes turned serious.

Samantha was home alone with her mom. Sitting together at the long computer desk in the great room, they were filling out online forms for a summer soccer league. There was talk of getting Samantha a car for school in the fall, so windows with car safety records were also open on the screen.

"I don't understand how you have sex with two guys at once."

Her mom didn't seem surprised by the question,

"If I had to paint a picture, I'd have a lot of trouble." Catherine sounded so young when she talked about really personal stuff. "I was in the middle of it all. Rob was always around and he'd speak for me and make sure I was okay. When I think of it now, a lot of memories are fuzzy, but they're not bad memories."

"I guess I shouldn't ask whether Anton was making sure you were okay."

Catherine smiled. "I remember I got kind of upset one night when things were just beginning, and I told Rob I wanted to be alone for a few hours, and he let me go back to my apartment. I kept paying rent at my old place because I worried my parents wouldn't approve if I told them I was living with Rob."

"But they'd be fine with you living with two guys?"

"No, I kept everything from them. I was nothing like you." Catherine smiled wistfully. "But anyway, Anton showed up at our door. My roommates had the strangest looks. You know how he can be … imposing."

"Did he wear suits with waistcoats back then too?"

"Yes, it was probably weeks before I ever saw him wearing anything else." Her mom chuckled softly. "I couldn't believe it when I got up and there he was, standing in our drab hallway, all by himself. He wasn't smiling. We went to my room, which was quite disconcerting. It was the first time I was alone with him."

Samantha closed her eyes for a moment.

"And there we were. I barely said a word. And then he started talking … a lot. He apologized for scaring me. He said something about how he was glad he met us, that we were the "kind of people" he didn't get to spend time with. He said that the couples he knew were nothing like us."

Samantha saw grief on her mom's face, as if she wished she could figure something out but just couldn't.

"It was strange to sit there calmly talking to him about these serious issues after what had just been happening back at his place, but it was nice too. He said something about how it was a new situation for him also."

"The threesome thing? Or the experimenting with something involving another guy thing?"

"The experimenting. Both of them said they hadn't done anything like it before …. Anton told me I was wrong if I thought it all started because Rob didn't really want to be with me … or that Rob wanted to be with a different sort of person than me. He kept saying that there was no doubt in his mind that Rob would end up married to me … that there wasn't anything inconsistent about what was going on and Rob wanting to marry me. The way he said it made the whole situation seem like it was about *me*. That they weren't interested in anything unless it centered on me."

Samantha's nodded, breathless.

"We went back to Anton's apartment. It ended up being a turning point for me."

"Uh huh?"

"I'd never really been able to completely let go and be okay with myself. Do you understand? Things improved that night."

Anton surprised them all by showing up at her house in the middle of the afternoon, asking Samantha to go to lunch with him. Her sisters eyed her with suspicion. Her parents were going to have to tell them the truth about Anton soon. She was pretty sure she saw something like realization in Stephanie's eyes.

Anton drove himself this time in a silver-grey jaguar. He changed gears with a forcefulness that differed from Delaney's laid-back operation of a vehicle, yet he didn't seem on edge as he turned to look at her with a taut grin. She felt chatty as they passed the sign on the side of the highway that read,

Darcy, CT
"One hour from NYC and worth the drive!"

Looking at his etched profile, she said, "As if people from the city visit Darcy to ride around looking at giant houses no stranger is ever invited into."

At a tiny café in Greenwich, his height created a shadow that extended out the opened floor-to-ceiling windows and shaded the flowers in the garden.

"You want to go for weekend visits with him in Manhattan?" he asked.

"I wonder who told you that."

"Your mother, of course."

"Dad is trying to tell me I shouldn't go without a friend, but I'm going. I have to."

"Do not do anything dangerous, Samantha. You have a credit card, correct? You could manage to take a car service back to Connecticut if you needed to?"

"Yes. I have a credit card for emergencies."

"Perhaps he should visit you at your home. I think your parents are concerned about how his roommates will look upon you when you visit."

She frowned, feeling defensive.

"If your parents agree, I will give you the keys to my building on Central Park. If you get into an argument or feel pressured by him, you can go there."

"Okay," she said softly, looking at the self-assured expression of his eyes. He never seemed to hesitate before speaking.

"It sounds like she plans to let you go."

"She never lets me do anything unless Dad agrees."

"That is why they are still married while so many other Americans are divorced."

"What do you know about marriage and parenting?" She felt fearless. What couldn't she face if she could face being in love with Delaney Troy?

"I have learned some from speaking with you."

The waiter arrived and took their order. She thought of his first visit when her mom had become so dejected. She thought of how her mom was still not sure what he felt about her way back when.

"Why is it that you can't tell my mom that you cared about her... before?"

"It is not that I cannot but that I do not see the benefit of doing so."

"It would make her feel better."

"I think she is happy as the situation stands."

Samantha stirred sugar into her iced tea, creating a vortex. "You never knew your mom?"

"No." He brushed his sleeve, although there wasn't any noticeable lint. "I do not know anything about her, not even her name."

"Do you know if she's Italian?"

"I assume so, yes. I suspect she was a servant."

"I guess you're not as high class as you think you are."

"Perhaps, but no one has ever said that to my face."

"Sorry." She swallowed her grin.

"Apology accepted," he replied calmly. "Recently, I have wondered if she might look like you. I doubt she was an educated, accomplished woman. If I met her now, we would have nothing in common. I know for certain that I do not approve of several of the choices she made."

Samantha blinked several times and felt her pulse sprinting. "Who are you to lord over people like you do … that stuff you said about how girls in *your* family are required to do X, Y and Z? Using the word 'servant.' Who says that?"

"Your parents' families have a lot of history where you live, many connections. Your grandparents have strong beliefs. I also have family obligations."

"I think you've defied a few."

"Not publicly. Not openly."

She grinned. "I guess I have some good blackmail material on you."

"Yes."

"I'm sure my parents are going to tell my sisters about what happened. Someday Stephanie and Annabelle will crash the de' Medici family reunion and embarrass you."

"I do not think so," he said, as if his wishes made it unlikely.

"Yeah, eh, I'm just warning you, so you can have bouncers on hand to rough them up."

"You never cease to amaze me. I have very great respect for you *and* your sisters. I would not do anything to hurt any of you. And if anyone tried to hurt one of you or anyone else in my family, he would be in serious danger."

"A mafia hit," she laughed, not taking him seriously.

"No comment. But the Troys are included in that threat."

"Do you ever go out with anyone your own age? Like my mom. If you met her tomorrow for the first time and she was a never-married school teacher, would you want to be with her?"

"Why are you asking me that?"

"She asked me to," she said archly. "No, just kidding. I'm curious."

There was a long pause as he leaned back in his chair. "I do not see how I can answer that because she *is* married and I *do* know her. And if I did not, I do not see how we would ever meet."

"That's a no, but at least you're honest." She concentrated on her food, waiting to see if he'd let the subject drop.

"If I had the chance to get to know her somehow, then I think I might possibly ..." His last words weren't audible.

"Really?" she exclaimed.

"I do not understand your question."

"What makes her attractive enough to tempt you?"

He took a deep breath. "Almost all people are kind in order to get something they want or to convince others they are good. Your mom is an anomaly."

"What?" She almost knocked over her glass. "I... I might have to tell Dad not to let you visit anymore."

"Please do not. This is a private conversation."

"Alright. Your secret's safe with me, although perhaps guilt made you say it."

"Guilt? No. I do not have any guilt with respect to you... or your mom. I think you are an incredibly privileged young woman. Plucky, and all four of you out of control at times, but extremely blessed."

"While we're at it, maybe I should tell you what I think of you."

He laughed with closed mouth. "You need not bother. I have heard your criticisms and attempted to address them."

"Really?"

"Yes, and, as for being wild, you should always be aware of your tendencies."

"Yeah, but back to you, why don't you move on and get in a real relationship with someone … do like you're supposed to … pass on the family name? Mom and Dad say you're stalling but there's a lot of pressure from your father."

"I'm glad they are concerned about me." There was a strange, annoyed-looking grin on his face. "But, truth be told, I realize my incapability when it comes to something like matrimony. My lack of interest as well."

"But, wait it a minute. You said … You seemed to say that you might *not* be incapable when it comes to my mom?" Her voice rose at this shocking implication.

He shook his head. "What I do know is that I cannot be the close friend she desires."

"Why not?"

"But I would have helped her if anything awful had happened to her … and you."

"How?"

He exhaled. "I will discuss whatever you would like, but please keep this between the two of us."

She nodded. The idea that Anton actually smarted over losing her mom. It was so … couldn't he get someone else if he wanted? Samantha caught herself assessing her mom's allurements. She was great and everything but … "You were in love with her?"

He did not deny it, or even look away. His gaze was steady.

"So you would choose to be with my mom if my dad was out of the picture?"

"That is much too simplistic."

"But you don't deny it."

"If something happened to Robert, your mom would never recover from that."

"But if she asked you to be there for her, to hold her hand, you would do it."

"Yes. Of course."

"Would you marry her if she wanted a companion, if she asked you for more ... yet all the while you're aware that she'll never stop missing Dad?"

"It is difficult to speculate about tragedy befalling your family."

"Or would you pursue her, realizing that she's not okay being alone?"

He was smiling a little, shaking his head at her interrogation.

"Or maybe you'd just want to *be with her* once in a while."

"Is your investigation coming to a close?" His voice betrayed no exasperation.

"Yeah. You're guilty. But I'm not sure if it's real feelings or just nostalgia for old times' sake."

"I will say *to you only* that if your mom had been alone with you, I would have tried to be her *companion*, as you say."

Chapter 33:

She looked up at Delaney, and he kissed her before coaxing her head back onto his shoulder, brushing his lips against her neck. Swaying, her fingers drew an oval on the shoulder of his black dinner jacket. She closed her eyes, relaxed and calm.

Her dream had come true. She was dancing with Delaney, surrounded by the Midsummer's Night Dream décor of Darcy Senior Prom. He danced well for a guy, neither overdoing it or awkwardly stiff.

Immersing herself in the feel of the music, she tried not to be self-conscious as his hand rest on the exposed skin of her lower back. His friends were at a table nearby; he'd already danced with every girl in his group of friends, including Nicolette, who had seemed overjoyed by the gesture.

When he'd come to pick her up, Samantha had received a talking to about staying cool. She would get a reward if she didn't go ballistic and call his friends "big meanies" when they got out of line.

"You're planning to ditch me if I do something embarrassing?" she had asked.

"When do you *not* do something embarrassing?"

"What's my reward?"

"I'm gonna use my mouth to make you come."

The music changed to an upbeat song with blaring horns. Closing all gaps between their bodies, they moved to the thumping beat. Hoping it wasn't too noticeable, she tried some arm movements from Indian dance class as her hips grazed his pelvis. He pulled her against him, his tight grip causing her back to arch.

They skipped Nicolette's afterprom party and went to Manhattan for a late dinner, thanks to Anton's driver who chauffeured them around all night long. Sitting at a cloth-covered table with a plate of spinach gnocchi in front of her, Samantha felt grown-up. She was dining at a restaurant near Lincoln Center with a beautiful 6' 2" Calvin Klein model, at least that's what the maître d' had said as she walked them to their table. Holding her hand, saying nothing, Delaney reached over to play with her loose updo. His eyes were disconcerting as they focused on her slinky orange dress, which already had several wrinkles caused by him.

After dinner they found a small private park in the middle of a quad of high rises and managed to slip in the gates without being hassled. On the grass, he spread out his rented jacket and they looked up through the trees at a row of riverside towers illuminated with a random pattern of lit windows. The height of human artifice was filtered through the foliage, set against a backdrop of sky and the Hudson River.

Samantha clasped her arms around him, twisting her dress. Relaxed, she was dying to let it all out. "Remember that party I went to with you, when everyone was talking about that girl at school who's pregnant? Sometimes I think about that. What would we do if I got pregnant?"

"That's not going to happen."

"It's an infinitesimally small possibility." She reviewed her private thoughts on the subject. "What if I regretted not having the baby? What if

I had trouble getting pregnant later and felt really bad that I didn't have a baby when I had a chance?"

"You've got to be kidding. Are you intentionally trying to freak me out?"

"No, I'm just wondering. Just thinking out loud."

"First of all, you're too young to have a kid. Second, you're not going to get pregnant because we're extremely careful. And, third, when you're older and want to have a kid, you're not going to have any problems."

As he fingered the thin beaded straps of her dress, she decided to stop holding back. He could accept her or reject her. It was not just that he was leaving, living in the city and seeing other girls; it was that she was so crazy in *love* with him. He was everything she never knew she wanted until she met him.

She wanted to fully acknowledge it, address it. She wouldn't be able to move on and be interested in other guys. How could she sleep with another man without comparing him to Delaney at every step? She would never get over him. It didn't matter if she met a Rhodes scholar or a brilliant scientist or a professional athlete; she'd always want Delaney.

"I know you might not want me to say this to you, but I think I have to tell you something. I have to say it."

He turned his face toward her, his eyes still and balmy.

"I'm in love with you. I mean that absolutely ... in complete seriousness. I want to have kids with *you* someday. Only you, no one else, ever. I want to be married to you someday."

Eyes closed, long lashes quivering, he said, "You better give me a minute -- I don't want to say something stupid."

She tried to chuckle, but it came out like a cough. "Go ahead. Say something inappropriate. I just did."

Taking her by surprise, he jumped up. "You have to give me a minute." He walked ten feet away. She felt a minute of agonizing stomach pain, which seemed like fifteen minutes of agonizing stomach pain. She decided that her declaration of love wasn't poetic. If only she'd thought up something like Jane Eyre's I-may-be-poor-and-plain speech.

She sat with her knees up and buried her face. He bumped into her side as he sat down. "Actually, I'm not surprised to hear you say that." His breathing was loud. "And, it is incredibly flattering to hear that from *you*."

"Okay," she interrupted, suddenly wishing she could let him off the hook, let him not have to say more.

"Believe me; I'm not trying to let you down easy ... not in the least, Samantha. I want to see you, as we've talked about. I have no plan to quit you."

She nodded.

"There's just no saying what might happen in the future. Right now, I can't give you anything like a guarantee. It would be asinine to do that, as much as I'd love to say what you want me to say."

She nodded, looking at the towers, a sprinkle of lights on the middle floors went out. "I know that you like that people want you ... like to look at you. You love that you can go around having sexual experiences with scores of different people. It's this huge ego trip for you to walk into a room and feel like you could end up screwing around with anyone you want.

"But I love the whole of who you are. I would give up everything, except my sisters and my parents, to be with you. I would move to Tibet and live in a shack in the mountains."

"I understand. I understand. You don't have to explain. I've thought about it a lot already -- I knew how you felt, before you said it. Although, I can't say I ever expected any of this to happen, especially not after I did everything I could to make sure it didn't. I was honest with you about who I am.

"On the other hand, I'm definitely not interested in a relationship with anyone else. Maybe I'm interested in experimenting and living on my own, but I won't be getting 'involved' with anyone else."

"But I'm not enough."

"There's nothing lacking between us that makes me think you're not the one for me -- you're amazing. We're just way too young to be thinking about what you're thinking about. I'm not even sure if I'll ever be able to say, yes, I can be a good dad or anything like that. It'll probably take me a while to figure that out … years.

"But, like I said, I do know that I want to keep seeing you a lot. Whenever you can make it to the city, I'll free things up. I just can't be certain about the future and whether I'll ever be the kind of person who would be good at the life-long commitment thing that I know you want -- that I know you would be good at."

Solemnly, she said, "It's not that I want a life-long commitment now or that I want one in general. It's that my feelings for you make me want it. From the first time I noticed you, I felt this potential love for you. It was impossible not to think of you, like if I didn't get to know you, I'd be missing out on the best thing I could ever have. Now that I really do know you, all my instincts are confirmed. I was right about us. I don't think I will ever get over you -- I don't care how sappy and pathetic that sounds. Even if you get over me, I won't get over you. I won't be able to move on."

"Okay, okay," he sounded like he was trying to sooth … *himself.* "Samantha, I do love you. You've made me think about this stuff I never considered before. You've got me thinking about you and me and some kind of a future; I admit that. We have, like, perfect chemistry -- at least I think so. I think you're a dime. You're mad, and you're unbelievably smart."

She shook her head dejectedly, feeling his praise was a consolation prize. "You were close with Nicolette too once, but you got over her."

"Samantha, I not sure why this is such a sticking point for you, and I probably shouldn't tell you this, but you're totally off base when it comes to Nicolette and me."

"I guess I just feel intimidated by her."

"Nicolette and I only talked about partying and friends and stuff like that; we never talked about the personal stuff that you and I are *constantly* talking about. That's one major difference." There was a pause. "And also, Nicolette doesn't like sex with me that much. We were really good *friends*," he said succinctly.

"You guys didn't have sex?" She was completely shocked

"Yes, we did. She did it for me."

"She didn't like it at all?"

"A little, I think. But it was always, 'Don't touch me here' or 'Don't touch me like that.' A lot of instructions. We *didn't* have chemistry."

She was quiet for a minute. "But, you've gone out with other girls who liked it."

"Yes, probably, but you're different, Sam. You don't fake anything. You don't even know how."

He stretched his legs out along the side of her body, moving as close to her as possible without embracing her. "I can separate sex from feelings. So, as odd as it seems to someone like you, there's no reason to worry about things like who I've had sex with or who I will have sex with in the future."

"So if you have sex with Meghan or some model in New York, I can feel fine about it."

"Listen. I promise you, I will never have sex with Meghan or Nicolette or anyone else you know. And, whatever random girl I might hook up with backstage at a concert, that has no effect on what I think of you. I want you in my life; there's just no saying how things will end up. Maybe when you get out of college, when you're like 22 or something, then we can talk about the future. I do love you, but I'm not ready to be what you want. Not now."

Breathless, she nodded, trying to accept. "I needed to tell you, even if it's much too soon for you."

"I don't mind. Nothing that you said bothers me ... anymore. But please, don't use my feelings as a weapon against me. We can talk about it but I can't handle ultimatums."

"I won't, Delaney. As much as I want you, I don't want you reluctant."

"The baby thing was sweet -- it's a very sweet sentiment, telling me you want to have a baby with me -- but it's totally out of the question now, Sam. You know that. We can't force things."

She nodded, trying to keep her countenance.

"Don't be upset. I'll call you once a week at least. You can tell me about everything that's going on. You can talk non-stop about your family."

"Are you going to tell me about what's going on in your life?"

"Yes, school and friends and the internship and stuff like that. But I'm not a moron. While I'm not going to lie to you, I think we should focus on us."

"I don't know if there's anything else I can say right now."

He nodded, and then leaned his head all the way back, looking at the grey, cloudless sky. She lay down next to him, not avoiding touching him but not reaching for him either.

"Okay, let's make a commitment," he said. "I promise not to sleep with anyone you know, to only have sex for the thrill of it, no relationship component, no heart-to-heart talks, no overnight guests hanging out at my place. I have no problem hitting the brakes and telling someone I have a serious girlfriend back home.

"*And*, when we're in the same place, New York or Connecticut, we're exclusive. We can do Christmas and holidays with your family ... as a couple.

Your crazy sisters. Your Burning-Man parents. I'm theirs to do with as they please." He grinned. "We'll make appearances at my dad's place -- he's starting to be much more accepting of things than my mom is. He approves of your academic transcript.

"I'm willing to meet the Italian guy. Also, I promise to listen to you moan about me sleeping around as much as you want. And when we both graduate college we will reevaluate things. You can tell me all over again about how you want me to knock you up. How's that?"

The warmth in his voice made a tear materialized, gravity pulling it down her cheek.

He pulled something out of his pocket. "I have a present for you, but right now I'm thinking it's completely stupid. Maybe later you'll appreciate it." He handed her a small velvet pouch. "It's supposed to go with that car your parents are talking about getting you."

It was a keychain with an engraved oval charm.

**I always thought that if I were popular
I must be doing something wrong.**

"It's Suzanne Vega," he said.
Her chest felt heavy as she read it again.
He told her to turn it over.

**To SCM
From DWT**

Her middle name was Catherine and his was William like his dad.

Emptiness. Longing to have sex with him. Fear that she never would again. She worried this was all she'd ever experience again for the rest of her life.

Then he phoned. "I told you I'd call right away."

"Yeah." She was silent, awaiting what he would say, not wanting to betray her desperation.

"I got a cell phone. Are you stoked?"

"Really? Your dad insisted?"

"No. My decision." He paused. "What's up?"

"Not much."

"My roommates are all college kids, but they haven't even managed to get the gas company over here yet."

"What are they like?"

He talked about his living situation and his internship. The hours were going to be long, but there were some other interns to hang out with, including a farm boy from Iowa. "What have you been doing?" he asked.

She leaned back on her bed and turned her face toward the pillow, hiding from the openness and light of the rest of room. "Thinking about what you might be up to."

His voice was steady and clear. "My room will be livable enough for you to come in a couple weeks."

"Okay," she said softly.

He mentioned an upcoming Friday and went into details about the train schedule, when he expected to get off work that day, and a meeting place -- the information booth under the zodiac ceiling at Grand Central Station. "We can go for a picnic in Central Park."

"Are we going to have sex?" she asked nervously, her muscles clenching.

"Either way, I want to see you."

"It might be hard for me. I might get really emotional."

"Don't worry, I can handle it. We can spend the whole time lying in bed and talking if you want. I know what you're thinking ... what you're worried about."

"I miss you so much already. I..."

The sound of a door closing came through the earpiece. "If we end up having sex, it won't be as complicated as you think," he said. "I'll be able to get outta here to come visit you. I can stay with Gun or my mom ... or with you." He chuckled, clearly not expecting that. "We'll see each other a lot."

She was silent, and then breathed deep. "I think I want to do it."

"Same here," he replied in a low voice. "We have to learn to have phone sex."

After he detailed several acts of sodomy he wanted to perform on her, she was out of breath and sated, cuddled up in her comforter. He made an exaggerated panting noise and laughed a little. "Feel better?"

"Yes," she laughed.

"I'll call you in a couple days. By then I'll have an internet connection, so you'll be able to send me those dirty letters you've been composing."

She smiled to herself.

"Oh, and call me if you want. Anytime. If you need to talk. If I don't answer, you can start blowing up my cell. I promise I won't complain. I'll get back to you ... the same day. I've decided to get over my aversion to talking on the phone ... *just in your case.* That's true love, right?"

Epilogue

She'd been through so much. Endless discussions with her dad about Delaney's carousing in Manhattan. Feeling scared that she'd accepted too many of his assurances about what might happen someday. Worried that she was putting off the inevitable heartache. Their quasi-open relationship was a constant trial.

Only the regular visits to the city sustained her. They were together every couple of weeks as a real couple, an exclusive couple. Exploring neighborhoods, sampling pastry shops, checking out free exhibits and half-priced theatre, eating street food, browsing hipster shops and used bookstores. Whatever happened when Delaney went out drinking -- to whatever seedy places he accompanied his friends and coworkers when she wasn't around -- Samantha was the only person who had a toothbrush at his apartment. She was the only woman to spend the night.

Delaney's parents soon learned that the best way to get Delaney to visit was to include Samantha. She bit the bullet and put up with their coolness, becoming closest to her former most-hated, Mr. Troy, who was undeniably intelligent and impressed by her academic transcript. Delaney was a staple at Montclair family gatherings, crossing Samantha's grandparents' doorstep for many holidays and special occasions. He got death glares from Robert for his off-color remarks, but never pushed it so far that he got kicked out. Both Robert and Catherine were won over by the fact he didn't push Samantha into risky situations, such as taking trains late at night or going to places in the city with drugs in the bathrooms. Delaney didn't want to change her into a seedier version of herself. He adapted himself to fit in with the Montclair family dynamic, admiring her relationship with her parents. He opened himself up to a new sort of family life where people never got falling-down drunk, drove recklessly, snapped at each other without apologizing, or manipulated passive aggressively.

Once she got to Yale, Samantha spent hours tucked away in a library cubicle. She kept away from distractions, so she could get her work done and take off to go see Delaney almost every week. Late at night she debated philosophy with her housemates, sitting on the floor of the hallway outside her dorm room, she but never felt much interest in inviting any guy other than Delaney into her room.

Delaney didn't have any other girlfriends to keep up with while living as a bachelor in New York, but he cherished his freedom to "do whatever he wanted," including casual hook-ups backstage at concerts or in dark corners at parties. Samantha had free access to his phone, which he used to keep in touch with his boss and call her; no women texted him about dates. But it was always a sore spot that he wasn't 100% monogamous when they weren't together.

Delaney and Anton had an open antagonism, which never boiled over into hot war. A general disapproving affect on Anton's side collided with snide remarks about hot secretaries from Delaney. Yet, Sam managed to have chatty dinners with the two of them when Anton was in the city. The outings had to be kept to two-hours max. After each, she hugged Anton goodnight and exhaled in relief as she and Del walked back to NYU.

★★★★★

Her eyes followed the squares of glass up to the ceiling as they curved over an inner atrium. On the table beneath the dampening sunlight were garlic pickles and canapés from her favorite local deli. Everyone was mingling behind her -- in the great room of Anton's dark-floored condo -- as she looked through terrace doors to Central Park.

Delaney picked her up and swung her around, not really taking her by surprise although he'd snuck up on her.

"Congratulations," he beamed, dressed in jeans and buckled shoes that screamed Greenwich Village hipster.

She kissed him, the only natural thing to do when she was near him.

"You never have to set foot in New Haven again," he grinned.

"You're late," she said. Anton was hosting a party to celebrate her recent graduation from Yale.

"Sorry, it was work." He handed her a gift bag with a vintage I Love NY logo on the side. He looked tan, even a little reddish below his shirt collar. Last weekend they'd gotten back from a jaunt to the Jersey shore. Their longest trip together, just the two of them, so far. Two weeks at a friend of his dad's small house on a romantic bay near the crowded beaches. She hadn't wanted to leave. He agreed their digs were beginning to feel domestic – "Should I got out and chop wood for winter?"

She pulled him over to greet her parents who were mingling with Anton and her sisters amongst the settees, all drinking champagne although only she had reached the age of 21. Annabelle jumped on Delaney, and he pretended to be injured. Stephanie was giving Anton instructions on what music to play as he merely nodded in Delaney's direction. Gretchen stood frozen like a doll in a yellow sundress.

Samantha noticed Delaney was sweating a little, around his brow. He glanced at the gift she held in her hand. She lifted it and peered inside but saw only white tissue paper. She looked up at him as he began speaking to her mom about his new job. Oh my God, why does he look anxious?

Looking down at her favorite linen pants, she tapped the feather-light bag against her thigh, swinging her leg. In an instant everyone was staring at the present in her hand.

"Open it!" yelled Stephanie, who'd said the exact same thing earlier about other gifts.

Samantha reached inside and felt soft fabric.

"A shirt? A tiny shirt. I think it's the wrong size," she said, looking at Delaney's stone-faced look of discomfort. His hands were jammed in his pocket and his mouth was seal closed like the last time he'd visited Yale and they'd run into the graduate student she liked to sit with during physics lectures -- the first ever sighting of Delaney's jealous side.

The infant-sized shirt in her hands had lettering on it. Inside her head, she read, reread, and finally, spelled out each letter of the two words embroidered on the shirt: soccer baby.

"What is it?" Gretchen asked, sounding excited and nervous.

Robert and Catherine looked confused but were smiling and interested.

"OMG! You're pregnant?" screamed Annabelle.

"No," laughed Delaney in reply. Glancing at Robert, Catherine and Anton, he added, "Seriously. I swear."

The room was spinning a little as Samantha tried to speak. "Ummm, ... I think you're jumping the gun a bit." She puckered at Delaney. "Where's my ring ... my marriage proposal?"

"I already know your answer," he said, smugness returning to his eyes. "Del!"

His grin turned into a huge smile. "I can't afford a ring suitable for the Montclare/de' Medici dynasty."

Everyone laughed. Samantha focused on her mom's happy calmness as little flashes of silver stars obstructed her vision. Annabelle started dancing. Stephanie joked with Anton about a wedding in Italy,

"In Capri! You pay for it … but put mom and dad's names as hosts on the invitation."

Anton replied, "He will have to agree to an unbreakable prenup."

Samantha reached her arm out, grabbing Delaney, who moved to her side, holding her up as she asked for a glass of water.

Her parents did not conceal their eavesdropping as she sat on Delaney's lap in the dining room, looking down on Columbus Circle where pedestrians challenged yellow cabs.

"Now's the right time? … Because I graduated?"

"Sort of," he said with a squint. "For so long I was scared to death of trying something I couldn't do … and making you give up on me."

"I don't want you to do this out of fear…"

He held her hand supplicatingly. "It's a true compromise. I got to indulge that part of myself for a while, but I want to be with you and we can't make this work if I never stop playing around like it's meaningless."

"But if you're denying part of yourself, that might be a mistake."

"I get something in return." He squeezed her and his voice lowered. "And I want it all. The kids stuff I never got to do because my dad was missing in action. Awful soccer playing … like the way you used to play. Camping. Skateboards. Surfing."

A giant grin again took over his face. He smiled so much since landing a full-time job in concert promoting. He was no longer dependent on his dad. After years of moving from one apartment share to the next, he'd recently got his own studio downtown.

"I can't believe you're the one bringing up having kids. Where's my Delaney?"

"I want to see you with stretch marks." He laughed and then his grin faded. "But I don't want our kid to feel like he has to be bagging a bunch of girls to be cool. I just want him to be a kid. Or, I just want her to be a normal kid."

"Right, I agree." Her voice was trembling.

"And when we have kids I won't need an assist like your dad."

"Stop! This is serious." She smiled as he glanced at her parents, who were good-naturedly grinning – they were used to him.

"You're sure now?" she asked. "You're sure you're never going to be … you're never going to have regrets, right?"

"If we do this, we're never getting divorced. I will not get divorced. I won't sign the papers. You're stuck with me. You're the one who loves marriage counseling, right?" She was interested in child psychology for at-risk kids and had applied to grad school uptown.

Her eyes overflowed at the thought of the crazy stuff he did, like flirting with models behind the scenes at photo shoots and partying with the band. "I shouldn't say it, but no matter what happens, we'll get past it. But do not make me put up with too much."

"No. No. It's not kinda, sort of, we're trying to be exclusive. It's completely, totally exclusive. Never apart. Like your parents."

"Oh my god, Del. We ought to live together for a while before we start planning anything permanent."

"It's not such a big deal actually," he continued, "I wasn't going to tell you, but it's been on for a while now." He shook his head like he was laughing at himself. "I've been testing the waters to make sure I'm ready. I get home earlier. I'm not so hungover. I want to come home to you. And whatever shit goes down, you can handle me, Samantha. I know you can."

Acknowledgements

Thanks to my husband for encouraging me and for being the irreverent, hilarious, beautiful and giving person you are. Thanks to my kids for being so cute. Thanks to A. Jenkins, Leigh Michaels, and Floyd Kemske. Thanks to my first readers, Kelly, Ellen and Janet. Thanks to Alyson, T.F. and E.F. for listening to me ramble on and on about my book.

Visit Elizabeth Famous online at

www.ElizabethFamous.com

Facebook.com/ElizabethFamous

Twitter: @ElizabethFamous

www.ingramcontent.com/pod-product-compliance
Lightning Source LLC
Chambersburg PA
CBHW071248170626
46809CB00001B/133